SOUTHEASTER

SOUTHEASTER

Haroldo Conti

Translated from the Spanish by
Jon Lindsay Miles

LOS ANGELES · HIGH WYCOMBE

First published in the United Kingdom and the United States by
And Other Stories in 2015.
Los Angeles – High Wycombe
www.andotherstories.org

First published in English translation as *South-East*
by Immigrant Press, Spain, in 2013.

First published as *Sudeste* in 1962 by Fabril Editora

ISBN: 9781908276605
eBook ISBN: 9781908276612

Editor: Ana Fletcher; Paratext Editor: Sophie Lewis; Copy-
editor: Tara Tobler; Typesetter: Tetragon, London; Typeface:
Swift Neue Pro & Verlag; Cover Design: Hannah Naughton.

A catalogue record for this book is available from the British Library.

Supported using public funding by
**ARTS COUNCIL
ENGLAND**

MIX
Paper from
responsible sources
FSC® C013056

Printed and bound in Great Britain by
TJ International Ltd, Padstow, Cornwall

CONTENTS

SOUTHEASTER

Between the Pajarito and the river that's an open sea, turning sharply northwards, narrowing and narrowing at first, to almost half its size, then widening again and drawing curves towards its mouth, coiling in on itself, secluded in the first islands, is the Anguilas Stream. Beyond the final bend the open sea breaks into view, rucked up by the wind. Even in all their vastness, the waters here are shallow. From the mouth of the San Antonio to the mouth of the Luján, everything is sandbank. The Anguilas empties out into the middle of this sandbank, amidst a field of reeds. Depending on your viewpoint, the place looks pretty bleak, and on a day that's grey, and with a blow, it disquiets any man.

Far off to the left, dark and silent like a ship, lies the isle of Santa Mónica. Far off to the right, fading blue into the distance, the shore. And if the day is clear, towards the south, like a lattice, the planes of grey and white of the highest towers in Buenos Aires can be seen, under the oppression of a constant grey cloud.

When strong winds from the north or the west cause a *bajante*, the water level plunges, and an area of sandbank rises up above the surface; after the *bajante*, it seems that terra firma has extended its dimensions, the springs that cross the reed bed feigning newly settled streams. There are fishermen who venture onto this new land, which is wet and desolate, but if they don't lay out the lattice matting from their boats, they sink into its mud, and almost to their knees.

The most recent of the charts marks the mouth of the Anguilas with a fish's silhouette, to show abundant catches here, but this is rather doubtful. In any case, there's nothing more daft than taking note of references like these. If there are certain fishermen who come to lay their nets here, at night, and in the week, it's owing more to the fact that the area is little frequented at those times. This wretched habit makes them think the place is theirs, and the unsuspecting soul who takes advantage of their head rope runs the risk they'll sink his boat, and with gunfire, too. Once upon a time, Polo had to shoot his way out, letting fly at either bank, and then towards the reeds, with that aged English shotgun, the 1903 Purdey with its sawn-off steel barrels that he kept for such occasions. He bottom-trawled his nets across this very stretch of sandbank, seizing on a surge, and once out on the open sea he pulled the catch on board. He sold in San Fernando when a little time had passed. But this is now an old tale. It's a long time since Polo disappeared. The fishermen are still around, though, and in the week, at night, they lay their nets.

He was working with the old man almost until spring. It was nine years or so the old man had lived on the Anguilas, and for seven he was living from the reeds. He came down from the Romero in the year of '48, where, from '34, he'd been working in the apples. It was the year of '47 that the *Elbita*, a six-ton fruit barge, foundered, drowning the only son who'd stayed with them. So then in '48, and already getting old, he came to the Anguilas in the *Elbita*'s little rowing boat. He made two journeys. One with their belongings, and the other with the old girl and Urbano, the dog, and two or three chickens. They made themselves a home in one of three empty cabins, the one closest to the river mouth, just where the Anguilas joins that blind little stream that peters out a little further on, often thought to be a prolongation of the Anguilas by those who don't know any better. He'd been confused himself in '48.

The cabin had two rooms, or really just the one, which was divided by a mud wall. As the years went by, the old man added two more rooms and put up a latrine, which he sited at the far end. Time made a group of the various parts, bringing them together in a dark and bulging mass, with two or three little openings, even darker still. Its base was very high and pretty badly bound together, with several rotten cross-beams. Over time it gave way on one side, the weakest, so the cabin gently leaned in that direction.

The stream was so narrow here you couldn't build a jetty. It was doubtful that the old man would have built one even so. Instead of this, he fixed a willow gangway to the bank, and tied the little boat from the *Elbita* to a cross-beam.

Everyone's aware that the more you crop the reeds, the more they will grow. When many folk are cropping them, and cropping them too hard, a market glut will follow, and no one's going to pay much for another shed of reeds. There's nothing more accursed nor more wretched. And, sad to say, there seem to be people on these islands who do nothing else.

Something like this happened just a couple of years ago, and the year after that, this last, no one cropped the reeds, or didn't try to sell, at least. The old man didn't either and hunger almost killed him. But he faced it all with dignity, on most days eating catfish, or, come the winter, silverside, which he called *latterino*, or else *lattarina*, and which are, after all, the rations of kings.

And so, the following year, the last one for the old man, the reeds picked up a bit.

Boga came along when the cropping had just started, and they'd worked together since, until this spring was almost here.

In the dead year, which is to say the year before, the old man finished work on the straw-and-willow refuge he'd begun three years earlier, which was when Urbano died. He built it very low and didn't put in any walls, but placed it on a rise, beside a solitary *ceibo*. The old man dug the floor out to a depth of half a metre and built a sort of stove into one corner. They used it at midday or when the weather turned inclement. They ate a piece of pork belly with sea bread, then they drank some maté. Sometimes Boga grilled a catfish, when they'd caught one on the line, but really he preferred to take them home. Then they slept a while. The old man slept sitting up, with his head laid on his knees and his arms around his legs.

Neither the old man nor Boga ever said more than was needed. And yet they understood each other perfectly. At dawn, they walked into this green and humming solitude that swayed with every gust of wind. Each one made his own path, stepping through the water. At times it reached their thighs, but they didn't seem to notice. Beyond the wall of green, out towards this River Plate which the folk here call the open sea, they heard the water murmur as it rolled tirelessly across the sandbank. The distant, sorry screaming of a limpkin. The suffocated din of a motor launch, still further off. The sand boats with their rhythmic beating diesel engines as they travelled the canal. The boiling of the Glosters in the clouds as they leapt the sky in one, chased by their own din.

The old man had a skill – never mind his age. When he gathered up the reeds from where he'd laid them to dry, spread out on the rise around the refuge that he'd built, he did it with a briskness that was staggering to see, and even with a certain elegance. He caught them in one swipe and, continuing the movement, shook the reeds out straight and then bound them in a sheaf, tying each one round with another reed in a final little flourish. Boga had neither this skill nor this degree of devotion to a matter that he didn't think called for artistry. In fact he felt a little bored, although he had a patience or, to call it what it really was, an indifference that never tired. What gave him pleasure was to gaze out from the refuge at the carpet of reeds, which he'd spread out with the old man and which now shone darkly in the sun, giving this lonely corner the appearance of an island in the tropics.

When it was the time, the old man swapped the reeds for cat's tail or bulrush. It didn't look the same when there was straw laid on the ground, but it served them just as well.

At times they took along with them the cream-coloured dog, but the old man would get angry when it went off in the reeds and barked all the time, so he preferred not to bring it. But the dog would turn up in any case, at some point in the day, and start with its barking. The old man would let it go a while, as if he hadn't noticed. And then he'd stand up straight, like a spring, and fire off a curse that seemed to land right on the bullseye. They heard the rushing noise from in among the reeds, and listened as it went away towards the house. The old man didn't feel much real fondness for this dog, although he saw it had its uses. The old woman, on the other hand, was fonder of the cream-coloured dog than of Urbano.

When Boga asked the old man if he'd lend him the double-barrelled shotgun, which had been hanging near the headboard since the day he'd arrived, the old man looked him in the eyes and didn't say a word. Two months after that, when you'd imagine he'd forgotten, he took the shotgun off its hook and put it in the passage, leaned it up against the wall right next to Boga, who was lying there, puffing on a cigarette. Boga took the gun onto the boat from that day on, and kept it on the floor between his feet while he was rowing. He worked out in the reeds with the shotgun there to hand, hanging on a forked stick that he'd pressed into the mud. When a limpkin or another bird he thought was worth the trouble paused nearby, he gathered up the shotgun with a straightening of his arm. The shot rang harsh and sad, like a punch across the vastness, rolling on and on across the undulating field, and then across the water, and after that the nearest islands. Once back in the house, down on the floor of the veranda, he cleaned and stripped the shotgun down, absorbed in his meticulous attention to the work. It was a Belgian shotgun, a Pirlot & Frésart, that took 12-cal cartridges of 65 mm. He would have given his all to own this gun, but he knew that the old man prized it just as much as he did. What he might instead dare ask him for, at some point, was the Sheffield knife he used to cut all kinds of things, including his cigars.

The old man did his work barefoot, in trousers that were worn out, cut off just below the knee, and wearing two jackets which he tied round with sisal. Boga himself wore a sweater with a high neck and a pair of long johns with a fly that was sewn closed. It was dirty work, and hard, and it numbed them by degrees. The wind buzzed round their heads continuously, on most days, rather like a swarm of wasps, dizzying them and stabbing at the skin on their faces.

Boga took the lines in when the light began to fail, and then they would go back to the house, dead tired and ill-tempered. He didn't take his long johns off but pulled trousers over them and lay down in a corner of the passage. The old man, on the other hand, gave himself a wash that seemed to go on an eternity, then put on a clean, fleece, collarless shirt, full-length trousers and a pair of Pirelli boots. Then, on the veranda, he sat and used his Sheffield knife to cut one of his Avantis and smoked it until dinner time, very slowly, with the cream-coloured dog beside him, looking at the river, looking at the heavens, looking at the night begin in silence. The old woman lit a lamp.

The old man would get up first, in the grey light of the dawn. Boga listened to him prowl around the house (the only time he did seem old), until the slow, heavy steps grew loud towards his room. He let fly with a kick against the door, then went away. It was his one show of authority, and Boga understood it as such, for it made no other sense. Both knew it was useless. He'd been awake a long time, and knew just how the light grew in the cracks that lined the door, and how, at a certain point, the light and the kick would meet.

But this day, just before the spring, the light rose past that moment and he didn't hear the kick; he hadn't even heard the footsteps, slow and rather heavy, make their way towards his room. He'd only heard some muted steps at dawn. And now he doubted even that. Then the steps had stopped and the light grew on alone. Now the day had come. The vague shapes of his feet were there, opening in a V. He was still lying on his back, his ears alert despite himself, looking at a small hole in the roof that shone like money.

He heard the half-past-seven plane that came in from the south and seemed to roll across the roof, then he got out of bed. He stood there in the half-light with the silence lifting from the floor, or seeming to lift, before it flooded through the room. He went into the passage then, smoothing down his hair with both his hands.

He saw the old man there at the far end of the passage, sitting in the reed chair with a blanket on his legs. He was looking at the river.

Boga paused and looked, still standing in the doorway of his room, his eyes half-closed, but his face betraying no surprise. The cream-coloured dog was lying close beside the old man and, sensing him there, it raised its ears. He went into the kitchen that was always left in darkness, with its soot-layered walls that smelled of smoke from long ago, and had a feeling the old woman was waiting in a corner, looking out at him and the old man and, beyond them, at the river. The old woman had put the kettle on the range but not quite on the flame, so the water wouldn't boil, and left the maté ready in its upturned lid. Just as every day. He reached up to the bag that was hanging on the wall and took himself some sea bread, which he stored under his sweater. He went into the passage with the maté and the kettle, and sat down on the floor.

The old man's face was thin and gaunt and unshaven, his beard now growing as if sprouting from an overhang.

Boga threw some sea bread to the cream-coloured dog, but the dog merely sniffed at it and went on with its sleeping.

'Those reeds,' the old man said, 'they must be dry by now. They can come inside today, in what's left of today.'

The dull hum of the fire could be heard here in the passage, stirred up by the suction of the chimney.

'Ok . . . '

'They can come inside today and then tomorrow go to San Fernando.'

'Ok . . . '

'While you're there, you're going to bring back several things we need.'

'Ok . . . '

They heard a launch out in the distance.

'It's nine o'clock.'

'Shit!'

'You'd better make a start.'

Boga got up from the floor.

'What's wrong with you, old man?'

'I'm not going. No.' He made a gesture of annoyance. 'You'd better make a start.'

'Ok . . . '

Going down the willow steps, he paused and turned around and clicked just once with his fingers. The dog got to its feet with no visible transition from total relaxation to absolute mobility, and jumped aboard the boat before he'd got there.

He gathered in the reeds and killed a pair of scrub-hens that he came upon near the sandbank, and he returned when it was dusk.

The old man was still there, sitting quietly in the passage with the blanket on his legs. He'd listened to the barking of the dog out in the distance; he'd heard it through the day until the time the shots rang out.

Boga crossed in front of him as he went towards the kitchen.

'The buggers with the net were there.'

'Fuck 'em!'

'And Old Bastos.'

'What did he say, seeing I wasn't there?'

'Nothing.'

The old man sat there thinking. Boga took the pair of scrub-hens into the kitchen and held them out at arm's length, towards the corner where he felt the woman waited.

'And the reeds?' the old man said.

'They're done.'

The old man sank back in his thoughts. Among other things, he was tormented by what that lousy Bastos might have said.

The old woman came out from the shadows and leaned down across the range. Boga touched her shoulder and, when she turned to face him, he gestured to the old man.

'He says he's going to die,' she said, and shrugged.

Boga gave a frown.

'It's what he's saying now.'

And Boga gave a shrug before he went back to the passage. It struck him as hilarious.

'Hey, stop mucking around, old man,' he said, and brought a snigger up from somewhere very deep inside and laughed it in the old man's face.

'It's true,' the old man said.

'Where'd you get this idea from?'

'I know exactly what I'm saying.'

'Yeah, don't make me laugh!'

'I'm on my way out, son. You can believe me or not.'

Boga felt a bit disturbed.

'You'll soon put this behind you. Whatever it is you've got. I can't see anything wrong with you.'

'There's nothing to put behind me. It's time for me to die . . . that's all.'

Boga gave a shrug.

'All right, whatever you say.'

The next day he went down to San Fernando with the reeds. It was something that the old man did, but now that he was busy with his dying it was down to Boga. Up to now, he'd simply loaded the bundles on the boat and gone along. It wasn't easy work fitting them all onto the barge, owned by Deaf Angarita, but they always did it in the end. The old man would get dressed as if to sit there in the passage, in his clean, collarless fleece shirt, and then he'd put on his waistcoat and knot on his neckerchief, both of which were black, and then came his black and very wide-brimmed hat, which had a high, round crown and which he pulled down straight onto his head, and then his pocket watch with its heavy silver chain. Boga, for his part, put on trousers and a coat, and then Pirelli boots, the same kind as the old man's, but his had two red patches. He did the steering on the way out and then, when they were coming back, the old man insisted on his turn at the tiller. He would wander round the town while the old man pursued his business, and sometimes went as far as Pona's, where for fifteen pesos he could take her to bed, or else one of her two daughters, depending on whichever of the three was in the house.

Now it fell to him to do the whole job on his own, the old man's part as well, and it all became quite difficult.

*

Old Bastos showed his face when a couple of days had passed. As expected. He roamed around the sandbank with his boat that was half-rotten and the rod he always fished with.

'What does that man want here?' said the old man, to say something.

Old Bastos was his only friend, and yet they seemed to loathe each other, going by appearances. There'd never been a time when they didn't end up bickering, as if they were possessed, and once the old man had emptied both the barrels of his shotgun through the air above his friend's head.

For a time the Pajarito was where Bastos lived (the New Canal, to use its proper name), between the Pacú and Anguilas, but then three years ago he'd made the move to the Anguilas, where the stream is at its narrowest. He had been living on his own ever since Cabecita – a halfwit he'd picked up on the Antequera during the 1940 flood tide, when he'd seen the idiot clinging for his life to a canoe already sinking in the middle of the river – had drowned on the sandbanks. No one ever knew quite where this Cabecita came from. Not that it concerned them much. Since Cabecita disappeared, he'd lived on his own with his two mottled dogs, just skin and bone.

They heard the sorry squealing of the rowlocks in the gloom long before the little boat came into view. The squealing rose and fell with an exasperating rhythm in the sleepy quiet of dusk. Boga had arrived back shortly before they heard him coming, and flopped down in the passage just as Bastos hobbled up the rubble path. He looked up at the old man from the bottom of the steps, peering out from underneath the wide brim of his hat.

'Hey!'

'Hey.'

'What is it you're doing there, sitting like an old man?'

'Being an old man.'

'It's the first I've heard of it.'

'Who says you have to hear it?'

Old Bastos scratched behind his ear and spat into the distance.

'Ok, ok . . . so what is it you're doing?'

'You can see what I'm doing.'

'I can see you're sitting down.'

'That's what I'm doing.'

'Which isn't saying much.'

'I do what the hell I want. Is that all right with you?'

'It seems all right with me.'

He started up the steps.

'I don't see why it's anybody's business,' said the old man, shuffling himself forward as if he meant to jump.

'There's no talking to this chap, then,' said Bastos.

'Don't you call me chap.'

'It's just a way of speaking. There's no harm in it I can see.'

'Well I can see the harm!'

The old woman came out then, and looked across at Bastos.

'I asked him what he's doing, nothing more than that.'

'Don't give me that!' the old man yelled, and turned his head away.

'What is it he's doing, sitting there?' Bastos said.

'He says he's dying.'

Bastos looked hard at him and he frowned. He looked worried now.

'He could do it, to be awkward,' he said at last, and scratched behind his ear.

*

The river spreads wide and silent, and is bleak on the sandbanks.

He worked the season on his own, although the dog came with him sometimes and became his only company. He went into the reed beds a little after dawn and, most days, didn't even stop at midday for a break, to take a rest back at the shelter. When the water level dropped he made himself a bed of reeds and lay down for half an hour. As a rule, he went back to the shelter when the water rose, or else he stopped just long enough to chew a piece of sea bread with a slice of pork belly, and to smoke the longest stub that he could find in his pockets.

The wind pulled at the river, and above its rippled surface was the changing sea of green in which he worked. He heard the whistling curl itself around him, like a serpent, and then the beating heart of this colossal solitude. He took this world around with him, wherever he might find himself. The wind had aged his hands and face of tight and weathered skin. The distance emptied out his eyes, the isolation turned him pensive, melancholic.

The droning of the aeroplanes first blossoms and then withers overhead from side to side across the sky. After that, the silence. The engine of a motor boat is howling in distress somewhere far off in the distance, which teases the sound. A dark bird vents a lonely screech and rises into flight. Then he hears the dog bark, all the notes astonishingly uniform and sad. When at last the barking stops, his ears continue throbbing. Closer by, the constant chafing sound of the reeds, and the mud that gurgles underneath his feet. The thick and steady booming of the sand boats on the channel gives a warm sense of bonanza.

*

He returned to San Fernando on two or three occasions, and once down to the Tigre, to the River Corporation yard, where he'd picked up a two-cylinder Ailsa Craig engine – this was some time back in the autumn – which, in short, did not do the job they'd had in mind for it.

The old man, at that time, was involved with Colorado Chico, trying to buy the hull of a seven-metre fishing boat. Its keel was of *lapacho* and its planking made of *viraró*. Built by José Parodi, it had been on sale in '39, but with a British 40–50 h.p. engine and new gaff sails. All for 2,800 pesos, cash in hand. Now Colorado Chico wanted 15,000 pesos, and that just for the empty hull.

While they were in talks, the old man bought the Ailsa Craig for 4,500 pesos, thinking of the fishing boat. To summarise what happened, it was Colorado Chico who ended up purchasing the Ailsa Craig; the old man sold it on to him, together with two camp beds with woodworm in the legs.

There was a week of rising waters while the weather was still cold. He gathered the trammel nets, loaded up the *Elbita* and went out on the Sueco, for the last few days of the silverside fishing. This time, when he came back, he found the old man somewhat changed. He'd been changing all the time, but it took those days away for Boga to see it for himself. Perhaps the old man had been right after all. He seemed to be much skinnier, and yellow.

He went back to the sandbank, but this was when he started to neglect the work in hand. He fired the shotgun far more often than he had before, and set up two more fishing lines, with five hooks on each. He anchored one as close to the river mouth as possible, and then the other two, which included the one he'd started with, at twenty-metre intervals.

He was baiting the lines on the morning when he heard Colorado Chico's boat coming from the Pajarito. He'd stopped off at the house, most likely.

He heard the engine once again a half-hour later but now, instead of heading west, the droning grew towards him.

He'd gone into the reeds. It was coming here for certain. So he headed for the shore.

When the boat came into view, as it turned the final bend, he was some way from the bank, standing up there on the top beside the shelter, to be seen.

Colorado Chico cut the engine of the boat – the same craft that he'd used when he'd brought down the Ailsa Craig – and let its momentum land it very gently on the shore.

The man waved.

'Hello!'

'Hi!'

'How you getting on?'

Boga shrugged his shoulders. Colorado rubbed his neck. He had a heavy build, with a reddish face and hair.

'I've just come from the house,' he said. 'That old man's really buggered. I don't know if you've realised that, the pair of you . . . '

Boga shrugged his shoulders.

'I'd take him down to San Fernando Hospital if I were you.'

'They'll kill him there and no mistake.'

'This isn't some kind of joke.'

'How would we do that?'

'I've explained it to the old woman.'

They stood there in the silence for a while.

Boga shook his head. 'We'll have to see.'

'If you want to, you can use my boat.'

'We'll see.'

'As you like. If it's decided that you'll take him, come and get it at the house . . . '

He started up the engine and reversed out at full throttle.

'Hey!' he shouted then, from the middle of the river.

Boga cupped his hand behind his ear.

'I sold on the Ailsa Craig, to Della Vedone!'

'Didn't that old codger die?'

'Not yet, no.'

'I'm glad.'

That can happen with these engines. You pass the dud on to someone else. And everyone makes something, except the one who tries to get it going.

'See you!'

'See you!'

At first he showed some interest, but then as time went by he didn't ask about the reed bed. Sometimes Boga told him this or that to let him know, but when he saw the old man didn't listen to his words, he said no more about it. He was thinner still by now, and yellower.

Old Bastos came more often, but he tried, if he could, not to argue. He spoke of very general things, or else he didn't speak. He also grew to understand the old man didn't listen. The three stayed in the passage, dispirited and silent, as if they were expecting that the night would bring some news.

The sight of the old man became etched into his big eyes that were like those of a dying fish, so even when the shadows came he'd see the old man's face before him, looking rather awful, eaten by some inner flame. The old man was a long way off. It was a while since he'd died and now only his spirit remained, but turned away to other things, towards a point so distant that the others couldn't see it.

'Spring is here already,' Bastos said, to say something.

It would have made them glad to see the spring in other times, but now they were so gloomy that it seemed to be for others in the world, not for them.

Boga felt a jolt, notwithstanding all of this, in the depths of his being, a kind of dark call. It really was the spring. October is the end of the winter fishing season. Now the *patí* season starts. The colour of the light would now be different on the river, on the sandbanks.

He shifted in the shadows, feeling suddenly unsettled, something in him restless, and reached out with his toes to brush the cream-coloured dog. The dog got up and moved to lie a little further off.

No one said a word but no one could forget the thing that Bastos had announced. He felt the spring had started with that unforeseen revelation. A tingling that unnerved him ran around inside his body. He braced himself against the boards and lit a cigarette. He'd been too long among them. And now they felt like strangers. The old woman scuffed around in the darkness of the kitchen. The fire's glow made its way out through the doorway. Now she'd light the lamp.

When everyone was finally convinced that the old man was dying, Boga noticed something faint, a note of pleasure on his face, perhaps a note of jest. It seemed as if it pleased him that they'd finally agreed.

Spring was now advanced and Bastos, to say something, said:

'I'm thinking of putting an engine in this little boat.'

No one said a thing.

'What do you think, friend?'

'That it's rotten.'

'It's not in its bottom, and that's where it counts ... They've told me there's one going, in the Corporation yard.'

'It wouldn't be an Ailsa Craig?'

Bastos gave a shrug.

'If you're going past that way, I'd like it if you had a look.'

'No harm in that.'

When they first spoke of taking him, the old man cursed them all. The second time, he drove a burning look into each one, a look that was condensed, as if two flames had lighted in the depths of his eyes, but so deep it was incredible.

This last time it was mentioned, he neither said nor did a thing.

They dressed him in his best fleece shirt, his wide-brimmed black hat, his waistcoat and the neckerchief that matched it.

Boga had gone off to look for Colorado Chico's launch. The cream-coloured dog began to bark when he appeared, as if it didn't know him.

Bastos helped him down the steps, his arm around his waist, while the old woman shut and barred the doors. The sky was cool and limpid and the morning shone below it. The gently leaning house, all the trees, the little path, they seemed strangely still and silent, made sleepy by the sun. Men were setting out. Silence would move in, and a peaceful kind of sadness. Something, like a secret veil, kept men and things apart.

The old man stopped along the path, halfway to the bank. He patted at the pockets of his waistcoat.

'My watch,' he said at last, in a whisper.

His voice was strange and deep and, in a certain way, urgent.

The old woman turned around and went back for the watch, and they stood there without moving, not knowing what to do, slightly annoyed, as if they weren't really needed.

The old woman reappeared and shuffled her way sideways down the steps, as she always had, leaning on the handrail. She was holding the watch and carried a blanket on her arm. It was the first time that he'd seen her in this floral-print dress, cut too short and just a little youthful for her age. It was sure to be her only one, and dating back forever. She also wore a straw hat that was wide and flat, with cloth flowers stuck on one side. The ensemble was a little sad and also rather comical. She'd put on woollen stockings but she kept her brown ankle socks over the top and was wearing a pair of men's shoes. Signalling the journey was her black, enormous leather purse that hung down from one arm.

Once they'd put his watch on, the old man moved again. This was the moment when the cream-coloured dog, which had gone back to the passage with the old woman and was shifting restively, let out a plaintive bark and tumbled down the steps. When they took the old man on the launch it started to whine, sniffing at the vessel from the bank.

'Watch that one, it wants to jump,' said Bastos.

Boga waved his fist and the dog backed off a little. There it stayed, fidgeting, until they moved away.

'Ok, let's go,' said Bastos.

Then the old man got to his feet. He cast his gaze one last time across the empty house, then across the trees, and then along the footpath. The dog had fallen silent, looking at him with just a glint of hope.

He sat down at last. Boga got the engine going. The old man stared ahead now, his eyes towards that secret point.

They left.

The dog followed on, running quickly down the bank. It got ahead at one point but fell behind before they'd made it to the outlet, as the launch gathered speed.

But they still heard its barks for some time to come, stubbornly pursuing them across the river.

They waited for an hour in that white room lit by sunlight. The old couple sat there together on a bench. She was barely on its front edge, her purse in her lap and both hands on the purse. Boga waited standing; he moved his hands around at first, not knowing what to do with them, then stood completely motionless. They looked somewhat defeated.

A nurse asked them two or three times what they wanted, and two or three times they answered slowly and laboriously.

Boga at last said, while searching for a stub:

'That bitch thinks she's the boss.'

They listened to her cluck behind a door of frosted glass. It opened once or twice, and through it they could see a bit of trolley and a glass case, above it an electric clock. At last the door opened for them and they made their way inside.

The doctor went on speaking to the nurse for quite a time, as if they were alone. He hadn't even given them a look when they'd come in. They waited, still and silent, watching the pair without the slightest interest in their words. Then the doctor stopped and turned, awkwardly, to have a look.

His look confronted Boga's for something like a second, and then he turned away, his composure rather lost.

'Well, and what's the problem?' he asked the nurse instead of them, taking up that cold-blooded tone that public servants use.

'You're asking me!' the woman said, with a shrug. 'I can't make them out.'

'So you will have to tell me,' the doctor said, turning round to face them.

Boga tried again, still more slowly and laboriously, certain from the outset that they wouldn't understand him.

He signalled at the old man. 'He said that he was going to die. It's some time since he said it . . . '

The other man stood and waited. Then he made a gesture as if to say, 'And what else?'

'Well, I think he's doing it . . . '

The doctor glanced at the nurse as if to make a joke but turned back without speaking, and searched the old man's face with a sudden look of kindness.

'And what have you to say, old chap?' He approached the old man as he said it.

'I don't think he'll answer you,' Boga said at last.

'Well, that doesn't matter . . . I think we'd better take a look.'

They crossed the giant ward, between two lines of beds, pre-ceded by the nurse and a nun. They walked close together, as huddled as possible, not daring any sideways looks but feel-ing all the eyes in those gloomy faces turned towards them. Bastos smelled the medicine and instantly felt ill.

They went into a side ward that only had four beds, two already occupied. Like animals in wait, the patients pulled themselves up and observed the new arrivals with a look of some resentment. The old woman set to stripping the old man of his clothes, then they put him in an empty bed.

'The padre will come to see him later on,' said the nun. 'I'm certain that the old chap will have many things to tell him. Isn't that so?' she added, trying to make it friendly.

'And what padre's that?' said Boga, believing she was joking.

'What padre do you think?' Bastos said, trying to set things right while not quite sure himself. 'The Heavenly Father, probably.'

The nun was dismayed and gave them a look, believing in her turn that this was some kind of joke.

'It's not a laughing matter,' she said, maintaining her decorum, and smoothing down her habit with her hands.

'No, madam!' Bastos said, needing to say something, and feeling that the smell would drive him mad. 'Not on your life.'

The nun's skirts rustled as she slipped out of the room. Bastos thought she looked just like a boat with all its sails up; he felt quite relieved as he watched her move away, as if she were walking among clouds.

'It's better if you go now,' said the nurse after that. 'Visits are on Tuesdays and Thursdays, two till four, and Sundays, one till five.'

They felt bereft as they listened, and she seemed to understand.

'Don't worry about the old chap. He'll be fine here with us.'

The old woman went to smooth the sheets on the bed, and also the old man's hair and his best fleece shirt, which he still had on in bed. He looked like a small creature captured in a corner. She tried to delay, begging his forgiveness with that look of desolation, astonishingly meek and sweet and sad. And then at last she kissed him on the forehead, and went.

Boga paused beside the door, his fingers on the handle.

'See you then, old man!' he said, forcing out a smile. 'There's no need to worry about anything. It will all turn out fine.'

The spring was almost over. He continued in the reed bed, all the time working his way closer to the sandbanks, along the open sea.

The singing of the islands sounded more intense each day. It was always in his ears.

Now he also stayed there by the lines all through the night, stretching himself out in the bottom of the boat, looking at the stars as they made their steady journey. A curious disquiet was eating him inside. The summer wasn't far off.

As long as it continued, the old woman went to San Fernando every Tuesday, also on Thursdays and Sundays. Most times with Old Bastos. On these days he was left with the older man's rotting boat. He could reach the sandbanks on foot if he went along the shore, but he might need the boat for something else. When he had a load he had to carry to San Fernando, he chose one of those three days or, to be precise, one of the two weekdays when visiting was allowed. He went all the way to the hospital with a half-pound of chocolate, a bag of sweets, a basket of fruit and some newspapers. The old man didn't touch them but he took them all the same.

He sat between the beds on a cast-iron stool and looked up at the old man, mostly saying nothing much. The old man seemed to overlook this presence by his side, but once he turned and fixed him with a long and steady look, as if he'd just remembered him.

He spoke from time to time for the sake of saying something, although not sure that the other would be listening.

'I brought three hundred bundles today . . . at eleven pesos a bundle. I've heard Fat Soriano pays two pesos more . . . I'm going to start the cutting on the other bank tomorrow . . . still the same sandbank . . . depending how things are. The moon brought the *bajante* this time. If it carries on like this . . . '

He looked at the old man through his big eyes of a dying fish. It was pretty clear to see that he wasn't listening. Even so, he said:

'I'd like your opinion, about Fat Soriano . . . '

No, he wasn't listening.

'I wouldn't mix with that old skinflint if I were you,' one of the other patients said. 'Not for anything in the world!'

Boga turned towards the haggard face.

'The last laugh is the longest,' the nasal voice insisted, shifting in his bed.

Boga shook his head, unable to decide.

'That scumbag always has some brilliant scheme on the go. Remember the otter farm?'

'They say he ripped off half the country.' This, from the second patient, came muttered in a thin, cracked voice.

'Not me.'

'You're one of the other half then . . . '

'And that business of the Co-op . . . '

'Ah! A cracking piece of fiction that was . . . '

'It was indeed, yes . . . '

'What a splendid chap! Ha, ha!'

'A son of a bitch, more like.'

And the voices gathered life on either side, like distant blinking beacons on a night out on your own, and he listened to them in a way, but only to the sound, to the sighing that they made, not even thinking what the words were, and much less what they meant, absorbed by these two faces, a pair of trembling smudges in the half-light of the room. The first voice was embittered, crushed into itself. The second a little shout, a sterile sound in fact, something odd and set apart that came from just in front of the shrunken face now fighting with the shadows.

'There are a lot inland who get rich with that business.'

'Inland's full of idiots . . . but here . . . when did it ever happen here?'

'Don't you believe it . . . '

'Come on! Everyone's a smart-arse here . . . '

'There's always one who takes them for a ride . . . '

'There are plenty of men shrewder than Fat Soriano.'

'The man's a real expert.'

'I wouldn't go that far.'

'An expert.'

'Do you think so?'

'Do I think what?'

'That he's an expert.'

'But what did I just say? Ha, ha! You're on another planet. Are you feeling all right?'

'Of course I'm feeling all right! Better by the minute.'

'Oh, yeah!'

'I'll be out of here any day now, rattling my bones about. Didn't you hear the nun?'

'I wasn't listening to the nun.'

'Any day now . . . '

And the voices sounded fainter all the time, and grew more distant, like the whisper of the heavy sea on a sandbank.

The same thing had happened every time. Every time he'd tried to have a talk with the old man.

He crossed onto the other bank just two days after this. The men with the net were back, and that was when he met them, in the middle of the river.

'Hi there!'

'Hi!'

They came from time to time, always busy and hurrying. He crossed behind their head rope.

They turn up here today, tomorrow over there. As if they sprung up from the river. They had a certain shiftiness, an air of something volatile. He didn't recall their faces when he saw them, in all truth. All he could remember was the shadows of the men and the gentle curve of the head rope. He saw them on the river and his feeling was of worry and nostalgia.

'Are you on some fish?' he said as he was passing.

'Nothing worth the trouble . . . '

'There's less and less here now . . . '

'For some time now on this part . . . '

'The nets of the fish-oil plant let nothing through at all.'

'It's not just that in any case . . . it's not as if they're close.'

'It's what I hear people say.'

'But all fish have their good and bad patches . . . '

Boga lit a cigarette and then, for the first time, he looked into their faces. They were toughened and inscrutable, moulded by the harshness of the winters. Their eyes looked rather dazzled, blind even.

'What happened with the silverside?'

'We've nothing to complain of there . . . this time we tried right next to Baldissera's hull, searching out the harder sandy beaches. It's a pretty decent place to drop a paternoster line . . . '

'So they say . . . '

'Then we took the trammels to the mouth of the Guazú, all the way beyond Martín García. There you find the Gran Paraná.'

'That's what they say.'

'You've never been up there?'

'Not to fish, no.'

'There's not much for a rod, in truth . . . there's isn't a bit of shelter for a craft in all those places . . . only drift fishing, and then in decent weather . . . '

'I see . . . '

'Nothing's for sure, of course . . . the silverside have their ways, like all these little fellas . . . '

'As everybody says . . . '

'To begin with, they don't bite in the same way everywhere . . . the Paraná silverside has a bite that's distinctive . . . it takes the line off one way first, away against the current, and then it sinks the float. You have to rod the other way.' He gave a demonstration. His speech was slow and satisfied. 'A bite on open water, far out from the shore, isn't always equal . . . you're not sure if it's silverside, or bucktooth, or the sea bream . . . '

One of the men was following the head rope back towards them in another boat, close in to the shore. The fisherman had stopped his talk, and watched the man, annoyed. The water now rushed powerfully out towards the river mouth.

The high points of the sandbank had begun to break the surface.

'At the start, you find the best bites happen at dawn. In the middle of the season, it's best at night. In the spring, it's as at the start.'

They heard the squeal of rowlocks coming on in their direction, getting louder.

'Of course, it all depends . . . if it's a cloudy afternoon, and cold, and then the south-east wind lifts and the river rises slowly, that's when the silverside are there . . .'

'It's what happens with the *tararira* . . . '

'They're woken by cool water . . . '

'I've seen it in late afternoon . . . the water rising evenly . . . '

The men had seen the lines. Sometimes just the lines and at other times him setting them.

'The time is getting close for going upstream, to the north.' The man had said it to himself.

Boga looked at him awhile.

'That's what I was thinking . . . '

'The dorado are upriver.'

It seemed as if he spoke of things that waited far away. He looked into the man's face, as if trying to read it.

'Anyway, it's not as if you have to go so far,' he said, with just a hint of bitterness.

'No, of course you don't . . . there are those who are quite satisfied to stay at Punta Temor.'

'That's what I'm saying . . . where the Felicaria joins the Aguaje del Durazno.'

'All along the sandbank is a good place for manduví and dorado . . . in their season . . . come in from the Paycarabí, you'll find a spot to anchor, and well sheltered too . . . '

'I've done it in a rowing boat and coming from the Sueco, along that very sandbank.'

'It's all good fishing there . . . where all those rivers drain into the Bajo del Temor . . . everyone agrees on that . . . '

'Punta Morán, most of all . . . '

'No doubt . . . '

The man stopped for a moment. It seemed as if he studied something far out in the distance, away above his shoulder.

'Even so, all of this is nothing in comparison with going to the rapids of the Upper Paraná . . . '

'I've heard some talk of that,' Boga said in spun-out words, in his whisper of a voice.

'Itatí, the Jupiter Strait, the shoals at Mboi-Mbusú, the Itá-Cuá Strait, the Corpus Falls, Apipé, the shoals at Paranay . . . '

The voice was growing distant. The sound of all these names in the spring, with summer close.

The other boat was near them.

'What is it?' called the man as if a bit annoyed.

'See you then!'

'See you!'

He turned the boat towards the other bank and set to row. He listened to the voices, close at first, then far off, blown on by the wind.

The old man died exactly when the summer came along. As if he'd been delaying it, waiting for this moment. Many things then happened, decisive in their way, and important even though they'd go unnoticed.

Colorado Chico came to find them on his launch and they knew the day had come.

'Let's go!' was all he said. And they went.

They'd put him in a small room, alone.

'Looks like you're a big shot now,' said Bastos.

It was two days since he'd known who people were. His eyes, even deeper now, were all that there was left, still shining while the rest of him had slowly drained away.

A couple of hours went by like this, the four of them just watching him, dumb and feeling sorry, not knowing what to do.

A pair of nuns then entered and began to cite the rosary. It made them feel still more distressed. What did they think they were doing? When they understood that the old man's time had come, the old woman moved towards the bed and stroked his hair. There was an unspeakable tenderness and care in it.

And then the old man sat up in the bed and looked at each of them with curious lucidity.

He seemed serene and victorious and stately.

He took hold of his wife's hand.

'Old girl!'

And nothing else.

The men leap from the grave and mop their sweat with their shirtsleeves. Recovering their breath. The small group and the men look at each other mistrustfully. Boga sees their muddy boots, splitting at the seams and very slowly sinking down into the wet earth of the mound. They hold on to the shovels with a small show of impatience.

The place feels quiet and empty, like the islands on the open sea. White gravestones and white crosses doze in the sun.

'Right!' one of the men says, and both take up the coffin, and then they let it run to the bottom on the ropes.

They stop then and they wait, but no one makes a move.

The man says:

'Throw the first earth in.'

The old woman picks up a lump and throws it on the coffin. The others use their feet. The clods land with a dead sound, a little like the rain, when they drop onto the lid. The two men begin to shovel strongly now. When they finish there's just a little hill of loose earth. No one understands how they've done it all so quickly.

The men leave, but the small group stays, uncertain what to do. The old woman holds the bunch of flowers in her hand, her eyes completely dry. They look at her in glances, waiting for a sign. Colorado speaks at last.

'It's best we go, old girl.'

She lifts her eyes towards him, with that ageless, gentle manner that resigns itself to everything. She bends towards the ground and puts the flowers on the hill of loose earth.

They go. Then when they reach the gate, Bastos says:

'Well, he got his way. Once he had an idea in his head, there was no stopping him.'

The river always changes. At times it's hard and brutal, at others it seems measured for a man.

The start of summer came at the same time as December's great *bajante*, lasting five days. They watched the waters falling and the river go on emptying as if it wouldn't stop. At night there were recoveries, but nothing much to speak of, and within a couple of hours the water turned around again and headed out towards the open sea, thicker all the time, dragging mud up from the riverbed.

Boga and the cream-coloured dog went about plastered head to toe in muck. The dog seemed pretty pleased with things. For the others, a kind of irritation was developing, suppressed, but always there. Now he spent the nights sleeping stretched out in the passage, the dog across his feet, with the mud stuck on his skin drying out and tightening. The cuts and drains that flowed into the watercourse were infinite, their soporific murmuring still louder in the night, so it got into his blood. The clicking of the catfish, trying to reach the open sea, caused the dog to start. Then he'd take the lamp down, and the dog would go out beside him to the midpoint of the channel. Stationing himself at the point that seemed the shallowest, he beat the fish to death. Their dorsal fins stood out a little way above the water, and he would aim the final blow just a little further forward. And so it went, every night.

When the sixth day dawned, all the world was under water. It was early in the morning that the south-east wind began, and the water flooded in at a rate you couldn't credit.

The first thing he did was to jump into the water and wash all the filth away. Then they went out further, beyond the river mouth onto the middle of the sandbank. The water stood so high now that the two of them appeared to be abandoned on an endless sea. But with the water high and the sky a solid cloud, every sound you heard appeared to come from very close.

He thought he heard some voices coming over from the river, until he saw the vague shape of a boat across the sandbank, advancing with its sails unfurled. He'd never seen a boat like that on this part of the river, which showed how high the water ran. The boat looked like a great bird making smooth, majestic turns. He thought, from its shape, that it was the *Pintarrojo*, a ketch rigged in the old style.

He stood there for a long time in the middle of his boat, watching it in silence as if dazzled by the sight. The south-east wind blew steadily, but now it wasn't so strong, bringing in that smell that made you think of the sea. The sky began to clear up on the easterly horizon and the light began to penetrate. The *Pintarrojo* slowly turned its prow in that direction. He watched it move away and then it vanished over the rim of light.

One could take it as a sign.

He went that very day to visit Bastos in his cabin and, as soon as he got back, gathered all his things into a tarred canvas bag. This was when the cream-coloured dog started whining, running everywhere in front of him, watching him uneasily. At last, when he'd got everything, he stepped into the kitchen.

'Are you there, abuela?'

'I'm here and listening to you,' said the voice inside the shadows.

He took some time deciding.

'I'm going, abuela,' he said at last, struggling with the words.

'Yes, I can see.'

He heard her as she got up and came towards him. When she stood there right in front of him, she looked into his eyes.

'As you wish, son.' She said it in that patient voice which nothing ever troubled.

He was standing there in silence, wondering what to do.

'Don't worry about me, if that's what's on your mind.'

Then he looked at her in turn. She knew them well, these men like him.

'I've spoken to Old Bastos . . . he's going to come up here . . . I think it would be best.'

'If that's what he wants . . . but don't you worry about me.'

'Yes, yes I know . . . '

'I think the old man owed you.'

'I don't want any money.'

'It isn't right.'

'No, I don't want . . . '

'All right, then take the old man's gun.'

'No, you're going to need it . . . I'm going to take the boat, Old Bastos' rowing boat, and the small trammel net and a couple of paternosters.'

'That's not very much at all.'

'It's fine for me.'

'The rowing boat's not ours, and besides, it's rotten.'

'It's fine for me.'

'Honestly, this man!'

Boga scratched his head.

'That knife, the old man's knife . . . what will you do with that?'

The old woman faintly smiled.

'What do I want with a knife?'

He took his turn to smile, and then he scratched his head again.

Old Bastos' rowing boat is a boat that has a story, as do all these things. Not many folk would give you something for it now, but in its time it really was a great little boat, and more than just a rowing boat. A ready eye can still pick out the elegance of its lines. The boat was old even when Old Bastos bought it, from the hands of Old Messali. And Old Messali bought it, in his turn, from Old Sotelo. It was round this time that some bottom timbers were changed. As for Old Sotelo, it seems that he received it from a Turkish man called Zarur, and in exchange for a cow that had a story of its own. But this is too far back in time and no one can agree the facts from Old Sotelo on. The boats are often mixed up and the stories get confused. You talk about a boat, at least you think that it's a boat, and in fact it's really two boats, or even three at once. Apart from that, a single boat gives rise to different stories. It will happen there have been so many changes to the boat, that you reach a point in time when it is taken for a new boat. It happens that a boat is quite another as time goes by, excepting for its shape or in the nature of the spirit that gives it life, because there's not a timber or a nail or any other piece that hasn't been replaced. There's nothing odd in a rowing boat of a certain length being turned into a little launch, a splendid one at that. So it was that Old Messali thought to fit an engine, a little Lauson 2 h.p., back in '38 when they were selling very cheaply as they came on the market, and complete with the propeller shaft, the screw and packing gland. But fate had other plans for this boat.

Some said that the boat was made by the hand of Don Juan Froglia. But this is saying a lot. Apart from any other doubts, Old Froglia died in '27. Some insist, however. And maybe there's some truth in it. Perhaps it wasn't by Froglia's hand but rather his apprentice's. Some can see the old style in it, rather like with paintings. Regardless of the truth, though, every time the matter of its sale came into question, the owner mentioned Froglia, and swore the boat was one of his. If this was even half-believed, the buyer asked for nothing more to come to a decision. This is how these people are. Even if the boat might fall to pieces at a kick. The very same Juan Froglia, of Austrian descent, whose boatyard on the Tigre's left bank quickly rose to fame in the first years of this century, for its motor boats and launches, its Tarpón cruisers, the *Italia* for instance, the *Titania* or the *Albatros*. It quickly reached the point where it was doubtful he would've had much to do with any mere rowboat at all. This was at the time when the internal combustion engines started capturing the market, burning 'Russian petrol' that was sold in crates of two drums holding eighteen litres each and at $3.80 the crate. It was at that time.

The boat, four metres long at most, was fitted out at first with a short Baltic pine mast, and a small lateen sail for when it went on to the open sea. It kept this mast till recently, but all that was in place now was the beam fixed to the keelson, which served you as a type of cockpit, and a seat there at the mast-hole right above it. There aren't many folk who would part with cash to buy it now, even if Juan Froglia really had built the boat himself. Half its planks are rotten and the transom's split as well. Even if her story was complete in every detail, it wouldn't be enough to patch the smallest of her holes.

Old Bastos turned up first thing in the morning on the following day, his boat jam-packed with junk. Working side by side, they stacked the whole lot on the shore and, when the boat was empty, he began to stow his own things. The Primus stove and kerosene lamp, machete, wooden box with all his odd tools picked up over time – all of this he put into the locker in the prow. He'd held on to the pincers, a pair of Doble Cañón, since the time when he was working on the Pancho Comercio dredger. You can't put your hands on a pair of Doble Cañón pincers now, not for anything in the world. With the kind of job he used them for, other brands of pincers would have done him just as well, even something made locally. But, when all is said and done, a pair of Doble Cañón is a pair of Doble Cañón.

He put the gill net in the stern, down underneath the seat, with the tarred canvas bag and the basket with the paternoster lines. He set the kettle for the maté and a box holding tins and bottles in the space behind his back, between the seat he sat to row on and the seat beside the mast-hole. Pushed against this large box was a bag that held some sea bread and a decent lump of pork belly. He covered up the bag and box with a canvas large enough to reach across the boat when fully extended.

The cream-coloured dog followed every single movement, letting out a whimper or a bark from time to time. He stood up two or three times, staring at it angrily. He found those gentle, pleading eyes disturbed him in his work.

The dog sat on the bank as if it had the shivers, shaking as it whimpered very softly. One time it got caught up between his feet on the path, and he removed it with a kick. When he had things ready, he called the dog and tied it to one of the house's uprights. Then, in the middle of the morning, he left.

From inside the house, Bastos and the old woman heard the squealing of the rowlocks and the slapping of the oars moving slowly off in the direction of the river mouth, but they didn't come to see him leave. The dog, on the other hand, was desperate in its howling. A howling choked off, in part, by the violence of its jerking on the cord, which only made its desperation greater than before, as if it were being strangled. He rowed on with a rhythm that was slow, just like the old folk's. A long way lay ahead.

He went beyond the final curve and then on past the refuge, and now across the sandbank, going in among the reeds.

The day was very lovely. His plan was to go out onto the open sea a little, to the far side of the sandbank, then carry on around it till the evening, when he'd land on Santa Mónica and stay there for the night.

Then the howling stopped and he knew the dog was loose. He saw it not long after when it ran between the reeds and then jumped out into the water. He went on with his rowing.

You can't say that the river changes one way in the winter and another in the summer. The river simply changes. The islands, on the other hand, seem different with each season. Not just for the striking green of summer, but far more subtle things. In winter, from the open sea, they vanish in a distant mist. They're there, and then they're not. You come to doubt the river and believe you'll never reach them, despite the faint uneasiness that cuts you off and rocks you and in a way distresses you. Their shores may prove illusory, a shadow out towards the west, swayed by the horizon. And if at last you draw near, they come to seem remoter still, colonised by loneliness, by silence and a sadness past repair.

The light hides high in winter. Dawn and evening come on at the summit of the sky, a long way from the surface. In summer it's the opposite. The light begins to rise up from the outline of the islands and, pushing out from there, spills its way across the day. The islands look like jolly barges rocking on the water in the middle of the morning. When heading towards them, one heads towards the light. And towards that strange commotion that has slowly gained intensity as summer comes of age.

It all takes place unnoticed. This business of maturing. The winter's there inside you, the summer's who you are as well. But, leaving this aside, it's plain to see that everything comes from the north. The anxiety and the hubbub and the very light itself. All this exaltation and this frenzy of the summer.

Between mid-morning and mid-afternoon, the islands lie there gleaming with a sharp and even light, dozing in the sun. They look a little flattened. A stroke of light, a stroke of shadow. Nothing in the mid-tones. The suffocating air. The sand along the beaches makes a quiet creaking sound. There is a thick and boiling silence. The atmosphere above is clear, but at the level of the ground it quivers strangely. Then the silence turns into a never-ending drone. But this is also summer. The crowning of the day is in its dawning and its nightfall. And then there is the night. The breeze at dawn is cool and draws a shiver from the fishermen. It comes in from the river and the islands give a shake. It's then that all the bustle and the boiling in the blood begins, the fretting that provokes a man to head for the horizon. An angel, something like that, has just skimmed across the water and around the wind-blown features of the man down in his boat, asleep. It moves too quickly to be seen, cutting through the dawning light that makes the world elusive. You barely feel the touch, but it's enough to leave you troubled. It's time to find yourself there now, away towards the north and beyond these early islands. It summons and impels you. You must go.

Even at its widest point, the Delta of the Paraná is barely seventy kilometres. But this is only the beginning. Things go well beyond this: 3,282 kilometres along the River Paraná and 1,580 kilometres along the River Uruguay. And it's not certain that everything ends there.

But then, it makes no sense to try to use this kind of measurement. An aeroplane, a P11 or else a tiny J3, taking off from the San Fernando airfield and heading northwest, sees the Paraná de las Palmas before it's climbed 400 metres, when it's still in its ascent, and then could shut its engine off and simply glide to the far side of the Delta. A sloop that leaves the shore in the middle of the morning, set for Punta Morán, in the mouth of the Paraná, does well if it arrives the following day, with all the snags it meets. Unless the wind is really kind, it starts out making long tacks, which will bring it slowly closer, but not so as you'd notice. At noon it sails the river that's an open sea, the shoreline always visible and probably appearing from a new direction every time. The shore grows ever smaller. It's a bobbing line, if that. Now it seems the sloop is in the middle of the sea. That it's heading not towards somewhere, but rather leaving all behind. Sometime in the morning it will stand off Buenos Aires. To starboard all this while, almost to the bow at times, the filmy hedge of buildings has been emerging like a grey ship, its funnels under the constant cloud of smoke that is the city's authentic sky. After noon, the sloop turns north. Now it sails close-hauled, heading straight into the wind. If things go on the same way it will come to Punta Morán at the end of this enormous tack. For now it's mid-river. Just like the middle of the sea. When the boat begins to pitch you hear a fleeting cracking noise from underneath the stem. The wind sings in the rigging as if this is what amuses it, and never takes a breather. The sails maintain their curvature and at times they give a shake. This constant, steady pressure makes its way into your blood. Inconclusive points appear, swaying out there in the distance every now and then, and you locate them feverishly on the charts. The effect of seeing a buoy, or a marker out in front of you, is something quite incredible. All of your anxiety is drawn towards that inconclusive point, which takes on so much significance. But if you look too hard it disappears.

Now it's getting dark. The points begin to wink. There's something in each glint of light that carries something warmer, even tender. The boat sails in the night, now. The river dark and baleful. It runs towards a buoy that has a white and flashing light. The jet-black silhouette grows large, and hovers like a ghost. You hear the water slipping around its sides as you go by. These buoys are so enormous that they startle you a little. Their light is kind when distant, but once you come up close and see them standing like a rock face, their look is simply dismal.

Even with no buoy in sight, you sense how deep the water is, how crushing. The sloop sails on the channel now, across the Paraná, and the pressure of the current here compels you to correct the drift. Now it is night. The sky seems more inhabited than all this empty solitude with its winkings in the distance. The stars seem low and very close. Sliding south, and slowly. Once across the channel you come up against the sandbanks, the water just a metre deep, and sometimes even less. Best to drop the anchor. Punta Morán will be there when you wake up with the dawn, directly ahead, but still a good way off. With the water on the rise you can sail across the Bajo del Temor.

Yes, this is another kind of time and another kind of measurement. Distances expand and one's objectives grow further away. When you're at the halfway point, everything is distant: the point from which you set out, the point of your arrival.

*

He had with him a kedge anchor, which he'd found at the bottom of the river. Not that he'd thought he would ever use the thing. But as it was still hanging where he'd left it, on a cross-beam that ran underneath the house, it had struck him that the anchor might be of some use after all, when he was on the open sea. So that when the night was falling as he drew towards the island, he didn't make for land and instead tied the anchor on the rope and dropped it, some way from the shore. He wasn't absolutely clear why this was what he did, but what really carried weight was that he simply had a preference for sleeping in the boat.

In the last light of the day, he took a paternoster line and baited it and threw it in the river. As far as paternosters went, he wasn't one for strewing them, nor using many hooks. A single twenty-metre line seemed practical to him, with only four or five hooks, of five-and-a-half size, and a good-sized sinker on the end. He was in the habit of tying this type of line onto the stern shackle, so all he had to do was add the bait and throw it in. It took seconds to gather in, and didn't slow his progress. He preferred to drag the line if the spot that he was moving to was relatively close, and even when he pulled it in, he threw it back again minutes later with the same bait on the line.

And so, in that last light, he was throwing in the line, and he didn't need to light the lamp to feel down in the bag and reach for the pork belly and then a piece of sea bread. When he'd eaten, he leaned out on the rail and drank some water from the river. Then he lit a cigarette and looked out at the night, with that faint little blinking somewhere just before his face. And then this brilliant little point drew a longer line, before it sank back in the darkness and left there behind it just the briefest reddish wake.

Boga checked the line and then he slipped down into the bottom of the boat.

In any case, the following day he was forced to land. He'd shipped a lot of water in the little rowing boat. All the things would get too wet, conditions that made the rowing hard. A boat that's holding water doesn't only weigh a lot, but it handles very badly and can heel at any movement. It's a curse in every sense.

He checked the line and felt the drag of something on the end. He decided not to bring it in until he reached the shore. He was looking at the boat, and did so for a good while, without deciding anything. He didn't know whether to turn the boat or use the tin to empty it. He wasn't very keen on having to take out all the things. He chose the latter course. But first he pulled the line in. He had two yellow catfish and a *patí* weighing a kilo. Thinking better about it all, it made a lot more sense to make a fire here and eat, and then go on his way. The idea perked him up a bit and so he set to empty all his things out of the boat. When he'd nearly finished, he went to gather branches and then he lit the fire. He filled the kettle half-full and he set it on the fire. He stuck two forked sticks in the ground and spanned them with a green branch, on which he hung the kettle.

While the water boiled, he finished emptying the boat. Then he drank some maté. He lay down on the beach and enjoyed the murmur of the sand, and the wind from the south-east that cleaved the air around his face.

He finished with the maté and set to clean the fish. If you haven't got the mood for it, there's nothing more disagreeable than having to clean a fish. He kept one of the catfish, putting it to one side, for later use as bait. Then he grilled the other one with the *patí*. In fact he'd cleaned them well. He sprinkled the fillets with boiling water to get rid of all the odour, salted them and pierced them with a stick to hold them open on the grill.

Now everything seemed better. From this moment on, out here on this empty beach, with his fish to cook and eat, he could feel himself a wanderer.

He didn't exactly think these words, but rather felt invaded by a curious serenity, a newfound sense of calm that put contentment in his smile. He was doing all the things it seemed he'd wanted to do for ages.

He ate the tastiest pieces and the parts which had most meat. The *patí* is a splendid fish, even if it's greasy. The old man used to lose his mind for a slice or two of *patí*, fried in just a little oil.

He got up to have a look around the boat while he was eating. He circled round it several times, and here and there he kicked it. The best thing he could do, if he wanted to go on with this, was put the boat in order now. He'd brought along a few planks, a ball of cotton wicking and a tin with dribs of paint in.

But he wanted to get just a little further on, before that. He wasn't a man to rush at things. He'd only just set out. The mouth of the Anguilas was still visible from here, and he'd landed on the sandbank he'd been working on all year, more or less. Nothing, up to now, had really changed at all. He was still really going round the circuit of before, and what he sought was hardly closer.

He lit himself a cigarette and turned to watch the river.

He wouldn't make his first stop yet, at least until he'd crossed the Paraná.

He went back to the river, but running north-west now, so by afternoon he'd sailed beyond Isla Zárate, all the way across its sandbanks to the channel.

The wind was getting up at bit. He ought to get a move on if he didn't want a wait. He'd been rowing facing forward for several hours now, with the stern advancing first, and watching where he headed. Now he turned the boat around, settled in a posture that was steady on the cross-beam, and set to row again with his back towards the channel.

He'd gone beyond the island and the current started pulling. The water was two metres here, and five soon after that. He'd keep buoy K42 along his left side as he went.

There, stretching out towards the right, was the island. The sandbank off its northern side is excellent for fishing. But he chose to sail on past.

The water took him on in the direction of the buoy, but by the time he'd gone that far it was behind him by a distance. He was now out in mid-channel. He'd probably come out quite near the Isla Lucha sandbank.

It's not the sandbank off the east end of the island, but another, smaller one, and separated from it by a current that's a metre deep.

And this was how it all worked out. He passed very close beside the winking scarlet eye of buoy K41. The channel was behind him now and so he dropped the oars. He felt a little tired. He wanted to go on, as far up as the islands, up to Nutria and Lucha, and go into the channel that ran all the way between them, and before the night came down, if he could. He remembered having seen, on the latter of these islands, just metres from the shore, a lean-to built for fishermen. The area all round here is popular with them.

He'd camp out in the lean-to. But first he'd set a line up at the entrance to the channel, and tie it in the reeds. He'd collect it on the way back, when he set out once again.

The river was now rising and the sky had clouded over. The wind was blowing steadily. It all seemed fiercely barren now, and lifeless.

These are low-lying islands, and it isn't very long ago they reached their finished state. Their warm and dampish tangling of ever-sprouting grasses makes them seem, from a little way off, rather higher than they are. One imagines it's a perfect place to land. But your feet sink in the mud and you feel the rock-like roots stab through the bottom of your shoes. There isn't one dry corner. The mud is always gurgling. His panting and his sweat wrap around him like a shroud.

The water had submerged the land a while before midnight. Boga heard the water come, and listened through the night, through the timbers of the platform, to its churning. He'd tied the boat to an upright on the shelter, calculating then that the ground was going to flood. In the middle of the night he took the rope up in his hands, and the boat came all the way in underneath him.

He'd only set one line because the current here is mighty, and if he had to leave when the level was this high, the work would not be pleasant with more lines to gather in. On more than one occasion, he'd had to fish out the end a line completely submerged in the water, ducking through the surface where he thought he'd tied it up. He ought not to have left even the one on the sandbank. If he wanted to set out in the morning, he might have to resign himself to losing it.

In truth, he didn't know quite why he'd climbed up on the platform. The lean-to was collapsing and the weather filtered into it from every side at once. There were holes across the roof where the straw had disappeared and he looked out through the holes at the soft light in the sky, a ghostly incandescence in the low cloud of the night. He would have been much better off in the bottom of the boat, and covered by the canvas – once he'd bailed the water out, of course. It wouldn't have filled the boat up to the point where it would wet him, not in a single night, if he stayed up on the deck planks.

Disregarding all this, he took several things out from the boat and put them in the shelter. There was a sheet of metal nailed down in a corner of the platform, on which to make a fire. Boga lit the Primus stove and, while he ate the left-over fish, he drank down several matés. Then he wrapped the canvas tightly round him, and lay down on the log floor.

At one point in the night he'd expected it to rain, but now was sure it wouldn't. He'd crossed his hands behind his head and watched the night sky gleaming through the spaces in the straw. The water made its way across the ground underneath him. He heard it coming in. He was lying in this shelter in the midst of this colossal space inhabited by no one. It was, in a way, like lying on a drifting raft. The feeling was of sat-isfaction, curious but real. He could feel his body breathing and the thousand little movements that he made inside his clothes, clammy now and cracking with the dirt that turned them hard; he smelled himself and heard himself, and all parts of his body, in a hundred different ways. His presence weighed upon him, like something that was sleeping, warm and quite alone. He was, right at this moment, the centre of this flooded world. One who had survived. The silence and the night and the waters overflowing and the loneliness of this river that was like a sea, all came to die around him. The feeling, not the thought, provoked in him a strange elation and an odd sense of security. He didn't have to journey out to anything at all. Things all converged on him.

The wind began to blow more strongly, damp gusts bringing in the smell of ozone from the river. This wind and smell aroused him.

He was lying there awake for the best part of the night. Suspended in the darkness, there above the water, in the wind brought on by summer.

Dawn had not arrived when he heard the muffled wailing of a launch out in the distance. There was no way to determine the trajectory it followed. The wind was toying with the sound, advancing or delaying it, or stifling it completely. Until a bellow rose up at the entrance to the Sueco, rather indistinct, and from that moment on swelled up in the night, drowning all else out, as if it were coming straight for the shelter and would strike at any moment.

The clamour of the motor launch abruptly disappeared, taken somewhere by the wind. The silence sounded more intense.

The deep and changing glow of night was followed by a flat and doughy light. The day was starting.

Boga gathered up his things and put them on the boat, then he jumped on with the Primus. He pulled his cap away and stuck his head into the water. It was pretty hot already, despite the early hour. The water was receding. The day was overcast, but with a cloud that doesn't sadden you. A yellowish resplendence seemed to blossom from the river, unusual spills of light that moved in lazy fluctuations.

He considered for a moment abandoning the line and going on along the Sueco, going round that side to cross the Bajo del Temor. It would be a longer crossing, but what he really wanted was to sail along the coast, between the mouth of the Chaná and the Chanacito Stream. He remembered all the handsome trees along that stretch of shore, rising up behind the reeds. The high and spreading treetops in the last light of the day are a sight you don't forget. It's a place that gives the sense of being larger than it is, and a kind of quiet joy fills up your spirit when you see it. And then it's good for fishing, there are several secret currents running in between the reeds that connect with little streams. The green veil of reeds hides the presence of these inlets, and some are marked because of this with long protruding stakes.

But then the open sea route, as well as being shorter, also has its special charm. And even by this way he'd get the chance to see the towering trees, straightening, or so it seems, and leaning back a little on the deep and brilliant sky.

He bailed out the water and ran quickly with the river down towards the open sea, driven by the pressure of a terrific current. He made use of this to smoke a cigarette, allowing the boat to drift along, correcting his direction from time to time with a quick blow from the oar.

He let the boat run on when he came onto the sandbank, until he reached the point where he thought he'd set the line. The water was still high and the reeds were barely visible. He couldn't find the line. Even with no trace of it, he spent a good while looking, for the simple joy of finding it, and, in another way, to quarrel with the river. The truth is that all feelings are alien to the river, but it often seems motivated by a mood that's very gloomy.

The river is magnificent and man feels mysteriously drawn to it. It's the only thing to say.

This man stands by its waters and looks out across its murmuring vastness with nostalgia, as if he had lost something very dear to him and absolutely primordial, here in the middle of this river that resembles eternity. It's this, perhaps, that makes him think the river is good.

But the truth is, underneath, this river is often devilishly astute and grim and even mean.

Its men, this river's men, this man who stands here now and is looking at its waters, his big eyes of a dying fish that hang above the water like two lenses in the air, these men are like the river in every way. It's why they still survive. It's why they seem so aged, so distant and remote. They don't love the river, exactly, but couldn't live without it. They are as slow and as constant as the river. More than this, these men are as indifferent as the river. They seem to understand they form a part of a stubborn whole, that goes its way inspired by a certain kind of fate. And nothing makes them rise up. When the river wrecks their boat and their cabins and themselves. And this is why they, too, seem bad.

After anchoring the boat, he stripped away his clothes and threw himself into the water. Part of it was feeling that he wanted to take a dip. But he was sure he'd find the line as well.

He dived down several times, but he didn't have any luck.

Diving in the reeds can be a devilish thing to do. The feeling when the stems chafe on your body is repugnant.

He went down for a final time and hit upon the line. He held it in his hand. It seemed the line was slack. He used his knife to cut the thread and got back to the surface with his final gasp of air. He dragged the line behind him as he swam towards the boat. It offered small resistance. There would be nothing on the hook, he thought.

He pulled the line onto the boat. It lacked the last six metres and the last three hooks as well.

He rowed all through the morning. It was only when he came close to the shore and his arrival that he stopped, towards midday. He would have made the journey quicker if he'd had a different boat, but he didn't mind the time it took, as long as he was there before the night.

The weather turned out splendid and the river barely rippled at the gentle south-east breeze. He liked to take his time along this section of the river, so shallow yet so wide. He felt as if he'd journeyed on a sea to reach this place, from somewhere that was infinitely vast and very deep.

He stopped his rowing several times. In truth the boat now travelled with the momentum it had gathered, encouraged by the pushing of the current. There it was, a small mark that was dark and rather complex, as if drifting in the air. Then the smell of the river and the sighing of the water, turning around him.

He'd felt a little chilly after diving in the river, but now he felt quite drowsy in the sun. But only in his body, as something that was more intimate was always keeping watch, glad eyes looking out across the waters and the heavens, at the long line of the shore, as if from the veranda of a solitary house, inside its shadows.

And now he saw the trees, just a little way behind him to the right. At first off in the distance and then impossibly close, isolated somehow, and casting their estrangement at the sky and on the river.

He stopped close to the shore and drank some matés at midday. If he got to Punta Morán before the middle of the afternoon, and went a little way into the Chanacito Stream, he might meet the provisions boat. If he had no luck with that, he'd go the following morning all the way up the Baldozas Stream, and back to the Chaná along the Piccardo Canal. The bakery is there, and a couple of holiday camps. There were certain things he needed to buy. He felt the wish, for once, to eat like other people ate, but still it wasn't a craving, and even if he got the chance, he wasn't sure at all he'd find much pleasure in the eating. It was rather that he sensed he was going to feel a genuine need to eat something more substantial, and within the next few hours. It wasn't the kind of thing he'd ever worried about before, despite, and when he got the chance, being able to put his food away with very little fuss. But up to now his body had resisted with a will on the maté and the sea bread and the other bits and pieces. It's the best thing you can do when you're wandering the river.

He got to Punta Morán just as the light seemed to be climbing to the summit of the sky, and many hours later than the middle of the afternoon. He'd got a bit held up back in the inlet of the Ancho, and had to bail out water on a couple of occasions. In any case, it wasn't that he'd settled on an hour for his arrival, and thinking on it now, it made him glad to arrive just then, as the dusk was coming in. It was rather like entering a temple, something of that kind.

Ever since the dawn, and like the circling of bees, he'd had, until a certain point, the murmur of the water and the sighing of the wind in his ears. This was on the open sea, and while its drone continued, he'd felt far out at sea and disconnected from the shore, however close it seemed.

But all at once it ended and he entered in this calm, in a second, and the River Plate was far away, infinitely distant, gleaming above the stern as if it formed a separate sea.

The water is much deeper here, much calmer. At its mouth the Chanacito gives the sense of being a lake. When sailing down the coast, the changes as you move into its mouth are very gradual, and you find you're well inside before you see them all around you. The shoreline on the starboard side is bare and prone to flooding, but on the other shore there is a darkened line of trees that grows increasingly dense. The water on this side, and at this hour of day, seems very deep and rather grim. The impression is of a place both gloomier and more silent; it gives the sense of some enormous amphitheatre. And only now you're here do you once more feel the islands – they've always been in sight and yet they've always seemed far off. Far off in an uncommon way.

He's here now, at a standstill in the middle of this calm. He's put aside the oars and has his feet in the water to his ankles. The scrub-hen calls from time to time, squawking like a thing possessed, as if there were an unseen hunter wringing out its neck behind the nearest of the trees. He lights himself a cigarette and dozes in the stillness of the dusk. Here, the night is falling. Not so on the open sea that's only just behind him, as if a thousand years away. A clear line marks the boundary. There, the open sea is agitated by the wind and its waters show another colour, shine a different light. He watches how they pucker in a million little points, in a movement that's mechanical, or almost is, but futile, and now and then he smells it. Here, these other waters lie quite calm and very dark. Here the night comes quickly.

It would have been a madness to land at this hour and try to make a camp on shore. Mosquitoes come in clouds and they drive you round the bend. It isn't even possible to go in close to shore. The best thing is to anchor just a little way offshore, gauging that a change of wind won't drive your little boat into the net of water hyacinths. This is what he did. And bailed the boat out one more time before he lit the Primus, before having a piece of sea bread along with several matés. Then he took a couple of lines and baited them and cast them, one on either side. He hadn't had the time to fix the line onto the stern.

The fish stirred up the water with a snapping sound like gunshots. It's not a sign that augurs well, despite what some folk think. When fish are making all this noise they won't be taking bait. He cast the lines in any case, trusting to the night.

Then he pulled the canvas out, wrapped himself inside it and slid down into the boat. Perhaps he could have anchored closer in after all, somewhere with more shelter. The southeast wind can rise at night, and when it does there isn't much to choose between the open sea and this. But he wanted to wake up right here, not further out, nor in. Everything is different in the morning when you wake, and it feels you really are coming in from the sea towards these islands that you've seen so many times before in dreams.

*

He caught the river's smell at dawn, opening his eyes and breathing through the sharp and acrid odour of the canvas. He didn't feel hot or cold, so he'd likely feel the coolness when he pushed away the canvas. He heard the wind whine overhead, the little blows of water knocking all around the boat. He couldn't see any more than a turbid show of light as he looked into the canvas with its blackened heavy weave, but he imagined all those details of the morning.

He pushed away the canvas and got up to his feet. The sun was just ascending from the line of the horizon, and the place was quite transformed. The river mouth and open sea were now one and the same, a water that had thickened and was milky-coffee-coloured, as if its bed had been stirred up, and folded in a million points in steady movement. And then the water's sighing and the water itself appeared to separate, with all connection broken. The sound was here around his head, a hundred thousand swarming bees, and then there was the water with its movement like a strange machine, a dislocated image.

He saw a little fishing boat bobbing in the distance, on the line of the horizon.

The light broke through the line of trees and areas of sand could now be seen in several places. These beaches, by the look of them, had surfaced in the night, for at dusk the trees had seemed as if they'd stood against the water.

He lifted off his cap and put his head into the river. Then stood up on the mast-hole seat and looked into the distance, across the brightened water. The wind soon dried his face and his skin felt taut and frozen. In time he grew aware of the whispering from the trees, and at length turned to the islands. The feeling that he had was of hanging somewhere over things, not standing in the boat, but hanging weightless from the sky on this fresh and radiant summer's day.

He would have liked to land at once, stopping where the shoreline gently turns away south-west, before it runs into the distance. Right here on this curve which folds just like a balcony above the open sea, at the entrance to the Chanacito Stream. But he was set on the Piccardo mouth, going up and bringing back supplies that afternoon.

He gathered in the lines that had been set as night came in. He took hold of the first and felt the movements of a fish. It was sitting on the bottom, pained, perhaps a bit perplexed to feel this cruel thing catch its mouth. He felt the gentle weaving of its protest underwater, and then the desperate fighting when it came up to the surface, and seemed about to free itself.

Now it came just below the water surface, and even skipped right out at times. He saw its flashing back two or three times while it struggled. It wasn't such a marvellous catch after all. A middling yellow catfish with a slightly swollen belly. Possibly a female. But a catfish swallows anything, and what you take for spawn can be entirely something else.

He held the fish a while before he took it off the hook and threw it down into the boat. He'd always been amused by this clicking of the catfish when it finds itself entrapped. The damp back of the animal shone brightly and it looked handsome, in spite of being a catfish. He looked down at its round and puzzled eyes. And, for an instant, he felt pity. This poor little catfish, with its barbels beating wildly, was the only friend the man had at this moment. But the man was not at all sure that he needed a companion. And a catfish isn't a dog, of course, or anything of the sort. Perhaps in other times he would have answered to this timid call, and yet it wasn't likely. He'd been hardened by the river. If anything was clear-cut in this man, if there was anything that really stood out, it was precisely this submission, this acceptance of or obedience to what he met along the river, the fine or dirty weather, the floods or lack of water, everything, when all was said and done, life or death.

He unhooked the catfish, took out the Sheffield knife and broke off all the fish's barbs before he threw it in the bottom, where the water in the boat would keep the animal alive.

It seemed as if the other line was empty. He'd noticed it was slack when he was dealing with the first. He leaned across the gunwale and began to pull it in. And there wasn't any drag, except that of the lead weight and the length of line itself. But when the first hook surfaced, he had a premonition and he pulled hard at the line. In truth he couldn't have said if it was really a premonition, or if in that moment the fish revealed itself, or if both things had happened almost at the same time, and with so little margin between them that the premonition held. He pulled and it pulled back in turn, at his hand. And he knew what he was dealing with at once and fought hard, with a sureness and a speed that were quite prodigious, while something still eluded him and he heard how he was panting and was laughing at the same time, and the water went on cleaving, shattering into pieces and he saw, for an instant, its body, like a dark scar, or a dark wake. He shouted:

'Now!'

And he noticed that his voice, which for so long had been silent, rebounded in the morning, as if it came from some-where else.

He struck, but not with violence. With a certainty of move-ment that was even and sustained, drawing on the line but also checking as he played it, his arm both spring and damper as he worked.

The fish paused for an instant with its body almost com-pletely out, as if the water held it there despite his greatest efforts. He felt the burning in his hand and was sure the line would break at any moment. The fish ran twice from one side then back to the other, beating at the water, and then rose in the air with a furtive shine. He held it in the air, but now above the boat, so that its weight, its total weight, that was hanging from its mouth, would keep it still. He watched, his breathing laboured, and whistled just the once, with aston-ishment, and then he burst out laughing as he held on to the fish, which doubled like a spring and made his arm vibrate from end to end.

The river has its ways. When you least expect it, it remem-bers you, or seems to. If he were a man who could hold in mind a thought with some persistence, this would be it, and he'd have thought a thousand times about something like what had just happened. And, starting now, he'd think of it more intensely still.

In these days, in these rivers with their dark and surly fish, it's pretty much unheard of for the man who casts his lines come what may, and with dogged steadfastness, to hook a three-kilo *tararira*. It's not a fish for deep or for fast-running waters, but he'd caught it with the line that he'd thrown across the gunwale closest to the shore, right in there among the reeds. Sometimes you can find it in a ditch with little water, filled with logs and branches, where you'd never think to find a fish belonging to this species. And then the thing is big, a fish right for the sea, you'd think, and yet it has a spirit that is really of the river. Sly, savage, pitiless. He looked with exaltation at its battle-hardened head, its sunken eyes, its fearsome jaws, and its gills that rose and fell with a rhythmic movement that didn't betray its pain. What manoeuvres had he not tried, what places and what hours had he not used in his bid to catch this fish? Now the fish had come to him without his having decided on it in any real sense, excepting for this state of being ready at all times. This is what the river's like.

He held the *tararira* up against the morning sky, feeling the exuberance of life there in its weight, multiplied by torment. He'd have liked to stretch this moment out to something quite impossible. And then he felt a little sad, and didn't know why.

He took enormous care when he was prising out the hook, and threw the *tararira* in the bottom of the boat. The animal began to fight and throw itself around, splashing water back at him. He couldn't believe its strength.

He sat and took the oars. He was still filled with excitement. The *tararira* gradually became a little quieter, and then he started rowing. He really couldn't believe it.

When he thought it over, the Chanacito way had to be a little shorter. But then, on the other hand, the time he saved by going up the Piccardo Canal would be lost on the Baldozas, which twists away south-west. And so he went upriver on the Chanacito Stream. He could have a look, in passing, up beyond the Ignacio, where at certain times of year the fishing turned out pretty good. He could even drop a line and pick it up on his return. But he didn't get as far as the

Ignacio in the end. He met with the provisions boat before he'd got that far, and was back at Punta Morán before the middle of the day.

He saw the boat come round the bend that meets the Caguané; it sailed out in mid-river with a judder in its engine and a blue plume of smoke rising upwards from its funnel. The boat was of the island type, special to these rivers, constructed with a double prow and flat bottom, a decent length and not a lot of beam, but with its overall proportions something larger than the standard. The superstructure windows had been cut out very large to allow for loading goods.

He heard it long before he saw it come out from the bend, in the middle of the river, its plume of smoke escaping from its funnel. It's rare to see a vessel of this class that has a funnel. There's usually an outlet in the stern, to the side. But this was a launch that at first had carried passengers, and as a rule a vessel of that kind will have a funnel. And then the boat had once belonged to Deaf Angarita, a man who had his own ways. A launch with a funnel has a different air entirely.

He knew it by its sound before the boat came into sight, and it made him glad to see its smoky plume above the river.

The launch stopped at a jetty, its engine still running, and he rowed across towards it. The man didn't see him as he made his way across. He was speaking to another man, standing on the jetty, and he opened up the throttle just as Boga came up close. He hammered on the side of the launch with an oar, and the man turned to look.

He stood there without speaking and just studied him a while, with the noise there in between them, rhythmic and intense, and didn't seem persuaded that he merited attention.

Boga got up on his feet and wrapped his hands around the gunwale, and then the man decided that he'd throttle down his engine, now that, by the look of things, he didn't have a choice.

'What?' he shouted from the wheel at the bow, and making it quite clear that he wasn't for wasting time.

'I want a couple of things.'

'WHAT?'

'I WANT TO BUY SOME THINGS!'

He was still looking back but he hadn't made up his mind. Then he came towards him, weaving down the boat between the crates and all the tins.

'All right then, all right. What is it you want?'

Boga fixed him with a stern gaze and the man looked disconcerted.

'I haven't exactly got much . . . you can see what I've got.' He spoke without ill humour now.

'I'll take a bit of sea bread to begin with.'

'How much?'

'How much can you give me?'

'I've only got one bag. I can give you up to half of it . . . '

'How much is that?'

'Five or six kilos . . . at ten pesos a kilo . . . '

'All right, as it comes.'

The man got the bag and began with the bread. 'What else do you want?' He was weighing out the bread. 'Have you got something to put it in?'

'A bag.'

Boga crouched down in the boat and lifted out the bag.

'Give me two or three of those chorizos.'

'Two, or three?' the man said.

'Two. When are you round here?'

'Every other day . . . usually around this time. Whereabouts are you?'

'Away down the river . . . at Punta Morán.'

'I can go as far at that.'

'I prefer to come up here . . . I'm not always in one place . . . Give me a packet of that yerba maté.'

'Which?'

'Whichever. A kilo. Better give me two.'

'Two packets of a kilo.'

'Now I'd like a bit of meat.'

The man scratched at his head. 'That's another matter.'

'Anything . . . a few bones with a little bit of meat . . . bones would be good.'

The man opened a metal box.

'I've got some *ossobuco*, then.'

'I'll make do with that.'

The man wrapped up the shinbone in some pages of a newspaper, then waited, watching Boga.

'Matches, several boxes . . . a packet of coarse salt . . . I'm sure I'm forgetting something.'

He crouched down again and took a five-litre can.

'Kerosene, for one.'

While the man was filling it, he wondered about buying a bottle of wine. Until now he'd been drinking only water from the river. When he thought it over, he could get by fine without it. It's not going to kill me, he said to himself. Back with the old man, he'd rarely tasted wine.

'Have you cigarettes?'

'Some, yes . . . these.' He placed a wooden box on the gunwale of his boat.

Boga reached in and rummaged among the packets. He took out five packets of light Particulares, twenty cigarettes in each, and two packs of Regia Italiana.

'I think that's all I want.'

He opened up a packet, and lit a cigarette.

He started with the stowing while the man made up the bill. The *tararira* flailed when he bent down just beside it, splashing up some water.

'You wouldn't like to buy some fish?'

'Why? Have you got some?'

'That's not what I'm saying . . . I mean the next time, if you might be interested.'

'It depends . . . what have you got there?'

The man came to the gunwale and looked down into the boat. He saw the *tararira*.

'Shit! What does it weigh?'

'Three kilos.'

'Bring it over here. We'll put it on the scales.'

'There's no need . . . I'm just saying, if you might be interested, in the future.'

'It's a matter of having a look. It all depends on what it is.'

Boga finished stowing the things and gave the man the money. The boat's engine had been running all this time. When he moved out from the launch, it seemed to him as if he'd gone into a silent, empty room. He found his ears were humming. He saw the man, his shadow, as it slipped towards the bow. The droning of the engine reached a pitch of desperation. Then the launch jerked forward, in the same direction, but within a few metres it turned all the way around and headed off towards the north. The man didn't look down as he passed him in the boat. He was rowing more or less in the same spot on the river when the launch disappeared around the bend. He looked at the smoke plume that still hung above the river. While the humming of the engine travelled ever further off, and was finally absorbed by the distance.

The water here inside was very bright and very still, and the dividing line that ran between the river mouth and open sea was visible again. The water there outside was folding up in little ripples, and had another colour. He saw the little fishing boat, still there.

He rowed towards the river mouth, veering gently right. He heard the murmur of choppy water further out, and then, in a moment, he was sailing it himself. He headed for one of the beaches dotted round the curve which folds like a balcony above the open sea. Right there the water gets much shallower. He saw the reed beds on either side, and straight ahead the measureless expanse of grey that, when you're far away, becomes confounded with the sky. He felt the morning wind that blew all the way across it, humid on his face. This wind and this murmur formed a globe or ring around him. He was at its centre and the globe or ring moved with him.

He heard the rub of sand against the bottom of the boat, and several metres further on he ran aground completely. This was the place. He stood up on the mast-hole seat and considered his surroundings with a certain satisfaction. He wasn't the kind of man who could easily be pleased, but what he saw now gladdened him. The murmuring and the wind and this beach in the morning, looking onto the open sea.

The beach was almost hidden by a covering of logs that had been rounded by the water, with not a lot of space between the water and the weeds. It was scarcely a few metres to the first line of trees. First a line of willows. Behind them, and much taller, there were other trees that rose between their stooping green crowns. He'd heard some talk about these trees. Many of them were missing now, cut down in the war, but the ones that still remained were those most hidden and protected by the shield of grass and willows. Wild vines ascended them and honeycombs stirred in their old, splitting wood.

He felt the silence and the damp, and then the kind of hum that rises up from any place that's been abandoned for some time. All of this emerged from the shadows of the scrub that was the heartland of these islands, and ventured out to meet him, the only thing so far to take on the murmur of the water, and the wind in from the river.

These are islands that rise higher, but have hollows at their centre, with tall trees hiding little lakes of still water. The ground is wet and overlaid with several layers of leaves, which give off tepid vapours.

But even though it's narrow, the dry, clear stretch of sand is bright and makes you feel alive, drawing all the morning light.

He rolled his trouser-legs up high and jumped into the water, then dragged the boat as far onto the beach as he could manage. This was going to be his first real camp.

He'd have to put the boat right if he wanted to go on. He would need to fix it while he was stopped here. He'd put it off till now, simply to avoid starting out on several days of work without a proper camp. Now that he was here he could see it as a pleasure, stopping in a place like this and taking all the time necessary to set a boat to rights.

The first thing he did was to make a fire. This making of a fire has a special kind of meaning to a solitary man. It's the same for any man lighting the first fire of a winter, whether he lives alone or not.

The fire burned in the morning with a riotous crackling, something like the water's murmur, but wild and more intense. He set the kettle in the flames, and when the fire got going he removed it with a stick and set the grill down in its place. The kettle went on top beside a five-litre tin that was half-filled with water. He threw a hand of salt in and the *ossobuco* pieces. He'd forgotten to buy potatoes. It was a pity this had happened, but he didn't regret it much, because he'd known right from the outset that he wouldn't remember everything.

He went to look around while the meat was on the grill, and his thoughts were pretty worked out by the time he returned. He'd clear himself a space between the nearest of the trees, and build himself a shed using branches laid with straw. He knew the spot already. Its full view of the sea and the stretch of sand before it was the best along the beach. He'd start to clear the land at once, and maybe have the shelter up tomorrow. Once that job was done, he'd empty out the boat and store the things inside the shelter, on a scaffolding of sorts that would keep them free of damp and safely up above the water, and then he'd turn his mind to the matter of the boat. He had big plans in mind for this little rowing boat. To begin with he'd thought he would do the bare minimum, only what was urgent, but little by little he'd decided on a scheme that was a good deal more ambitious. It would all take time, of course. But then he, in a way, was time.

Now, to get things going, he'd do, as quickly as possible, the things he couldn't put off; he'd change some of the planks, for one, renew most of the caulking, especially on the bottom, and apply a spot of paint. Once this work was finished, he'd deal with all the other jobs as something like a hobby, without the need to hurry things. What he had in mind was to bring this old boat back to something like it was at first, when it left old Froglia's yard, if in fact it had done.

He'd brought along some planks with which he'd thought to build the scaffolding where he would keep his things. These planks would make a rudder. A pretty little rudder with a pretty little tiller. Then, and when he stopped off on his travels round these rivers, he'd make himself a lugsail with the canvas that he'd brought. No rush, of course. He had, inside a metal box, needles, thread and pure wax, and a sailmaker's palm. It was the job he liked the most. Meantime, he would come across a pole along the way, or a boom or something like it, to serve him as a mast.

This, in general terms, was how he saw things in his mind. And when he came here next, sometime in high summer, he'd have himself a little yacht, or something pretty close to one, to sail out every morning on this river that is like the sea.

The boat was not as rotten nor as shoddy as it seemed. The opposite in fact, it was a splendid little boat put together in the old style. It had met with bad luck, was all. Perhaps because it lacked a name. No one wants to bother with a boat that has no name, or at least not take the same care as they'd take with one that has. To give a boat a name is in this way to provide it with protection. No, this boat had not found luck, in spite of its beginnings.

The problem of the leak was for the most part in the bow, at the junction where the timbers come together with the keel, and this part with the stem. Some caulking had worked loose and what was left of it had aged. It's the spot that gets the most buffeting. He stripped out all the caulking from the best part of the bottom. He didn't use the wicking, but the fibres of a hemp rope that he'd left to soak in diesel. But before he set to do this job, he changed three of the planks, and before he changed the planks he cleaned the old paint off the boat with a scraper that he'd sharpened, and which took the dirt off too. He thought it best, while changing planks, to bind one of the ribs that he noticed had split. He fettered it to either side, using screws of milled brass to secure the reinforcement, and then coating these with paint to make a seal.

He didn't neglect the fish while he was working on the boat, especially as this was what he lived on. He checked the lines he'd set at nightfall early every morning. There was always something on them, even if not much. Once he'd taken the hooks out from the fish, he put new bait on all the lines and threw them in again, but moving one or two to different places. As the day went by, and when the work began to bore him, he took a look around the lines, and if, when he came back to it, he found the boat still bored him, he made himself a new line, or else he had a swim. He was trying a dorado line he'd put a lot of faith in. He'd used *ceibo* wood to fashion all the floats himself. First were several round floats, standard-size and white, then came the final float, which was larger and cut square, rather like a half-brick, cut out from a lifebelt that had seen better days. He fixed every hook with a snap and a lead, and used triple swivels on a short length of leader, placed exactly halfway between one float and another. A pretty piece of work. To bait his dorado lines, he used, if he had them, eel and catfish pieces, knowing most dorado have a preference for the former, and placed them alternately.

Along the other shore was a lengthy stretch of sandbank noted for good fishing, in a kind of elbow, or perhaps it was a pocket, at the drain of the Diablo. But he had no way to reach the place unless he had a boat. Notwithstanding this, one morning when he got up, he swam across the river with a tightly rolled line that he'd wrapped inside a cloth then tied securely round his waist. He understood that somewhere round this spot there was a guard-post of the military command, so he made a sweeping detour on his way out to the sandbank.

Once he'd cast the line, he wondered if it wouldn't be best to stay there while he waited, so he wouldn't have to make another journey in the evening. He'd look around the sandbank and come back and check the line. If he didn't have a bite by then, he'd come back in the afternoon, or else the following morning.

He was gone for about an hour, going out and coming back. He went to check the line. He'd barely touched its thread when he knew he had a catch, and began to reel it in with a tingle of excitement. It's a thing you never get used to. The first two hooks were empty, but the water smashed like glass as the third came to the top. He pulled hard on the line. When he realised what he had, he gave a leap and then he whistled, and held the fish up high.

'Fucking hell!' he said, somewhere in among the whistling, feeling how his arm was already getting tired.

He'd caught a chafalote, over half a metre long, and something like four kilos. It must have followed bream as they'd gone into the reed bed. It was a handsome fish indeed and it looked quite aggressive with its bulldog lower jaw.

He took it off the hook and crashed its head against a log, so he could take it back across the river with him.

It was on the second day he was working on the boat that these strange, gigantic birds appeared. They came in from the south, at times a little west of this, and cut across the entire sky in a matter of just seconds, as if they were crossing a patio, or something even smaller. Sometimes only one appeared, more often two or three of them came over in a group. They flew very low, which made them seem quicker still. He'd heard somewhere or other that they had a base at Morón, and that sometimes they just exploded in the air, and were gone without a trace. You expected nothing less when you heard the noise they made. He stood underneath them as they charged across the sky, 600 kilometres per hour they went, chased on by their own din, and waited for the bang. They were the Air Force's Glosters, and one time he thought they'd seen him, because they'd wheeled on the horizon and flown back across the beach, so close overhead that he'd dived onto the sand, quite deafened by the noise they made, and had made out the pale, strangely peaceful face of one of the pilots.

As the work on the boat advanced, he felt a growing appetite for working here one day on the building of a real craft. It was just a passing thought at first, but then it made him think that he was wasting time on this job, that he'd never really wanted anything else in life. Now this job was really only holding up his plans, it was nothing but a pretence, a pale imitation. Finally, he began to get fed up, his longing for a boat mixing up with his longing to move on. It all became one thing.

And so he finished up and left, as if, by moving on, he would in some way start his boat as well. As if, behind these rivers that he had in mind to travel, his boat was out there waiting, and the only way to reach it was by going out to meet them. Even so, he'd managed to do the rudder.

And he left.

The man sailed up the rivers until almost the middle of the summer, and then came back in much less time, arriving at midsummer proper, at its height. In truth it wasn't very far, some ninety kilometres. But for the man, in his small boat, it was what you called a journey.

Setting out from Punta Morán he went up the Diablo, and reached the Paraná Miní in only half a day, although he hadn't set a time for his arrival. Then he made his way out to the Pozos del Barca Grande, and sailed across these sandbanks from buoy K47 to the unlit, black K50. It was here he left the Pozos and entered the Barquita, crossed the Barca Grande and, going up the Pantanoso, Borches and Camacho, he finally came out onto the Paraná Guazú. This is a river. In this part of the world, you have to come this far to know what river really means.

He stayed here for a day before he set out for the other shore, sailing a completely quiet river. Across, he took the Ceibito, and then down what remained of the Ceibo to its mouth, and the River Uruguay. There, he was thinking about skirting all the sandbanks, between the Argentine coast and the Canal Principal, or else to make his way down to the Alférez Pago, and then on by the Bravo, up the Paciencia Chico to the Gutiérrez Chico, and come out by that way, and in between the sandbanks, beyond Nueva Palmira at Punta Chaparro, on the coast of Uruguay. He settled on the Bravo, but, once he found himself on the Gutiérrez Chico, he went round to the left and then upriver on the Delta. He took

the Brazo Chico and then the Brazo Largo, and after that he
sailed on by the Brazo de la Tinta. From there he took the
Sagastume Chico to the sandbanks, sailing out across them,
and in between the currents, to the mouth of the Ñancay at
the Delta's northern limit.

He sailed upriver all this time without the slightest hurry,
and stopped off here and there for several days along the
way. What he liked above all was to let the currents take
him, running with the waters. He was going up towards the
north, and after the dorado, after fish in general, but with his
mind on the dorado, as if the fish and the king of all these
fish were running on ahead and he had to catch them up. He
wasn't yet aware of the extent to which this fish, this one in
particular, had for him become a myth. He'd fished it several
times before, but still lived with the feeling that he hadn't
really fished it, as if what he'd been fishing hadn't really been
this fish, but a kind of imitation. And somehow not the fish.
He felt its best was over when he raised it from the water.
And even just before.

The truth was that this man, if there'd been some way
to do it, would have wished to catch this fish in the fullness
of its element, in the deep heart of the water, not the fish
diminished, the dorado at the moment when it is no more
than a yellow glint, a folded line of gold in the darkness
of the water, that mere furtive brightness. It couldn't be,
of course. Perhaps, somewhere deep in things, the longing
of this man was to merge with the fish, in some way be
himself the fish.

He'd fought this battle several times, in several different
places, and it had only stirred his longing. What wouldn't he
have given to hold on to that moment that could never be

described, when with a spring it left the water, and he knew that he'd defeated the dorado! But then, once in the boat, he felt himself frustrated, as if he'd done things wrong and this wasn't the dorado, just a clump of time-worn gold.

He'd noticed subtle differences existed in the fish. Some possessed a longer snout and some a rising lower jaw, quite like *tarariras*. The former is *Salminus maxillosus*, the latter *Salminus brevidens*. He hadn't learnt these names, of course, but knew the variations, had a preference for the latter for its more aggressive look, that majestic head of gold that called to mind a sort of helmet. But finally, no matter, it might be the magnificent *Salminus brevidens* after all, but when everything was over and the fish began to die, in the bottom of the boat, he didn't feel the joy that he'd imagined, but rather, sadness.

It was partly due to this that he fished on just as intensively, but not as keenly now. And then, as time went by, this intensiveness diminished too. It wasn't that his feeling changed from one day to another, but that his irritation grew. And by the time he was almost north, he only fished to eat.

He went up with the river and, of course, with the dorado. And as he went upriver, his interest in anything but wandering from place to place, and always further north, dried up. The days were getting hotter, and not simply for the season, the summer now maturing, but because of his direction, towards the season's provenance. Between the middle of the morning and the middle of the afternoon, everything was sleepy. The squealing of the rowlocks and the slapping of the oar blades stretched out longer in this torpor, acquiring a strange nature. The sounds didn't come from near or far, but seemed to come from everywhere, the very air itself, and he was sure if he stopped rowing that the oars would sound all the same, as if they were an aspect of the summer.

He often disembarked in the middle of the morning, and lay there on the shore until the height of afternoon, in the shadows to begin with, and later, as they moved along, he lay out in the sun. He felt a curious pleasure when he stretched out in this manner, abandoning himself, oblivious to everything, even to the heat and to the presence of mosquitoes. At times he felt surprised at his capacity to bear it. At other times he thought this was the way to live these hours, there wasn't a better way but in a kind of partial stupor. But for the most part at these times he thought of absolutely nothing.

The heat and the mosquitoes were always there on top of him and got mixed up together, until they were the same.

It's true you can be driven round the bend by the mosquitoes. The only way to stop this is to clear them from your mind. Some folk say they bite those who get flustered or take notice of them. Just as with the skittish horse that knows which rider fears it and decides to throw him off. Others say they leave alone the folk who live around them. The best thing you can do with them is not to think at all, whether or not there's truth in this, and even as they stuff themselves in handfuls up your nose. And this is what he did.

On more than one occasion, if anyone had seen him there abandoned on the shore, they'd have taken him for dead. He looked as if he were dead. But he kept a hazy notion of this sleepy, silent world that encircled where he lay, mostly an awareness of sensations that defined it: the heat or, rather, something of a sticky warmish liquid, and this humming of the heat that was the product of ten thousand buzzings mingled into one, the rubbings and the dronings and the acid smell that rose up from his body and his clothes.

His beard had grown and often itched, as if his face were dirty. In truth, it was a little, even though he took his daily dive into the river. His clothing was disgusting, as was his whole appearance. Over time, his clothes had come to have the smell of canvas, in which he'd slept at first, and now, and still quite frequently, on top of which he lay.

On two or three occasions, lying on the ground like this, the rising water wet him and he didn't move away until the clothes stuck to his stomach.

But in the early morning and the late afternoon, when the heat was not as fierce, he seemed to come alive, and was pleased that it was summer. And then he had the night to come, in spite of the mosquitoes and the heat from the ground. Especially the moonlit nights, the splendour of the islands. It was enough to have a little moon to go out for a swim, unless it came up late and when the air had grown too chilly.

Living in this way a while, he got used to the notion that he travelled and was living with the summer and the river, completely in accord with them, that he was himself the summer and the river.

When his fishing interest waned and other things could interest him, other than this languid life of wandering the river, he dedicated time to the sail he'd planned to make. He made a good beginning, but he didn't get to finish it until much later on, before he made his way back, in the clearings of Ñancay, when he roused himself abruptly from the lassitude of summer with a will to make his way back for midsummer at Morán. Here, at any time of year, the winds in from the sea are strong and throw up stormy waters. These winds have curious powers and tend to feel quite personal.

Thinking of this wind brought back his memories of the open sea, and with them his nostalgia. There isn't a man among them can resist this smell of the sea.

It wasn't long before this that the nauseous event took place, which maybe was related to his longing.

He was tired of eating fish. If you don't prepare them well, all the fish out of the river taste the same. And even well-prepared, it's the sauce that whets your appetite. Doing what you can to hide the constant taste of mud is what it comes to.

In Boga's case, it wasn't this taste of mud that put him off, in time he came to like the greasy taste of certain fish, like the flesh of yellow catfish, and the *patí*. If this is how you are when you live in such a region, you can count yourself a lucky man. But nevertheless, he grew a little weary of it all, and as fish goes down quite quickly, he was always hungry.

A little way beyond where the Paciencia Chico meets the Paciencia Grande, he saw a band of Pekin ducks, and thought that somewhere nearby there must also be a house. He stood up on the mast-hole seat and looked in all directions, all along the riverbanks, trying to locate it. He couldn't see it anywhere, but knew there had to be one, and not so far away, somewhere hidden in the trees. The ducks went paddling on ahead, about five metres from the boat. Four Pekin ducks, smug and very white, and two of them at least were clearly still very young. The duck is not good for eating if it isn't three months old, nor after it's a year.

He'd put down both the oars and the ducks moved away. He bent down for the sea bread and he threw them little pieces. The ducks left off their paddling and gave him sideways looks, with their long necks stretching upwards. They began to come towards him, and at length they ate some bread. He went up to the stern, then, and laced a length of line around the gudgeon of the rudder. The movements that he made were all deliberate and careful, and every now and then he threw the ducks a bit more bread. He took the length of the line that was sitting on the water and fixed a fine hook onto it, an Alma Captiva. He baited it with sea bread, a decent looking lump that also had a bit of crust, and threw it on the water. He went back to the centre seat and tied the other loose end of the line around his leg. The point of this device was for the duck to take the sea bread and the hook to catch the duck. Then he'd pull the line, and the duck, which couldn't quack, would be pulled down under water as the line ran round the gudgeon. With the duck below the boat, he would then unlace the line and retie it round a rowlock, to keep the duck from coming up, and set off with the oars again until he felt completely sure that no one would observe him. Rowing was a pleasure with the thought you had a decent meal assured.

He would untie the line when the moment came to do so, and gather in the duck.

With a little bit of practice you can pick the duck you want and entice it to the chosen spot, an inlet or a bend or a reed bed, for example, away from prying eyes.

He'd just thrown in the bait. It was comical the way the duck first swallowed down the piece of bread before it stood up straight in the water and, with big, astonished eyes, it stopped and looked at you, perplexed by what had happened. The line trailed from the bird's beak like a worm or something similar, and looked both very funny and horrific all at once.

But he gave the line a pull, and the kind of death the duck must face, down under the water, and how long it would take to die, didn't cross his mind.

He did this once. And then once again on the Brazo de la Tinta, when he managed to hook the duck that he'd selected. But the third time that he did it, on the Sagastume Chico, things didn't turn out well.

It wasn't a Pekin duck, but a Muscovy this time. Perhaps this had its influence, one never really knows. He saw the ducks, he found the house, he worked out where to lure them to and then prepared the bait. He rowed in front of the house very close against the bank, which is the best way to stay hidden, having put a little bit of water on the rowlocks, so they wouldn't make their squealing. He carried on a way before he waited in an inlet for the ducks to come along.

Then the ducks arrived and he threw the bits of bread. Next he threw the line in and he hooked his chosen duck. It took a bit of tempting, but at last he had his bird. He gave the line a pull and the duck disappeared through the surface. He tied the line in place and gathered up the oars.

And that was when the air around him shattered, or it seemed to, and he felt a furious burning in his left arm, near the shoulder. He didn't understand what had happened at the time, but an instinct made him dive into the bottom of the boat.

He stayed there, pressed against the planks, panting hard and swearing, while the burning grew more angry, then impossible to bear. He felt his hand grow wet where it was lying on the wound, and then he saw the blood, leaking thick and dark beside his face, and dropping little splashes on the dirty bottom planks. He looked up at the clear blue sky, framed inside the gunwale, as if out from a well.

What would he do now, the bastard who had shot him?

He strained his ears to listen, but the silence grew still thicker, and then he started listening to the humming of the summer. He noticed that the boat went sliding on atop the water, bumping several times against what must have been the bank. If it would only move out from the bank! Perhaps it would be better if he jumped onto the bank and disappeared among the trees? No. He'd wait here for the son of a bitch. He wasn't going to kill him for a common Muscovy duck.

He waited in the boat for an excruciating time, until at length events took on an air of unreality.

The sun had risen high. He was being baked alive there in the bottom of the boat. And this burning in his arm, the very devil.

The boat still made its way along. At length his senses dulled and he fell into a stupor, and the pain drifted off a while, or else it took a form that he could reasonably bear.

The sun had disappeared from its frame when he awoke. But the heat was just the same. He'd lost all track of time. The pain was there again, now strong and well defined. His sleeve was soaking wet and the blood flowed underneath it, and out across his hand, but thicker now, and more slowly.

Was the man still out there? Why didn't he check the boat? Perhaps the man was frightened, imagining he'd killed him. He'd be hiding on the riverbank, spying on the boat and trying to work out what to do with the body.

It would have been much better for the man and for himself if the boat had been dragged far off by the current, but, as a rule, these boats don't drift far, unless there's a freakish surge.

It could also be the case that the man had washed his hands of the matter. This dead bloke in a boat would at some point be discovered, but time would pass before the coast guard came to be informed. People don't want trouble. A few days would go by and the man would see their launch appear, the rowing boat behind it with its pestilential smell. An officer would ask him, without a lot of interest:

'Do you know this chap?'

'No. Don't think I do. Can't be absolutely sure, considering the state of him. What a fucking smell!'

'Do you have a shotgun?'

'Yes, a 1916 double-barrel . . . like we all do round these parts.'

The officer would speak in a small, sarcastic way.

'Nobody knows anything.'

'Someone roaming round, then.'

And they'd take him off curled up inside the boat, beneath a canvas.

The man might also come at night and drag the boat a long way off, or, more likely, he'd bury him in the middle of one or other of these islands, where not a soul is seen. Then he'd smash the boat to bits and burn the pieces one by one, in daylight.

The boat bumped into something soft and then it seemed to halt.

He'd wait for nightfall anyway, to raise himself and row as far as possible from here. What could he do in any case, suffering this pain? Nothing much, for now. How close was the house now? He held his breath and listened. No, not a sign. Not dogs, nor voices, nothing. But the man could have tracked him from the bank, and in the trees. And things were even worse now, for now the man would fear him. No one in these parts wants a dead man on their hands, and even less, in this state. And if that man's just wounded he can think of coming back. It's an outrage, after all, to kill a man for nothing but a common Muscovy duck. A man who's spent a whole day in the bottom of a boat, suffering in the sun in the middle of the summer, and then is dragged off in the night – as long as there's blood left in his veins that man cannot take such a thing calmly.

What a bastard pain! And now, when he tried to, he couldn't move his arm. It seemed he had ten thousand needles buried in his flesh. He was going to try to rip his sleeve off, have a look beneath it.

The boat still wasn't moving. There were branches or some grasses brushing gently on one side. He must be at the bank.

He was tugging at his sleeve when he heard the sound of someone in the grass, coming closer. It's a noise you can't mistake. Impossible to advance through pampas grass without making this kind of noise, and much less on a quiet day. Not even little birds can do it. The noise was not continuous, as when a man moves easily and doesn't think of safeguards. The man took several steps and stopped. The place was wild, without a doubt. If there'd been some kind of path he wouldn't have made this noise.

The man had stopped some time ago, and seemingly close by. He held on to his breath. How long could he hold his breath and how well could he hide it?

At last the man moved on again, and now he was beside the boat, and watching him, the shotgun surely on him. He felt the dreadful presence of the other man above him, he didn't need to look.

The man bent down and put the shotgun barrel to his head. It was a trick. And yet he couldn't bear it. The man stepped into the boat from the other end, taking every kind of care. Boga had fallen near the prow. The rocking of the boat had now become a real torment and he had to make an effort to keep still.

The man came close and poked him with the barrel of the gun. He jogged him with his toe. He tried to turn him over with the barrel, but he couldn't. This really made him nervous.

At last the man put the gun down, propped against one side, and leaned towards him. He clearly heard the sound of the gun against the side, and made a calculation of the moment when the man crouched down. He leapt up like a spring and seized the man around the arms, as he came towards him, and pulled his body to him using all the strength he had, and clung on tight. Now he saw the man's face, its tension and surprise, while his body shook inside his arms, immobilised completely, and then began to hit him in the face, with his head. The man's whole body shuddered and he uttered little noises that were strangled in his throat, he heard the man's teeth cracking, and the bones inside his jaw. The man was trying to shape himself to knee him in the stomach, but they'd fallen in the bottom and he couldn't find a way. Then he butted harder still and then at last he felt the other's strength begin to fail. He still fought back a while, thinking how to free himself and make it to the gun. It seemed as if he'd fainted, but he wasn't going to trust a fellow like this.

He pushed the man away from him, as far as he could manage, and in the same thrust grabbed the gun. He stood up in the stern and aimed directly at the man.

But now the man had fainted, and he looked quite badly injured. His face was all messed up.

The man was getting on a bit, his face was gaunt and hardened. Boga left him on the bank, sitting propped against a tree, with the empty gun beside him, as if he was a hunter who'd sat down to take a nap. There was his face, of course, but you couldn't see it from further off. The two of them were quits. It was possible the man would come to see it that way too. Neither of them wanted any problems.

The pain made him demented. If he hadn't been a man who accepted what life brought him, he'd have cursed the day he set out from Morán, and further back, his setting out from the Anguilas.

Pain for him, quite naturally, was not the same as pleasure, and yet the line between them, the line that kept all things apart, seemed anything but clear. Life went through him like a river. Pain and pleasure came and went when neither was expected, one led to the other, each thing brought what followed it, and if you stopped to think about it, all things were at root the same, a dark and wild water in a never-ending current. He accepted every part of it; he was all of it in some way. He couldn't have risen up against it, couldn't have forced this life, this river, in any way at all.

When he'd put the Sagastume Chico well behind him, he made himself a camp in a secluded spot. He built a fire in which he made his rigging knife spike red-hot, and removed the pellets one by one.

He couldn't understand how those black dots in his flesh could be the cause of so much pain. His soul raged in those little dots. He felt their very pulsing and, if he closed his eyes, he could imagine that his arm was growing infinitely larger.

He'd heard it said that myrtle leaves were good for wounds like this. But he didn't make his mind up what to do for quite a time; he preferred to bear the pain than have to raise himself and struggle through the scrub. At last he did get up when the pain became unbearable, but stayed there with his eyes half-closed, lurching like a drunkard as he stared out at the river. The water glittered fiercely. He walked towards the brightness and stepped down into the river. After this he kneeled and put his head into the water. It brought him back to life, a little.

He moved along the shore until he came across a ditch. He followed it a fair way up, and deep into the weeds, and he didn't find the plant because he didn't pay attention. He travelled like an idiot, conscious of the smarting of the grasses on his hands, and at times he lost all sense of things, like walking in his sleep, and feeling in some vague way he'd been doing so for ages. He finally sank down onto the margin of the ditch, beside a willow, utterly exhausted. The heat and the humidity and his panting enclosed him like a cloud. And that old, bitter smell of the vegetation.

When he'd calmed a little he at last picked up the other smell, sweet and persistent. He must have been aware of it for quite a while, in fact. He looked and saw them there above his head, the little pointed leaves and blue-coloured berries of a myrtle plant two metres high, maybe even three. And a little way beyond it was another.

He went back to the boat and crushed the leaves against the seat, until he had a kind of paste, which he spread on a section of the sleeve that he'd torn off. This is what he'd heard, that you make a myrtle poultice, and he did his best to fashion something like it. Then he cut some line and tied the poultice on his arm. Now he had to wait.

At first it seemed to help a bit, but after that it seemed to make the pain even worse. At last he tore the poultice off and threw it far away, cursing everybody else for swallowing this nonsense.

He wished he had a decent lump of unsalted pig fat, the only thing he trusted, he'd seen for himself how it cured the wounds on dogs, however bad they were. The old man always had some, hanging from a kitchen beam.

He spent two days and nights like this, lying on the beach with his back against the boat, or else beneath a tree in the hot hours of the day, and living with his pain alone; he didn't know what the time was, he was smothered by the atmosphere, and there between his eyelids was that giant shining slick, like a ball of fire that rose up from the middle of the river, and which left him at a certain hour of day completely blind.

Time ran slow and fussily, as if it were an acid trickling from his wound.

He felt sick all the time and his annoyance was tremendous, a rancour of some kind against a thing he couldn't identify, something in the river, he felt, perhaps the river itself. And each attack of pain was succeeded by despondency. Compared with this, though, what he feared was when the pain announced itself. And then it fell on top of him, the real pain itself, summary and cutting. And always there was a part of him left to be surprised that he could take it at all. Then the long despondency, a thick and blackened water. And after this the rancour and the feeling of malignity he felt on every side, and he might have come to hate this endless river, really hate it, if it wasn't for the fact that nothing moved him very deeply.

At last he would fall asleep. But his body never quite forgot the pain lodged in his arm.

He came back far more quickly and he only stopped off once. He'd seen a boat aground as he passed the Pantanoso. It must have been there quite some time, and wouldn't be worth much now. The vessel was a wreck. Some use any excuse to take a boat out of the water, but in truth this is only ever a death sentence. A boat that's getting old can't hope for any happy outcome when it's taken onto land.

Instead of being up on props, it lay there on one side, as if it were asleep. He reckoned that the side on which it rested would be rotten, the timber soft and black with the consistency of cork, and then completely warped beneath the full weight of the vessel. He didn't remember having seen the boat, which must be old, before; its lines were clearly from the past, though it was not as old as some you still saw sailing on the rivers, the *Gorrión* for instance, and then the *San Pedrito*.

The mast and boom were still there and he stopped off for the latter, thinking it might serve him as the mast his boat was needing.

This is what he said to the man now on the jetty, who was kicking at some dogs.

'I've been looking for a mast . . . I thought perhaps that boom might do . . . '

'It's made of fir, same as the mast. You won't find anything better . . . '

He lost a little heart when he looked into the man's face. He wished he hadn't stopped at all.

'I just saw it and I wondered. It's a boom in any case, and not a mast.'

'I don't know what it is you want. You say you want a mast.'

'A small mast for this rowing boat.'

'You won't find anything better, then.'

He had his head on one side and he watched him with one eye half-closed. There was no doubt that he saw him as an innocent.

'Depends on what you're asking . . . '

'Well, selling it like that wasn't what I had in mind. I want to sell the whole boat, as a piece, and nothing else.'

'I can't see what a rotten boat is good for.'

'A lot more than you seem to think . . . it isn't in such bad shape.'

'True; it could be worse . . . the thing is that I only want a small mast, not a boat.'

'It doesn't do me any good to sell it off like that. It serves no use at all. If you start taking bits off, then you'll never sell the rest.'

'You wouldn't sell that boat even if you put bits on it.'

'That's only what you say.'

'There's nothing more to say, then, if you don't want to sell.'

'Fine by me as well. It doesn't do me any good.'

'All I want's a little mast. Forget I even said it.'

Boga took his seat again, as if to start to row, and the man looked away and put his hands into his pockets. So Boga had to start to row.

This was when the man said:

'And how much for the boom? Just for asking's sake. I was curious to know what you think these things are worth. It seems you're out of touch.' He spoke in an affected tone to make light of the matter.

'I don't have a figure. It's your boom to sell.'

'But just in general terms. Tell me what you'd give, and in whatever place you've been to, for a boom that looks like this.'

'I don't know. You tell me.'

'It's a boom that's made of fir.'

'Whatever the wood.'

'It's not the same, you know that.'

'Ok, let's agree it's gold, what is it you want for it?'

'I hadn't really thought. I want to sell the whole boat.'

'You've told me that already.'

'Well . . . I think . . . and just for argument, and giving the thing away . . . five hundred pesos.'

'Yeah, and the rest. I could buy the boat for less than that.'

'What do you mean! That boom is fir . . . any old stick would cost you double.'

'If it wasn't rotten.'

'Now just hang on a minute!'

'There's nothing more to say.'

'I won't say a word.'

'You were never going to sell it; am I right?'

'I was going to sell the whole boat.'

'Who're you trying to fool!'

'Not another word.'

'Forget I spoke. See you around.'

He gathered up his oars.

'Five hundred pesos! How much is that today?' Now the man was shouting.

'I haven't got that much.'

'Who are you trying to kid?'

'I don't have the money!'

The man scratched at his head.

'In that case . . . I'll take four.'

'Too much.'

'Are you mad? I'm doing you a favour.'

'You can keep that kind of favour.'

'So you want it as a present?'

'I didn't say that either.'

'Four hundred pesos.'

'It's far too much . . . three hundred too.'

'You're bloody mad!' He was spluttering and choking, and banging on the rail of the jetty.

'Not another word. You can stick it up your arse!'

'Stick your shitty three hundred pesos up your arse!'

'I wasn't going to pay you that.'

'So how much was it then?'

'Two hundred at the most.'

'Yeah, don't make me laugh!'

'Do you want the money or not?'

He hadn't for a moment thought to pay in cash. He suggested to the man that he work the money off, on whatever jobs there were. And so he stayed the two days that he'd planned on from the start, because, and in his turn, the man had haggled a bit from his side, getting him to do a little more than they'd agreed. But in the end they both came out ahead.

The days are even longer now, and if wasn't for this wind that blows from the river, the heat would do you in. Boga turns his mind back to his fishing once again, but the enthusiasm's gone. He knows now for certain that he can't fish the dorado.

Not, in any case, in the way that he would like to. And it saddens him a little. It will go up to the north, soon, that's if it's still around, if it ever swam these waters, and would that this splendid summer fish had never come down.

The condition of the lean-to was exactly as he'd left it, and he had a sense of coming back; it was the first time that he'd felt this. Someone else had been here, and not so long ago. Perhaps a man out fishing, perhaps Lefty La Rocca, who seems to turn up everywhere, as if one spoke of God. He looked down at the remnants of a fire that wasn't his, some newspaper pages that had started turning yellow and an empty tin of corned beef lit up by the sun. Seeing it like this, the place seemed even lonelier, this place set on the river.

He finished fitting the boat that afternoon, as Froglia had pictured it all those years ago, and set out in the morning for the deep heart of the river. He rowed for a bit and after that he raised the sail. The wind was a northerly, blowing from the land, and he let it run him on to the Las Palmas Canal.

The wind had gone by midday, but he went down with the water to buoy K33, right at the bifurcation, passing very close to the hull of the *Macá*, sunk in 1924, the same year as the *7 Hermanos*, which is a little before, except further out. It was swaying at the centre of a large, deep stain, and the buoy's isolation made him feel a bit uneasy. These enormous, lonely buoys always have the same effect.

The sun was shining high and it seemed as if it watched him there. He took a cigarette and looked above him to his sail, feeling rather anxious at the rag there on his mast. So this is where he was, at the mercy of the river, on a little boat in which he'd placed a little too much faith, perhaps.

He came back with the evening, running with the south-east wind, fleet before the night.

This was how he spent what remained of the summer. He met a boat from time to time, and Lefty La Rocca twice. He slept out on the beach when there wasn't any wind, lying down beside the boat. All he could accomplish was to draw large boats in the sand, or whittle points on sticks. He found he'd grown a beard such as he'd never had before, and looked a real castaway. Loneliness had matured on his face, and this life had made him brutish, in a way.

On nights when there was moonlight, and with a bit of breeze, he ventured on the river out to where he saw the channel lights. But one night he was caught out by the wind from the south-east, and was fighting with the river until the water threw him on the beach. The sail was torn up first and then the mast was snapped in half when the water knocked him down. The shreds of sail were flapping like a woeful bird's wings overhead, and when they tore the sound was quite tremendous. He couldn't see much of anything, just these couple of whitish patches flailing in the gloom, but he heard the water churning, boiling all around the boat, and twice he fell and rolled into the bottom. It seemed the boat had taken in a large amount of water. He felt the wish to stay there, in the bottom, like a just-caught fish. But he sat back on the seat and tried to hold things with the oars, knowing the river could knock him down again at any moment, and regardless of his skill, if it wanted. Now it even entertained him, fighting in the darkness and with not a hope of winning, pitching up and down in the night, as if he rode a beast, mounted on its giant back.

Angry at the river at first, he'd wondered what to do, how he'd extricate himself. But then he didn't think at all. The wind that circled round his head and all that devilish whirring like a siege of buzzing wasps, it had left him in a daze. It was the only thing he heard, and all he felt were his tense wet limbs, his feet stuck underwater, and his hands, holding on or even tied to the oars that seemed to circle on their own, suspended from the noise. He went on riding up and down. He saw a light at one point, but he couldn't tell its distance, though it wasn't on the channel. And everything at last seemed strange, held there in the darkness, and then his breath was taken by a feeling of euphoria, at times he didn't know where he was, or even what he did.

Until the water picked him up and threw him on the beach. He'd trusted in the river. Nothing riles the river more.

It was some time since he'd lost track of the passing of the days, but even so, he clearly saw the end of summer coming. It wasn't a question of dates, but from a sign, and then another. Perhaps it was because of exactly this that he saw it when others didn't; because he didn't go calculating the days, which aren't a line of numbers, but rather, a constant and deliberate movement of the light.

He knew it was a Sunday from the number of small boats that were appearing on the river. He'd seen them springing up, white and frail and silent, like a flock of doves along the shore, when sailing on the channel. But now he didn't have the little boat to go out when he liked, he saw them from a distance as they sailed towards the east, and with a lot more space between them. Some went round the outside of the Bajo to Punta Morán, and others through the

Sueco. Here come the Sunday sailors, he was thinking, with a quiet laugh.

The boat hadn't suffered too much damage overall, but the sail had had its day. As it was, these circumstances suited him quite well, now, for he changed with the seasons, and the river at this time became more distant every day. Things might change from one moment to the next, they were changing even now. The summer was still here, it seemed. But now the light was different and the colour of the trees had turned quite lustreless and murky. This was one such sign, and so were all the insects that were rising from the weeds, as if the world were too ripe, almost rotten.

It didn't seem possible that winter would ever arrive, on the face of it. But it would come in the end, without a doubt. It was already arriving, in a way, if you could see these things. Now, when the night fell, a light mist rose to lie across the surface of the water. And as a certain hour went by, a saddened light that came in from the south traversed the evening, and the twilight, if you looked at it, was docile and silenced, a realm between two seasons.

He stayed here for a good while yet, without deciding anything, in spite of all these changes, sometimes feeling restless and at others even grumpy, as if everything he waited for would be resolved by time.

The south wind came one afternoon and swept the beach of sand, and he saw his shadow lengthening grotesquely on the wasteland. Everything seemed desolate, so sad and beyond repair, that he turned back to the land, towards the islands, and set sail at once.

In this very season, but at another time, he'd spent a night inside a ruin that he found on the Riestra, quite close to its outlet. It's a perfect refuge for the winter, if it's still there now.

All these streams that drain into the Bajo del Temor offer shelter and seclusion. Their inlets are concealed by an extensive fringe of reeds, which also shields them from the open sea. In the case of the Riestra, you have to find a current that runs out between the reeds, and trace it through until you reach the stream. If you take a careful look, and from the open sea, you might just see a marker buoy that indicates the entrance. But if you've been away a while it's difficult to find, for there are many of these markers and not all of them mark inlets. Quite the opposite, in fact: some of those most visible are placed here to mislead those who might use them as a guide.

Lately, he'd thought often about the place. Every time he'd thought about the winter, you could say. Until he came to see this place and winter as the same thing. It's a good spot for the silverside, which turn up here in April with the first cold-weather days. And from here, across the Bajo, it's straight into the Sueco. He could use the days till April to inspect his trammel net, to have it ready for the silverside. But aside from doing that, perhaps the time had come to put an old plan into practice.

He'd brought along the otter trap, the one he'd bought two years ago at San Fernando Fair, when he'd felt the urge to hunt them. The trap was very sensitive, the teeth it had were frightful and his pleasure at the time had been to tease them with a stick.

He'd always had the notion he could be an otter hunter, a first-rate one at that, in the style of Old Manito. It's a somewhat curious life, and suited to a loner. Speaking of Manito, who lived up on the Gélvez, he was otter-like himself. He moved around the scrub all day, shoving through the grass and sleeping out among the undergrowth, ever more the otter. It was difficult to find him, if that was what you wanted. He had seen him just the once, and that by pure coincidence, in San Fernando Harbour, just before he'd disappeared.

He was short and strongly built, with a very hairy head, and went barefoot in all weather. He held two sheaves of otter skins, one below each arm, at the time when skins began to make a decent little profit. He entered El Progreso, Basque Arregui's store, and everything he said in there was heard across the street, because he shouted like the damned and he didn't control his voice at all, and stammered a little, accustomed as he was to being alone, and to the silence.

If a pelt reached seventy centimetres from the eyeholes to the tail, and if he skinned it well, it could make three hundred pesos. He was going to put a pen up on the land behind the house. For now he'd get things started with his trap and with the pen. Then he'd buy more traps and make extensions to the pen. The trick was getting started. There, in the middle of the islands in the winter, it was just the job.

One part of the house had fallen down when he arrived, but most of it was standing. It must have been a fine house in its time. It was constructed on a regal scale, with plentiful high rooms and a veranda right across the front. Most of this veranda had already lost its balustrade, and half its floor had given way. It was a pretty spot to sit out and admire the afternoon. Its steps had disappeared as well, but someone had replaced them with a log cut from a willow.

It was a house of a specific time, not only for its style but because of something subtler, something ill-defined and that perhaps explained its dying. The piece of land in front of it, right down to the river, was a garden in its time, which isn't something common in these parts. Several handsome trees remained, like maritime pine and monkey puzzle. The scrubland and its undergrowth went right around the house, and yet, for all the time gone by, no weeds had moved inside it in the way that one expects. Something sad and docile, languishing as time went by, persisted in the place. The memory of other men still lived inside its limits and was stronger than the land.

He sensed it all around him, and in the early days he felt he didn't live alone here. His footsteps echoed strangely up and down the empty house, as if he walked across the deck above an empty boat. The silence was surprising in the late hours of the day, and all the sounds he made seemed disproportionate around him.

He liked the place in spite of this, and very soon he'd start work on the pen.

The same day that he lit perhaps the first fire of the winter, something strange took place. He'd been here for a while now and the pen was underway. It happened then.

He'd just hung up the trammel net between a couple of trees. He was going to light the fire now, and then, first thing in the morning, he would start to check the net, with the daylight. Busy as he'd been with the pen, he'd snacked on a bit of cold fish in the middle of the day, eaten with some sea bread and a drink of water, and only now, with nightfall, was he lighting the fire, at this auspicious twilight hour.

He'd brought a lot of firewood to the middle of the garden, or what had been a garden once, including several timbers from the house, where it was falling down, and lit the wood with a handful of dried grass he'd doused in fish oil. The flames expanded quickly and he circled round the fire a while, as if around a party. Any good-sized fire produced this feeling when he saw it. It seemed like something living, with the sparks of many lives. It's great company, without a doubt.

His hands and face were burning, but he stayed there and withstood it. He was dazzled by the brightness and could only just make out the very highest of the treetops, which seemed as if they nodded at the bidding of the flames. He made his way up to the house and lay on the veranda. He watched the fire from there. Some branches that were still green made brief explosions as they burned, and the crackling of the flames, as it came across the distance, sounded rather like the sighing of the water on a beach.

The darkness had set in, but there was still a little light far off, high above his head. He lit a cigarette, and when he raised his head again he saw the dog there, looking up at him, watching from the garden; its tail was wagging urgently as if it stalked a rat, or an opossum, something like that. He couldn't see it well because the fire blazed on behind it. So he leaned forward a little and the dog began to bark.

It was the first dog that he'd seen round here. Just two or three times, when the easterly was blowing, he believed he'd caught the sound of several voices in the distance, and the noise a household makes. On the Piccardo Canal side. This dog must be from there, because it didn't look like a stray. It was small and very skinny, and its coat was short and white, but with one or two black patches, and it had the look of all the dogs that live here on the islands – unhappy and resigned.

He spoke to it, but didn't move, so as not to scare it, his voice was sweet and gentle and sounded almost festive.

'Hi amigo! What's with you? Amigo, don't make so much noise! Hey, hey, amigo!'

The dog gave up its barking, and stood and watched him carefully, stretching out its neck with its head down, like a tortoise.

'Come on now, amigo . . . here, say hello . . . '

He slowly straightened up. The dog sent out a growl and moved away from him a little. He was up on his feet now, at the rail of the veranda.

It was then he had the feeling that a man's head had appeared, behind the maritime pine. He waited without moving, looking all around the tree. Now he was convinced that there was someone there behind it.

'Who's that prowling round out there?' he called into the shadows.

He'd taken several steps back now, looking for the shelter of the area in darkness, and he took out and opened up the knife. It was then he saw the man's head quite distinctly.

'You can come out now, my friend . . . there's no point . . . I can see everything you're up to.'

The head at last came right out and it stayed there for a while, looking up towards the house. He couldn't see it clearly, but the face looked rather childish. It even looked amused. He'd be thinking he was doing something very funny.

The dog had almost joined the stranger beside the maritime pine, wagging with its tail as it barked first towards the house and then away, behind the tree, to where this person hid himself.

'Ok,' he said. 'You've had your fun. It's time to come out now.'

He waited for a while yet. Then he made his way towards the end of the veranda, but keeping in the shadow. He could drop down from this end and make his way around the house, and not be seen. He was just about to jump down when he caught sight of the other man, on the move as well. The dog moved back behind the pine. He knew the man was leaving. He jumped off the veranda and went straight across the garden, to the pine.

There was no one there.

The dog turned up alone the next day.

Two days after this, he was finishing off the pen when he sensed that they were watching. He turned around and saw him, this little fellow with his gigantic smile, standing right in front of him.

He stood there for a good while, looking back without a word, but feeling ruffled. There the fellow stood and watched him in the half-light of the evening, quite undaunted. He was small and very skinny, rather like the dog. There are those who say a dog will end up looking like its owner. It's right what they say.

He wore a small white hat pulled right down on his ears, a grey, coarse-weave jumper that was buttoned to the neck, black trousers tucked into his socks, and basketball slippers. He looked pretty funny. His face still had that smile, but underneath, it held something sad. He leaned a little forward, looking up towards this fellow, and tried to decipher what was written on his shadowed face, which seemed to hang in silence from the sky. Now he thought he knew this chap from some place or another, and was trying to remember. He really looked just like a child. But the truth was very different.

'You're Cabecita,' he said at last, from his crouching position. His voice was quite contained and the words emerged slowly, in a tone of mild surprise.

The other didn't answer. He simply started scratching. He did so in a manner that was thorough and drawn-out, with the same neat attention as a cat does when it washes.

Yes, and now it came to mind. He'd seen this Cabecita just the once, and from a boat, but his face wasn't easily forgotten. Long and very lean and with a mouth that bulged with teeth, and those big glossy eyes that had no spirit. All he did was smile, and for no reason. Looking at him closely, it was just a fleeting movement of his large and silent lips, an automatic gesture that lacked any real meaning, for nothing else across his face expressed the slightest thing.

It could be Cabecita. Or at least, it might have been him, if it wasn't for the fact that Cabecita had been drowned, and several years before this, on the sandbanks as you're leaving the Anguilas.

He'd forgotten this at first. Although, if he was honest, he wasn't very sure now that he'd heard the story told in full. But anyway, he wouldn't have been the first man that they'd given up for dead. Colorado Chico was another case in point, and Ítalo Bordenave much further back in time, and then Lefty La Rocca, and several times in his case, so they came to think him immortal or a ghost or something like that, and no one came across him now without feeling suspicious, if they saw him at all, that is.

The river is immense. It's impossible to know of all the things the river does.

So there he was, that afternoon, this man who was like Cabecita and who could have been the man himself: Cabecita in the flesh. But things were less than simple, for you couldn't get a sane word from an idiot like this, who only grinned and nothing else, so never mind the time he stayed, you'd never really know if you were dealing with a dead man, or someone still alive, or even resurrected, or just some other nobody, in one of those three states.

'Are you Cabecita or aren't you?' he was still asking, just for the sake of asking really.

It was now growing darker and he heard the small uncertainty that got into his voice as it went across the garden like a solitary bird.

The little man's smile grew wider, and now he raised his eyebrows, and said nothing.

So he got up on his feet and put a hand on his shoulder. He felt a bit uneasy.

'Where's the dog?' he said.

And now he tried to think if he'd seen this Cabecita with a dog. Not that this would mean that much, necessarily. He could have got himself a dog later. The thing was that he now believed he'd seen him with this dog, exactly this dog. But this didn't carry a lot of weight either, if you consider that a dog lives fifteen years, if all goes well. It was the fact he'd thought him dead, or that he'd seemed so dead to him, and that now he was in front of him, like this – if it really was Cabecita – standing stock-still and mute in this garden lit by evening, watching from those giant eyes that looked just like a dead man's, even if he wasn't actually dead, as if it were someone else who gazed at him through those eyes, through that mask.

It struck him as a waste of time to ask him any questions. Not because he wouldn't understand, or wouldn't answer, but because his attention simply slipped across such things as these, to settle in a feeble way on something else completely, on the movement of his lips, it seemed, or else that look of puzzlement which played across his face.

He gave a shrug and turned and made his way towards the house, enveloped in the shadow of the twilight. He looked across the garden and, further off, the river, there between the uprights that were eaten through and blackened by damp. The river was in darkness.

He passed below the house and came back out around the front. Night was very close now. It felt a little chilly. The house, the boat, the trees were somehow plunged into a curious kind of languor. The noises from the scrub had dimmed, had almost disappeared. A great silence emerged from the darkness. He pulled up several floorboards and prepared to light a big fire that would keep the winter ghosts away. He gathered up some sticks and also looked back every now and then to where he'd left the little fellow. He couldn't see things clearly as the light was very pale. Perhaps the fellow had gone. And yet he had the feeling he was watching him from somewhere.

It was then the dog appeared again, right up against the house. Then he saw the little fellow was stationed up on the veranda. No more than a shadow leaning slightly down towards him.

'Hello there, amigo,' he called towards the dog, in defiance of the shadows, and his voice resounded very strangely in the solitude and silence and the half-light.

The little fellow left the veranda, and it seemed he'd gone to gather up some branches.

He built himself a new fire on the ashes from the day before. The ground was damp and cold now, but the spirit of the fire was there. He was tending to the ashes when the fellow came up next to him with his handful of sticks, and put them to one side. He made as not to notice him, although he used his sticks.

He got the fire going and then he didn't feel so alone. The little fellow had made him lonely. This hadn't happened once in all the summer.

Finally he looked at him, standing in the firelight. Of course, he was smiling. There was something very sad about this little man, something wretched. He seemed to see, behind him, all the long days of the winter, its sky of grey, the dried-up trees, the earth sunk in its sleep, the clothes that never dried out and the mud that got in everywhere, this mud that seemed the substance of the winter. At least he had the fire. When all is said and done, the winter also has its charms, even in these islands with their frightful melancholy. Every season has its charms, every season has its fish.

He lit a cigarette with a burning twig, and then lay down beside the fire. The frozen stars were twinkling high above, very distant.

'Don't stand over there, like an idiot,' he said at last.

He seemed to understand, because he came a little closer and sat down, though still apart. The dog sat down as well. Its look was very serious, and also seemed respectful. This caused him some amusement.

'What's it called?' he said.

'Ca-pi-tán.'

'Capitán! . . . Hey, Capitán!'

The dog picked up its paw and looked at both the men in turn. He had a little laugh.

'Where did these chaps spring up from?' he said, more entertained. 'Hey, Capitán!'

The flames were burning higher. He started laughing harder now, not quite sure why this was. Then both of them were laughing. The dog looked on astonished. Their laughter rang like gun shots out across the silent islands.

He didn't ask more questions. From time to time the little fellow heard him say, jokingly: 'Where did these chaps spring up from?' or, 'Where has this one sprung from?'

He took the boat beyond the line of reeds, one afternoon, and on the open sea, and he saw that little fishing boat which see-sawed in the distance, out towards the Sueco.

'It's them,' he thought. 'The time has come.'

He never came to know if it was really Cabecita, and neither did he worry now. He came most afternoons, when his interest seemed to centre on the trammel-net repairs. He hadn't yet decided if he liked him being around or not, standing there or squatting down, watching everything he did as if he were some rare species, but he was getting used to throwing him a word or two every now and then. He was just thinking things aloud, in fact, a frequent habit among fishermen and loners, since, as a rule, he answered too.

'You always know it's time, when your nose begins to prickle. The first cold days of April . . . it must be April, don't you think? I've seen the *Flecha de Plata* . . . you didn't see it on the Sueco?'

He didn't need to worry about the fire, now, not that it had ever really worried him that much. The little fellow took charge of lighting it each evening when he came. He seemed a bit impatient as he waited for the moment, as if it was the only thing he had to do in his life, and, scarcely had the sun gone down, he went collecting wood. He didn't mind the fellow building it, especially now that firewood was starting to get scarce, and you had to go into the scrub, and yet he still preferred to light it. The lighting of a fire is a lovely thing to do, especially in this season.

The two, or rather three of them, stretched out beside this bonfire and lay staring at the flames, dozy with the warmth, with their faces very flushed and their eyes dazzled. Every now and then they made their way into the darkness, returning with more wood. He'd barely make to stand up and the little fellow was on his feet. It riled him, just a bit.

'It's better if we take turns . . . and don't pull up more floorboards or we'll end up with no house.'

It made him smile at first to see him go off in the darkness with that kind of little trot, and the dog not far behind, and then, a short time later, hear the racket of him ripping out the boards. But lately he'd been worrying, above all after going out one night on the veranda, and putting down his foot where he believed it carried on, and his foot not stopping until it hit the ground, beneath the house. It was so unexpected, and it left him so bewildered, that at first he didn't know quite what had happened.

'All I need now is for them to set fire to my boat!' he'd said, shouting as he lay there on the ground beneath the house that night.

He'd said it rather vaguely, to no one in particular, as if it was the work of many, or of two, at the very least, and not an individual, perhaps to be emphatic or because he was thinking of the dog, which was there sniffing round him as he lay stretched in the mud.

He'd finally got sick of eating nothing else but fish, and now that it was cold he felt the need for something different. This little fellow, in contrast, gobbled up whatever fish there was, and no matter how insipid.

He'd twice been to the store on the Piccardo Canal, but barely bought the basics as there wasn't much money left. He had to get a move on with the business of the otters, and try to sell what silverside he could this coming season, regardless of the catch. He scarcely had one patched-up net, fifteen metres in length, but what he lacked in trammels he could make up for in time. By two or three more casts, for instance. This is what he thought about, stretched out beside the fire.

Cabecita, if indeed it was him, brought things back from time to time, but not so he could count on it. And then, when least expected, he was going to disappear in just the same way he'd arrived, and he wasn't really clear if this would help or be a nuisance, all things considered.

He'd turned up in the afternoons at first, and not stayed long. Then he spent a night, and after that he stayed for two, despite the freezing weather. He didn't have more shelter than the canvas from the boat, but he wouldn't have helped him anyway, to see where this was going. Lately he'd been staying there for several days at once, not doing much of anything but mooch around the place, and he gave him little things to do, to see if it annoyed him. But it turned out quite the opposite, for one day he arrived with all his clothes wrapped in a bundle, and with other kinds of junk, and every indication that he'd come to stay for good.

He looked at him a bit perplexed, and didn't know what to do. He was working on the trammel net and saw him, somewhat blurred, between the threads that formed the mesh.

And now here he was, having stepped out from the scrub; or rather, here they both were, watching him with that tame look that incensed him.

He let them see he wasn't pleased. He didn't like the look of this at all. He lived his life alone and he wasn't going to have this kind of burden on his hands. It was all so very clear, if you weren't so damned dim-witted. But he couldn't stand against it, or anything in fact, for things are as they are and come along when it's their moment. And he was really busy now, as well. Tomorrow or the next day he'd be on the open sea, on the way down to the Sueco, where he'd start to work the trammel net. He couldn't dwell on everything.

'Well, don't just stand there looking at me like that,' he said at last, when his threads began to tangle.

He wasn't really angry in the way one might imagine, rather he was worried. And it wasn't just this halfwit fellow, who comes and goes with the river, but for something that seemed to have turned up with him, or behind him, something dark and ill-defined that travelled through the winter and withdrew into the distance, and was like a silent bird that spreads its wings when night falls.

They didn't move, however, for they were obstinate and dim.

He went on with his mending, or pretended that he did, to show he wasn't bothered or, better, hadn't noticed them, which meant it wasn't seen if he approved of them or not.

'Did you hear what I said?' he asked, seeing that they stayed there.

But they still didn't move, and then he felt his blood rise.

'Must I spell it out for you?' he shouted out this time.

And then, a while later, in a suffocated tone:

'What shit have I got on my face, that makes you look at me like that?'

On saying this he went towards them, just a couple of steps. That was when the little fellow gave a laugh and came right past him, going on towards the house. He took a kick at both of them, the last thing he'd allow was that this pair would laugh at him, but he missed on both occasions, and he hadn't really tried to land the blow on either one of them.

'What's all that?' he called, once they'd gone past him.

The little fellow had brought a sack that was bulging with belongings and, when he made to run, it made the devil of a noise.

'I SAID, WHAT'S ALL THAT?'

The little fellow threw down the sack and then continued to the house. He opened it and rummaged through the junk he found inside, spied on by the little fellow, from the veranda.

It was a perfect pile of rubbish, and his face began to change as he was taking out the things, until he started laughing. There were several lantern batteries and all of them were flat, a lone blade from a hunting knife, a rowlock made of bronze and a spike knocked from a boathook, several ancient magazines, a useless sealed unit, various glass jars, a quantity of dried-up crabs, a lot of snail and oyster shells, a broken vacuum flask and some burned-out radio valves, empty toothpaste tubes, a necklace made from snail shells on a copper-wire thread, some spark plugs and a broken carburettor, and an Esso calendar from 1949.

He put aside the things that might be useful in some way, regretting, first of all, that he didn't have both rowlocks. The knife blade was a Solingen which, fitted with a handle, could serve him very well. The magazines would kill some time, even though he'd never been a reader in his life, or they could get the fire going, or even make his cigarettes, if it was needed. The boathook tip was good to have, and possibly the best thing there. He'd fit a decent handle to it, privet would be good, or perhaps he'd use bamboo, which even if it fractures does the job. The sealed unit made him laugh. It looked like something precious as it came out from the sack, with its shining yellow glass like a gold pot in the half-light. But the unit was burnt out. The calendar was years old. And it would have been quite useless even if it were this year's. But he stayed there for a while simply looking at the pictures, and despite the feeble light.

The little fellow left the veranda when he saw him start to laugh, and began to gather sticks to make the fire. He built the firewood up and waited quietly while the other was completing his inspection so he'd come and light the pyre. At last he made his way across, still laughing to himself, and set the fire alight in the way he'd made his custom, the match put to a paper twist, the flame from this applied to all four corners of the pyre of sticks and straw and leftovers of fish, topped by the logs.

He'd hooked a *tararira* on one line that afternoon, but nothing that he pulled out from the river that was fish-shaped was of any interest to him now.

The flames rose in the night, in the middle of the garden, like a kind of marvellous bush that was lit up by many lives.

And here they were, beside the fire, and each one with his story, as if they were two rivers that have just combined their waters after running for a distance, and now run on towards the open sea, pushed by a single force, a blind and darkened energy.

*

One early morning, he went out onto the river at last, looking for the silverside, as if going out to fight. Although the fight was with the season and the water and foul luck, because the silverside's a harmless fish. And it's not a fight at all, if you consider it a little, because the river weaves its story and a man is just a single thread, woven in with ten thousand others.

He'd made the preparations on the boat the previous evening, and the little fellow's concern to help him was completely overdone. He didn't like him helping much, these were things he liked to do alone, if truth be told, doing them unhurriedly, his pleasure in the details, in the way of older men. He put the trammel in the stern, folded in a way that meant he only had to take the tin, painted in bright yellow and that acted as a float, and throw it overboard for the net to follow on; the Primus and the kettle, a litre bottle filled with kerosene, a lantern, some rope, a bit of cold food, and his maté things and sea bread all went in the bow and were covered with the canvas; the tip knocked off the boathook with its new bamboo handle went on one side in the bottom, and the machete on the other, where he hung it on its strap, for whatever need arose; some matches in his pocket and some more inside the maté tin, very tightly closed; and this and that and other things.

He was wondering if he'd take the little fellow. It helped if you could count on having someone in the boat, to hold it in position while you gathered in the nets. It was a big help for all kinds of things, even with a dog in tow. But he wouldn't say a word of this unless it came from him, his plan had been to go alone and now he was too wedded to it. And then, he hadn't decided if he liked the little fellow or not, he likely never would decide, for things would run their course and he wasn't a man to stop them, which was why it had to come from him, entirely from the little fellow, if he came or if he stayed, and maybe it was better if he didn't come after all, because he still found him freakish or at least a very odd sort, and because there was that thing behind him, something like a hidden trap that might move on elsewhere if he left the fellow behind, although he knew he didn't think he'd do this, it was as close as being certain, at least not for the moment and, even if he did, it wouldn't change the slightest part of what was written down already, if this was how things are, and whether good or bad or otherwise.

The little fellow saw him jump aboard and seemed to be expecting that he'd say something to him, but he didn't even look, just pushed the boat out from the shore and rowed off strongly. The night still hadn't lifted, but he caught sight of his silhouette, standing on the shoreline by the white patch of the dog. At last they disappeared behind the first bend on the stream and he felt a little sorry then, as if he'd let them down in spite of himself.

Before he reached the river, he turned up his coat lapels and then put out the lamp. A chilly breeze was blowing and he listened to the reed bed as it shivered in the half-light, close on either side of him, as if an unseen animal were creeping through the reeds. He saw, as if through curtains, the river's pallid surface and the rhythm of its swaying in the dawning of the light, which seemed to rise straight out from it, cold and rather thick. The sky was high above him, it had almost disappeared out to the east, and in the west, what remained of it was sinking as if soaked up by the mouth of a storm, behind the horizon. He looked up at the morning star, a drop of gold that trembled there among the other lights, before it fell. He blew into his hands and then he rubbed them on his legs. Then he took the oars in hand, and went onto the river.

It was clearer now, and the water rising. It was the best time now, in April, to go after silverside, but it would be another hour or more before he cast the line, that's if he reached the Sueco. The cold air helped his rowing. He set himself and pulled with strength, not hurrying, but using all his body, rowing deeply. He had to make corrections for the drifting as he went, in this case with the bow turned just a little to south-east as he advanced, against the water, which came in strongly, pushing him away towards the Aguaje del Durazno.

The Bajo del Temor is wide, and with these heavy, sluggish boats, it seems as if the stern will never break free of the shoreline. You sail out from the reed beds and the coastline quickly turns into a lengthening grey line, growing hazy to the north-east, but then it never changes, a line drawn out as if pulled by a tug. It's best to think of something else, even though your eyes are always coming up against it, as if there's nowhere else: the toecaps of your shoes and then the seat set in the stern, the trammel with its yellow tin, and then a stretch of water and the coast . . . and the sky. But it all ends in the coast, because the heavens are a void.

It felt good to be alone now, more than in the summer when he went onto the river, and the cold air of the morning seemed to make the small things smaller still, the man and little rowing boat were now a single figure, an undetermined blemish that was making laboured headway to the Sueco.

The water here was choppy as it ran in from the east and met the wind set from the west. He felt the little blows against the starboard of the boat. It's a sound that is particular, an unremitting gurgle. It sounds, after a time, as if your boat were shipping water. If you listen to it hard enough, you end up dozing off.

Every now and then, there was the squawking of a scrub-hen or the whining of a dog coming over from the islands. Then he heard the sound of voices, other noises too, on the side of the Chaná. But the sounds were disproportionate, altered by the distance, and it seemed as if they came out from the air above his head. There was nothing that connected all the vast space there in front of him with all these sounds, familiar once, and now so strange and lonely.

It was then the sun appeared above the line of the horizon. He was almost halfway out across the waters of the Bajo and, by screwing up his eyes, he could make out the location of the mouth of the Riestra, of the Inca and Gutiérrez, and even saw as far up as the Medio and Chaná, despite the growing fog. But that was when the light broke in the east, as if the sky broke, and wiped it all away, just for a moment. Now he seemed to be elsewhere, rowing through the air between the long and layered cloud plumes. The water almost disappeared, it disappeared, in fact, because what lay around the boat now was a hard metallic framing that reduced him close to blindness, but he knew it was the sea when he saw its wide, black borderline, swaying to and fro before the giant, red globe, or half-globe, scarcely bright at all now, at the level of his eyes. He could observe it without squinting. It struggled up towards the sky and then it seemed to waver, and several seconds passed before it broke from the horizon. There was an instant when its lower edge, which rested in the water, seemed to stretch as if held fast onto this dark line of the border, which it briefly dragged aloft with it.

When it rose from the horizon and he once more saw the water in the fullness of its reach, he thought the sea had halted and turned into something solid, a sea of sand that puckered into millions of points, the light raking fiercely in and clinging to each curl, as if this was where it started, or this was simply light itself, a small cup of perfect shade behind each cup of light. In truth the water carried on, he felt it in the boat, but his eyes still held the counter-image, leaping out against the grey of dawn.

In spite of his precautions, the current had displaced the boat a little to the west, and now he had the Chaná inlet almost right ahead of him, astern. He saw the coast again. The fog had mostly lifted and the view was at its clearest. He saw a flock of lake ducks, black widows, as they called them, on the point of Punta Temor, and he launched a silent curse. They disappeared in twos and threes, to bob up not far off, either closer or more distant, as if they followed orders. They had to be positioned on a shoal of silverside. If he'd had the old man's shotgun he'd have let fly with abandon. When he looked in their direction next, the ducks had moved on east, onto the inlet of the Chaná. And that was when he saw it.

It seemed to be a boat. It was, in fact, a boat, but it was very odd to see it there. It was owing to the light he hadn't seen it there before. Until the sun came out and reached the entrance to the Chaná, it had been there but run together with the grey line of the coast, perhaps as a suggestion of a darker kind of mark, but not to be distinguished in the misty dawning scene, before the sun. But now the sunlight warmed the coast, it lay there clear and well defined, if strange, on the western shore, lying at the entrance to the Chaná.

He slackened off his stroke at first, but further on he stopped. He felt a little puzzled. He found himself a cigarette and lit it very slowly, feeling how the current took him towards the west, but not so strongly now, and with his eyes fixed on the boat. The impression that it gave was of a giant, wounded bird, or something of that nature. It made him sad to see a boat had got in this predicament. He couldn't get its measure, being so far off and on its side. But even with all that, it had the signs of being a handsome boat. The way the hull was lying and the angle of his view of it enhanced the bow projection, which gave the boat the look of being pierced by desperation, as if, and as it died, it reached an arm to deeper waters after being dragged here all the way across the sandbanks. All this forward movement, all this vain and final movement, was gathered in the prow boom, violent and cut in black against the morning sky.

How had it come to end up here? It seemed, from how it lay, that its intention was to sail into the Chaná from the Bajo del Temor. It's possible to do this, but it's risky. In this case, from the Sueco, you have to head for Punta Morán as you go round Isla Nutria, and then veer hard towards the north, lining up the stern with the island's eastern shoreline. The entry to the Chaná is marked by an extensive poplar plantation. It's all very shallow here, even though the shoreline scarcely rises into view, so you have go ahead with the engine speed reduced, and taking constant soundings. This seemed to be the route the boat had taken, but it had changed course at the last, and had fallen on the sandbanks. It was really odd to see it there, not wholly in the water nor completely on the land, but more than anything else, it was very sad.

There was also something else, the thing that really startled him. It wasn't just the fact that the boat had ended up there. Instead, a premonition or suspicion, or whatever – something more than just the fact – struck him when he saw it first, in that very moment, implausibly unfolding from the misty line of coast. He wasn't a man to see things that weren't really there before him. But he'd been going round alone too long.

The lake ducks had now moved on almost right up to the Inca. The water had displaced him and he found his boat was sailing on the shoals off Punta Morán, but things seemed calm for now. He heard the diesel engine of a launch of the Isleña firm, running at full throttle as it cruised into the Sueco. The noises from the islands had now come round to the bow, and also sounded close. He'd reach the Sueco soon enough.

He still looked at the boat as he was taking up the oars. Then he set off strongly, not hurrying, but rowing deeply, using all his body.

The water turned before he reached the Sueco. Now it ran down powerfully. His progress was laborious, close in to the reed beds to avoid the strongest current.

He started with his fishing once he reached the Sueco inlet, with the morning well advanced. At this hour of the day and with the skies completely clear, he could see the unlit buoy K50 off to the south-west, on the far side of the Paraná, sited on the limit of the Isla Nueva sandbank. Away and to the south-east, but a long way further off and looking filmy in the distance, was the tip of Isla Zárate. He took the float and threw it in, a little bit to his side of the middle of the current, and then began to row across towards the other shore, taking care to keep the yellow tin and boat aligned. The trammel went in smoothly. He'd run a fair way downstream by the time he reached the reeds that lined the far bank of the river. The boat and yellow tin, each one on its margin, were running near in line as the current took them on. The boat kept just ahead, because the Sueco draws a measured curve, turning to the north-east and dictating that you sail a little ahead around the west. The net fell in a gentle sag between the tin and boat. There was nothing at the surface but the corks along the head rope, plucking at the water in between the boat and tin.

The tip of Zárate and the black buoy quickly disappeared, and then a little later he could only see the entrance to the Sueco, where he'd started, as if the water ended there. When you're travelling on the water, the riverbanks go by in a strange kind of way, and the elements themselves, which seem disposed to change their nature, keep the scene in constant movement. He was only on the Sueco, which isn't very long, and even so he had the feeling that he'd crossed through several quite distinctive places.

Now he began to see some silver arrows leap the head rope.

He sailed on past the channel that runs out between the islands, looking at its inlet from the middle of the Sueco, and remembering the night he'd spent there, coming from its far end at the onset of the summer. He couldn't see the hut from here. He gathered in the net just a little further on. He hadn't reached the end yet, but he judged it far enough. By the time the work was done he found he'd drifted there in any case, to where the land on either side runs out. The silverside were small but at least they were abundant, and he'd caught a few sardines as well. He preferred to eat sardines. To him they tasted better.

He couldn't see the sandbank. He went back up again, but this time threw the trammel in when not as far upriver. By the time he pulled it in he'd come into the Bajo, and could see the boat.

He cast the net just twice in the passage of the morning, but with pretty good results. Then he beached his little boat on the shores of Punta Temor, and ate a little cold fish with the bread. He lit the Primus stove and drank some matés. All the time he did this he was looking at the other boat. It was difficult to see, not just because of distance, but because the sky was cloudy now, and when the sunlight reached the shore, its shine was just too bright.

The sky was overcast as he prepared the net that afternoon. The place looked bleak indeed now. The silence thickened round the boat as soon as he stopped rowing, and then his ears began to hum. He could feel the water level falling, and this falling, over time, possessed a tension that disturbed him.

He made some handsome catches, but even this, in some way, only fed his darkening mood. He'd allowed himself to stay too long and now had no idea what he would do with all he'd caught. As the time came near, he made a trip up to the Chanacito, hoping that he'd come across the provisions boat. Now he came to see that he'd invested too much hope in this. The conversation hadn't been clear, nothing that the man had said confirmed a real interest. In any case, he wasn't there, not this time or the next. The *Flecha de Plata* was another possibility, but meeting up with her in these parts was still less likely. Finally, and running out of time, he tried to speak to old man Polestrina, something that seems pretty daft in principle. He was as stingy as they come. He went round on an old barge, the *Rosita de Polestrina*, twelve metres long and as ruined as the man himself, but there was nothing lost by trying, however mean he was. He started out one morning for the Piccardo Canal, hoping that he'd meet with the supply launch on the way, or else when he was coming back, and he discussed things with the old man. Neither yes nor no. More likely no, however. Nothing he could count on.

'I don't see how it suits me,' the old man had said.

'By giving it a try,' he'd said.

'I don't think it suits me.'

He was known to be a sly one and you couldn't guess his thinking. He didn't seem to have the slightest interest in the matter, but this could mean the opposite. They finished up agreeing that he'd take just one day's catch, so he'd have a base to work from. They could talk about it then, if he had a real interest.

'I don't know what to think of this,' the old man had said. He was sitting on the deck of the *Rosita de Polestrina*. 'Bring me what you get and we'll see what we can do. What's the use of talking now?'

Perhaps the fish would bring him round, when he saw how much there was. But even if it did, he'd have to see what terms he wanted, albeit any deal at all would suit him at the moment. The way that things were looking now. If he had to face the worst, he'd take some to the store on the Piccardo Canal and try to sell it there, even to exchange it, getting other things for fish, and try to sell to Polestrina too, at least a little. Then he'd get fed up with eating silverside himself, the little fellow and dog as well, if he still had them with him. And then it wouldn't surprise him if he lost this batch of fish. If this was how it turned out he'd spend the next days seeking buyers, or a dealer who would sell it. Until he'd got that sorted out, he couldn't fish again.

He saw a flock of black widows out between the islands. The sky continued overcast, and now the light was sinking. It was also getting cold. This is winter: this sky and this silence, and the islands wrapped in mist. This vast, flattened solitude.

He rubbed his hands together and then he lit a cigarette. The boat and yellow tin were swept downriver by the current, which moved the silence to and fro, from one end of the channel to the other. He was going to let the net run on as far as possible this time, beyond Punta Temor. He'd set off once he'd pulled it in. And better to bring it in right now, going on like this would mean the night would catch him out, still sailing on the Bajo. Besides, he'd had enough. Yes, he'd pull the net in now.

He'd made a start already when he heard an engine coming, from the Honda Canal. The wind is turning round, he thought. The engine noise grew louder as he gathered in the net, and it went on getting louder still. It's coming over here, he thought. His mind was on the noise more than on anything he did.

'It's a four-cylinder Gardner,' he said then, out loud. 'Blow me if it isn't the *Juanita Florida*!'

He wasn't sure why, but the thought it was the *Juanita Florida* made him glad. She was and she wasn't a barge. And if she was a barge she had a very different air. He'd always seen the hull as belonging to a schooner.

He was on the last few metres when it came into the Sueco. He saw Long Fourcade standing up there at the stern, with his hands deep in his pockets and the tiller between his legs. Long had seen him, too, and he throttled down his engine once he'd passed the channel mouth and was in between the islands. He hugged the eastern shoreline, which is how you run the Sueco, but then he throttled down and turned the prow towards the boat. As he sailed in close he put the engine into neutral, and let his momentum bring him in.

'Hey!'

'Hey!'

'How's it going?'

'Well, you know . . . '

Boga caught the final length of net and pulled the float aboard. Long used his gears to bring his vessel right alongside. Boga took the boathook and used it as a clasp around the gunwale of the barge. The rowing boat and barge began to drift along together.

Long started speaking as he came up from the stern.

'I saw the *Flecha de Plata*, up by Isla Nueva.'

Then he leaned across the boat.

'Bugger me, you've caught a boatful!'

Boga didn't answer. He simply gave a shrug. He was taking out a cigarette. He looked at Long, through the smoke, standing there above him. It made him longer still. He was a fellow out of the ordinary, just as you imagined.

'What're you going to do with it?'

'I'm not really sure yet.'

'How's that?'

'I don't know . . . I thought that I could sell it.'

'Who are you going to sell it to?'

'That's what I'm not sure of.'

'That's really good! Didn't you make a deal with someone?'

'With old man Polestrina . . . but, you know, not a deal as such.'

Fourcade crouched right down, with his backside on his heels.

'And the old man said exactly what?'

'Nothing much at all, really.'

'So throw it back, for what it's worth. Has no one ever told you what an awkward sod he is?'

'Maybe I heard something . . . '

'There isn't a word that covers it.'

'Trying costs you nothing.'

'Even that will cost you if you're dealing with that piece of shit. Why didn't you fix a deal with someone else?'

'I let the time go by.'

'So I see . . . '

Long lit a cigarette and spent a while in silence, eyes towards the Bajo. The *Juanita Florida* and the little boat ran on slowly together.

'What price would you want for it?' he said.

'Well, it depends.'

'I'm not up with these things, you know.'

'It's all pretty simple.'

'How much are you asking?'

'Just a price that's fair.'

'That's clear enough . . . '

Long got to his feet.

'The water's about to turn,' he said.

'We've got a little while as yet.'

Long went back down to the stern and banged the tiller several times. He was a frank and steady fellow, and Boga liked him as a man. He'd seen him round the ports, where he would chat with all and sundry. A chap who never bothered you. Perhaps a little loud at times. He talked and joked in shouts, like a man who's just arrived back after many months away. He lived on the Ignacio, or else the Caguané, he wasn't sure. He'd seen him many times on the *Juanita Florida*, quite like him in its way, and exactly as he was now, with the tiller arm between his legs, his hands deep in his pockets, and with that worn-out leather jacket and a little bit of beard, and a black-and-white striped woollen hat.

'They're selling to the mongers now at thirty-five pesos . . . for a kilo, at the port. At least, that's what I hear.' He was coming from the stern. 'Isn't that the price?'

'I can't say that I know for sure.'

'Yeah, I think that's what it is.'

'Maybe so, it could be.'

'This isn't the port up here, of course. It's different up here.'

'I can't get it to the port.'

'No, I can imagine . . . '

Long crouched down and, once again, he looked him in the eye.

'I've had a thought,' he said.

He looked at him in silence for a while.

'I'll take it in there for you, if that's what you want . . . I won't buy the fish, because I don't want to mix in things I haven't got the hang of, but I'll take it into port for you and see what happens there.'

He was silent for a while. Finally he spoke.

'Seems ok to me.'

'I go right into San Fernando almost every day . . . I can pick the fish up here, when I'm on the way back anyway, and take it in the next day.'

'All right.'

'And on the way, I'll bring you back.'

'Yes, that sounds good. What I don't have is some crates.'

'That won't be any problem.'

Long stood up tall again, and rubbed his hands together.

'I think it might work out all right,' he said, back at his shouting.

'Why not?' he said, at heart not very sure.

'Let's get going now!'

They tied the rowing boat to the *Juanita Florida*, hooked onto its stern, and sailed out from the Sueco with the daylight almost gone.

In the middle of the Bajo, and as if he didn't care, he said:

'What's that over there?'

Long Fourcade looked at him, it seemed to be by habit that he looked you in the eye.

'You've haven't noticed it before?'

He was a forthright man at that.

'Only now, this morning,' he said, a touch annoyed.

The other showed amazement by a tilting of his head.

'It's been there for a while now. It turned up there one morning, after a southeaster.'

He thought about it for a while, remembering the storm that had ripped apart his sail.

'Since March, then,' he said.

'Yeah, I think it was . . . '

They were silent for a while.

'It's a shame.'

'Yes, it is.'

'It's a real damned shame!'

'Yes, it is . . . '

They were silent once again. Now the night had fallen.

'What boat is it anyway?' he said, a little hurriedly.

Fourcade gave a shrug.

'I couldn't say . . . it's not from here . . . it's got a funny name.'

'What name is that?' he said.

'I couldn't say . . . it won't stick in my mind.'

Long scratched his head.

'I think it's going to rain.'

He'd looked at the boat every time he'd crossed the Bajo, and then, as a rule, every time he pulled the net in out on the Sueco.

Fourcade took the silverside, and got a pretty good price in the port at San Fernando. As dusk came on each evening, he tied the little boat onto the *Juanita Florida*, and they journeyed back together.

The daft little fellow and the dog didn't move from where they'd ended up. He went on asking about the boat, now and then. You know how all these stories go. Someone tells it one way, someone else another. As a rule, too many stories, and with no real reason to put faith in even half of them. He heard it said, in the store on the Piccardo Canal, that the boat was from the north. Or rather, it was said that it had come down from the north. From the south, there's only wind. No one knew whose boat it was. Or rather, whose it had been. Old man Polestrina was inclined to call it his.

The only certain thing was that it had turned up there one morning, after the southeaster.

He decided, that morning, not to cross onto the Sueco. He had a mind to try out the Aguaje del Durazno. He hadn't let

Long know, because he'd made his mind up just like that. He came across him anyway, as night was coming down, on the Bajo. He had almost brought along the little fellow. But as it was a new spot, he decided that he wouldn't.

It took as long as getting to the far end of the Sueco, and even then it wasn't the Aguaje, strictly speaking. In truth, to reach its far end is a good way further still. And then, he'd stopped a while on the inlet of the Chaná.

Where the boat was.

It came out from the shadows, on a level with the Sueco, then glimmered in the fog a while, as if it might dissolve, until at last it settled on the morning.

It was half into the water, just a little tipped to port, and with the bow aimed to the east, giving the impression, when you saw it from the Bajo, that it sailed on still, close to the wind.

It was a cutter in the old style, with a very slender line, and with that melancholy air that disappeared for good around 1930. He couldn't stand those shining hulls they shaped into a knife-blade, without a forward boom and showing off Marconi rigging. They were the work of calculation, products made to measure for a man (for that subspecies of sportsman) and designed against the river. Not for the river and the man. He saw them come and go, and the same thing every weekend, not going very far at all, and knew, because he saw them, it was Saturday or Sunday. They went by, overloaded with technology and comforts. And, as Sunday evening came, they made their docile way back all together in a flock. There was one day when he'd seen its members climb out on the shore, get into their motors and, without a pause to take breath in their never-ending prattle, leave behind this world they didn't have the faintest notion of, had never tried to understand, their engines roaring off in the direction of the city, until the next weekend.

But this boat was distinct, despite its distant look of nobility, and of the folk who'd ordered its construction (forty, fifty years before), and of all that which spoke clearly of techniques from other days.

There was a lot of timber in the boat, as anyone could see, with a low-running gunwale and a sheer that was pronounced, and echoing a bird, and the gentle stern projection too, which stuck out like a balcony. The bow had no projection. The frame was low and short but the cockpit very spacious.

It didn't have much beam but it had a lot of depth, which was a feature of its time. Although the keel was large it seemed to fit well with the hull, and doubtless gave the vessel good stability, as well as lateral strength. A feature that was surely from the old days were its chain-wales. But they lent a certain elegance.

It was now a proper wreck, of course, and what he was admiring was its face in other days. That time of which the old ones spoke (that worn and melancholy splendour still seen on the river), as if all that could be done here was accomplished in the years between 1890 and 1925.

All the spars were lost with the exception of the boom, which looked to be much longer when you saw it from a distance. Of course, there wasn't a single strip of ironwork remaining. He could see the marks of chainplates where the chain-wale was fixed, three of them, long and wide, placed along each side. Several lengths of canvas were still hanging from the upper deck, all a dirty green shade, faded almost white. It surprised him that the tiller was still there in place.

It was a fine tiller with a fine handle. He'd never liked to see a boat of this bearing fitted with a wheel.

Studying it carefully, from the bow and slightly at an angle, exactly as he saw it now, the hull bore some resemblance to the form of a dorado. And then perhaps it was the case this fish had got into his blood, and it wasn't really like it, but evoked it in the same way it evoked in him the summer, so summer, boat and fish had come to be, in some way, one.

He went round to the stern and at last he read the name. The letters were cut in fretwork on a little cedar board, in the old style, and with the board fixed to the stern. Nobody had touched it for a boat dies with its name, it's a custom all get used to, and the least that one can hope for from this river and its folk. And so he read, with effort, and because the name was strange indeed: A . . . LE . . . LU . . . YA.

It didn't mean a thing, but he thought it sounded nice, and a name that was well-suited to a vessel of this type. *ALELUYA*. Perhaps, if he'd been capable, he would have made a name up that would sound a bit like this.

It was then a gentle gust of wind, coming from the southeast, folded up the never-ending murmur of the islands. And this was when he felt on his own with the boat. And felt it in a special way. Something like nostalgia and mistrust and also reverence, and all of this at once. However you explained it, a feeling of a gentle pain that, rising in himself, concerned the boat as well as him, as if they were in some way one.

A plaintive limpkin croak came through the air from the south-east, and barely had it reached him than its shadow slipped across the limpid sky, behind the call that went on quivering in the air, like the cry of someone falling through a chasm.

It was only at this moment, and now he thought it through, that he could say this summer's wandering, right from the Anguilas all the way up to Ñancay, was done, and finally had brought him here, to the *Aleluya*.

Yes, this was what he'd searched for all this time. The summer had matured in him this tame and stubborn longing for a boat, and had then brought the boat. What else could a man want on this river, with its solitude? Normally he dies with his desire, but nothing more, because it's hard to have a boat. Bastos often spoke of boats, and Deaf Angarita, whose words were for himself, spoke of nothing else at all. But he, he'd really wanted it, or else had made it happen, and now he had the boat.

It was old and beaten-up, and maybe it was useless. But was there any other way he ever could have found it?

He cast the trammel twice, and with a pretty good result, and the second time arriving almost back up by the boat. But what was in the net didn't interest him now, whatever it might be. And well before midday he turned the rowing boat to shore, where he beached it near the larger vessel, and had a little bit to eat. He hadn't landed right beside it, wanting to make sure that there weren't others prowling round.

It was a day of forceful wind and the reeds whipped in the air with a mournful humming. A Sandringham flew overhead, low, towards the aerodrome. He rolled his trouser-legs up high, took off his boots and jumped down from his boat. He preferred to walk in bare feet for his boots were rather low-cut and the shore was mainly mud. When he wore them he got stuck.

He walked around the hull at first, measuring the water. Twenty centimetres, you could think of it as dry. With its weight, the boat had dug itself in twenty centimetres more. It rested on the port side, but it wasn't leaning hard, simply tilting gently over. The timbers on the bottom had been flattened out a little. The screw had disappeared, but the shaft was still in place, and, most curious of all, the Goodrich bearing too, with its bright sleeve cast in bronze. He read the name again. This name Long Fourcade couldn't keep inside his head, and that he found so pleasing though he didn't understand it.

He lifted up his hand and gave the hull a gentle pat.

He stepped up on the rudder blade and climbed aboard the boat.

The engine had been taken, which is as you would expect. An old and loyal Ailsa Craig, or perhaps one of those Renaults, the two-cylinder model with its low revolutions which appeared around 1914 and was modified in 1920, the one Old Bastos spoke of with a certain veneration. (There was something mythic and pitiable in those endless conversations about engines. There was Della Vedone, for one, with his passion for any engine that was put into a boat and for the Kermath in particular, and which involved, as any passion did, an element of torment and a little desperation.)

A gust of wind blew in. He heard the water as it licked around the timbers on the bottom. The wind drove all the sounds in the direction of the islands, and for a moment all fell quiet, or it seemed as if it had. But this was when he noticed the persistence of the murmur that was coming from the islands, and surrounded him like the air.

He used his foot to push the cabin door. They'd thieved all the portholes, naturally enough. Even so, the light was faint, he had to wait a while before his eyes adapted to it. The grey and chilly light pressed itself against the ceiling. Level with his eyeline, it left him almost dazzled. He could barely see a thing that lay below the cabin line. He waited, crouching down, until his eyes adjusted. The door through to the lower deck was left a little open. He slipped up to the door and reached his head inside. He couldn't see a thing. The main deck hatch was closed. He reached into the gloom and moved his hand around the place the tank was fitted. They'd taken that as well. Some pay forty pesos for a kilo of zinc surplus, and sell it on for smelting. And then it might be copper.

He lifted up the covers in the deck and saw the water shine. He stuck his arm inside and felt his way around the timbers, to see if she was holed. No, if she was, it had to be the port side, and below the waterline.

Each one of the couchettes was a long crate with a lip to take the mattresses. There were doors on either side of them. He pulled them open on the port side. The deck planks had been thrown around and some of them were floating. He reached inside and felt the mud. This is where it was. He felt around the hole. Big enough to pass both fists through. And then there were the timbers that had split along their length. It could have been a log that had been covered by the water, a post, perhaps a house beam. There are times when an old buoy, or its remnants, does more damage than a buoy in good condition can prevent.

In spite of all he saw, he still couldn't fathom why the boat had been abandoned. They could have pulled it further onto land and then repaired the hole. Then they could have got it off the sandbank, with a decent tide. And if this didn't come, they could have opened up a trench, as when the *Doris* ran aground in the entrance to the Luján, in December of '15, or this was what he'd heard.

He went out to the cockpit. The wind was blowing harder now, with scarcely any lull. More water would be coming in. The Bajo del Temor, from here, looked wide as any sea. In moments when the wind let up, a silence fell across the boat, the sound of desolation. Then he felt this loneliness and death, and very close.

It was better to go back.

He went back to the Sueco in the days that followed this, returning to his fishing. Then the morning came he saw the *Flecha de Plata*, and decided to go out, in between the pair of islands, to the sandbanks. Sardines are abundant there. He spent the hour of midday in the hut he'd used one night at the beginning of the summer. There were the ashes of a fire here and some empty tins of food. In the afternoon he saw Lefty La Rocca, far out on the Bajo, on his way to Punta Morán.

He moved around a lot these days. But always had the boat in view, tilted on its side just at the entrance to the Chaná.

One day he came back early, without waiting for Fourcade. The little fellow saw him come, and in something of a hurry, and saw him jump from the boat and make his way into the house. He was quite a long while going round from one room to another, and making a fair racket. The little fellow was just below the house, standing with the dog, and watching with that docile look that drove him round the bend. He stepped into the passage and began to hurl some things into the garden. He was careful not to look at them, but knew their eyes were on him every second. It unsettled him to start with, and then it made him angry. But he couldn't say a thing. He was putting things that might break to one side, on the veranda. It started getting dark. This was when the little fellow began to sort among the things that had been thrown into the garden.

'Why don't you keep your fucking hands off?' he shouted in his fury. 'Did I say you could touch anything?'

He didn't even notice he was speaking to the both of them, as if the dog were human.

The little fellow stepped away and left the things there on the ground, and looked at him, upset. He felt himself turn red and he was even more embarrassed, seeing there was no reason at all to take things the way he had done.

He jumped down to the garden and went looking for the otter trap, the last thing on his list. He hadn't used it once and it was hanging round the back on a post, beside the pen. He lifted off the trap and, before he went back round the house, he kicked the pen to bits. The little fellow watched him do it, looking underneath the house.

Then he started carrying all the things out to the bank. The little fellow came with him, there and back, but keeping at a distance. He paid no heed at first, trying to ignore him. But the little fellow was just infuriating. One time, on a trip back, he got tangled with the dog, which was also trailing after him, and this was just the limit. He was carrying a tin and he threw it at its head. The little fellow just stood there, startled. He made no move to flee, but put his arms across his head, waiting for the explosion to come. Instead, he picked up all the rest and took it to the riverbank, thoroughly ashamed.

He waited for the daylight, and had a last look round before he went. Then he jumped onto the boat, and this time left for good.

He'd hardly slept that night and sensed the little fellow was even more awake, breathing very calmly, but watching in the darkness, aware of every move he made. He knew that his intention was to go away without him. Which was exactly right. He jumped onto the boat and started rowing with his eyes glued to the deck.

And yet it wasn't long before he saw the little fellow was following, coming on the bank. They disappeared from sight, at first, but as he reached the estuary he saw them almost up with him. He felt his fury rise again, but now not quite as fiercely. They'd more than likely turn back when they reached the river mouth. What else was there to do? Stand there like two idiots until they'd seen him disappear. Yes, that was it. He moved on round the coastline making headway to the west, and leaving them behind. And the pair of them just standing there, looking rather desperate. The dog had started whimpering, looking at the little fellow first, and then towards the boat that sailed away. He was glad and he was sorry, and both of these at once, but without either feeling going very deep at all, for the river made him hard. They'd soon be lost from sight. That's what he thought, at least.

The last thing he expected was to see the little fellow jump in, quickly followed by the dog, and begin to ford the river. He couldn't believe his eyes. He'd jumped into the water on this early winter morning and was doing some clumsy strokes towards the other bank. The coast obscured his view when they were somewhere in the middle, but soon they reappeared, and standing on the other bank. Now they walked behind him on the coast, and almost caught him up. He saw the skinny figure of the little fellow against the sky, looking shrunk and dark and dripping water as he came. He looked just like a lake duck, a widow dressed in mourning. His clothes were black with water and were plastered to his skin.

Again he wished he'd had the old man's shotgun with him, to fire above their heads and send them packing. It was madness.

And now he'd stopped his rowing. This really made his blood boil. He didn't want to show surprise, nor even that he'd seen them. He set to with the oars again and slowly upped his rhythm. They followed, but were held up all the time along the coast, completely wild here, and where they had to get across all kinds of hurdles. At times they disappeared behind some bushes or some trees. Most likely making detours. It made him glad each time it happened. Frequently the little fellow preferred to wade among the reeds, with the water to his waistline. When they disappeared from view, he took advantage of the chance to row as strongly as he could, to put some space between them.

And right up to the Inca, with him a little ahead. He saw them stop and disappear, and slowed up just a little, feeling suitably intrigued. It took a little while, but then he saw them on the other bank. He flew into a real rage and made his mind up there and then to move out from the shore, embarking on a detour. They stopped and looked, dismayed, when they saw his change of course. Then they sprang into the water and began to swim again. He swore he'd never pick them up, even if they drowned.

The river was on the rise. He could clearly see the boat from here. It wouldn't have taken long for him to make his way across, but if he wanted to get rid of them he had to hold his course, to convince them he was going across the Bajo. Then they'd turn around.

The advantage that they had was that the water in the Bajo isn't deep. Normally it doesn't reach above half a metre. Breaking through the surface here and there are lumps of trees, and branches that are sticking in the bottom. The little fellow went on wading. It was really odd to see him there, far out from the shore and with the water to his waist. Now and then he vanished as he fell into a pothole. So sometimes it was half a little fellow that tracked him through the water, at others just a quarter, and at others just a head. The dog, on the other hand, swam a decent stretch at first, and then the little fellow was forced to turn around and pick it up.

He couldn't make out that he hadn't seen them there, but he rowed as if he hadn't. And then, deep down, he started feeling sorry for the pair. Gradually they fell behind. The water went on rising. The flood tide had begun when it was quite late in the morning, and without a lot of force. But now, and very suddenly, he noticed that the water, instead of easing off was coming in a lot more strongly. He felt it in the boat, which began to move around. He looked back at the little fellow. It was covering him up. When he would at last have to swim, he'd be quickly swept away. He'd put the dog on his shoulders, and he had to stop at times, but he never gave a sign of turning back. And even if he had done, the water would have covered him before he'd reached the shore.

Now he wasn't rowing, but he moved the oars in such a way that, looked at from a distance, it would seem as if he was. He couldn't go on like that for long. At last he rowed towards the little fellow, leading with the stern. Besieged as he was, the other wouldn't be sure if he was approaching or moving away. While he rowed towards them, he cursed them under his breath.

When he came up close, he called:

'It's best you turn back now!'

His voice was swept away across the morning by a gust of wind. And it wouldn't be any use, but he'd said it as a threat as much as anything.

'Can't you bloody hear me? Don't think I'm going to pull you out!'

Now the little fellow was swimming, or rather, he was splashing, because the dog made his clumsy swimming style even clumsier, and then, and with a frightening speed, the water started taking them.

'Good! I'm bloody glad!' he yelled, but now a little wildly.

He began to row towards them using all the strength he had, and swearing at them both.

The dog had come adrift and was quickly disappearing. He pushed the boat up close and waited for the little fellow to grip the stern. He didn't let him climb in but rowed straight after the dog. Only when he'd reached the dog and pulled it on the boat, did he go to help the little fellow.

And now they were sitting there, together in the stern, with the water running off them, both shivering with the cold. He looked at them, frustrated, and said, his teeth clenched:

'Fuck the bloody pair of you!'

This was how Boga, in turn, moved onto the boat, the old, dejected *Aleluya*.

It was as if he'd searched all summer long, and only now, in the middle of the winter, had found it, with all its past forgotten.

He waited for a day when the *bajante* reached its limit and he set to right the boat, with the assistance of the little fellow.

They set it up on wedges so the water wouldn't reach it. It had a second hole further back towards the stern, right up against the keel, put there by a log that had been buried in the mud. He pulled away the timbers that would have to be replaced, and discovered that the boat's wounds were fatal. There were ribs that were splitting, and several different places where the rot was wreaking havoc. The damage, overall, was of old wounds reopened, and quickly made a lot worse when the boat was cast aside. The water hadn't reached a level high enough to float her, but there wasn't any doubt that she'd been thrown about a bit, which had loosened up her seams. He couldn't do a lot, but he would try to do it anyway. He was determined to get her back on the water, as old and dejected as she might appear to be.

He changed several planks and he bound the splitting ribs, and used the cotton wicking in all the cracks. He scarcely had materials, but Fourcade got some planks and then a bit more cotton wicking and some leftovers of paint as well as other bits and pieces.

'I don't know what crap's got into your head.' It was all that Fourcade said.

He selected the place where he would anchor the hull, and told the little fellow to dig a trench to there. When he'd done the boat repairs, he helped complete the trench.

Now things were ready. It was just a case of waiting for a flood tide that was high enough. With the flood tide and the trench, they would get her off the sandbank.

The water rose and, sure enough, she came off with the water and the trench. They tied her up to two stakes, and then he climbed aboard and had a good look round the bottom. It wasn't leaking much. He had to wait a while, give the new planks time to swell, and then with luck the leak would slow. He could feel satisfied with this work.

He was sad at heart, despite this. There was something that was final in it. Something that was final for himself and for the boat.

The days go on by.

He went back to his fishing, and, at last, he took the little fellow along. The restlessness had disappeared. Now he was happy to be living on the boat. The boat and little fellow and dog. It's incredible the turns the river takes.

Summer seemed a long way off.

They entered deepest winter. Like crossing through a long and lonely valley plunged in shadow.

The flat grey days went on and on.

As June approached its end they had a week of warmer weather. He knew this season well, the little summer of San Martín, some call it, others, of San Juan.

It was a hot and sticky heat and thick with dangers. But the colour of the light remained. They looked out every evening on the trees along the other shore, and saw this ageing colour. They couldn't let this little summer fool them.

There were also very cold days in this same month of June.

He didn't hope for much from winter. Things had happened early on, but now the world was shrinking to a long and drawn-out languor.

July was long and cruel. July killed off all hopes. A sullen irritation gripped them. The river and the sky were one, a grey and muddy wall. The islands, drawn out smudges of a slightly darker grey. The mud and the humidity that gathered in the earth were just as hellish as the water. In either of the two, on land or in the water, you finished sopping wet. Your clothes gave off a rancid smell and stuck across your body. They weighed a bit more every day. The clothes and boots and cold all made their movements rather clumsy. They hauled themselves around, dragging all this and their grievances.

The single consolation was to make a decent fire. A fire wasn't only good for banishing the cold. Its flames, restless and boisterous, reminded them of life. But at times the cold and nuisance of it made them lose their nerve, so much so that they didn't have the will to light a fire. They climbed inside the canvas then, the dog pressed in between them, and they slept.

Each hour of the day was exactly like all others. There was no real change between the morning and the afternoon. The night came very quickly, without the lengthy prelude or the nuances of summer. It was a cold darkness coming from the east and like a tide, and it advanced above their heads with a silent swiftness. They knew no other moment quite as desolate as this, when the cold breath blew against them.

This was how July went by. Long and cruel, but all the same it ended.

August was a strange month. The month of August always is. It even came upon them in the figure of a stranger.

They returned before the dark, as was their habit. The night came later now and the cold was far less biting. But winter was so deep in them they didn't even notice. The light was still quite good, although the early stars were shining.

They climbed aboard and tied the little boat onto a bitt. The dog was very nervous from the moment it jumped up with them. It started sniffing round the deck and then jumped in the cockpit, where it let out stifled growls at the doorway to the cabin.

'What the hell's got in there?' he said, his voice a bit uncertain.

He knew the dog by now and understood it was alarmed.

Then he saw the little fellow bending down towards the deck. He seemed to study something. He was still up in the bow and the little fellow was halfway down the boat. There was nothing on the deck where he looked around his feet. And yet, a little further on, and when he looked more closely, there were several blackish smudges, starting at the starboard rail and running towards the cockpit. The little fellow stood halfway down the trail of smudges. He moved towards the gunwale, where they started, and he touched one. He was startled when he realised what it was.

He took up the machete and then edged towards the cockpit. He signalled to the little fellow, as he went by him, not to move. The dog began to bark like mad on seeing him draw near. He stepped into the cockpit, and nudged the cabin door with the point of the machete.

He couldn't see a thing. The inside of the cabin was submerged in semi-darkness. He should have lit the lantern that he carried on the rowing boat. He had another one inside, hanging on a deck beam, but out of reach right now. The dark was better anyway. The lantern would have dazzled him, making him a target. He'd also have to go back to the bow.

He nestled down beside the door and kept as still as possible. He'd think what he was going to do. The dog had stopped its barking and was stretching out its neck to reach its head into the cabin. He saw a few more smudges on the floorboards of the cockpit. He saw them even though the night was falling quickly, as if the stains were floating very slightly off the floor. They were thick and very dark. He felt a little giddy. Was it someone with an interest in the boat, or just a passer-by? And what about the blood?

He tried to peer above the dog. He leaned into the darkness of the cabin for a second. It wasn't longer than that. And he didn't see a thing. But now he knew with certainty that someone was inside. Waiting in that silence. He had the clearest feeling of another body lying there. What he felt above all was a cold and hardened gaze that wrapped around him like a draught, or a breath.

Looking far away across the gunwale of the boat, he saw that night was coming. He saw the stars above his head, close by. But there was still a little light down at the level of the deck. The dog was turning restlessly and rubbing up against him. He stroked along its back in an attempt to keep it calm.

He whispered to the dog.

'What's the matter, Capi?'

He heard a noise behind him and he turned around, alarmed. It had to be the little fellow. But he sounded overwrought.

He signalled him to move away. The blood banged in his temples. The little fellow was in the stern, and to someone in the cabin would be easily discernible against the evening sky. He must have stood out squat and black, and cut out on the piece of sky that fell inside the door frame. If he had a weapon there, the other could have brought him down in one. And shot him, too, when he'd leaned into the cabin. If he wasn't stupid. Although he'd done it quickly. Whichever way you looked at it, he'd acted like an idiot.

He remembered Sagastume and he didn't want to take any risks. Remembered many stories of the river, and their many stupid deaths. You never know what's coming from this river. The man might not be armed. It might be some poor devil. Whoever, it was possible he didn't want more problems, what with being in that state. A lot of things were possible. For one, that he was waiting for the right time to dispatch them both with absolute assurance. Even out of confusion.

He leaned forward.

'Hey there, friend! We don't want any trouble . . . it's best if you come out from there . . . '

He waited for a little while, holding in his breath. There wasn't any answer, but he heard the breathing now. It rose and fell inside the darkness, almost as a moan at times.

'Come on now, pal . . . we're not out to get you . . . has someone messed you up?'

He heard the breathing, nothing else.

He quickly slipped up to the bow and came back with the lantern and the boathook. He signalled to the little fellow. The dark was almost total now. He took the lantern, lit it, and then hung it on the boathook. He fed it through the side hatch, right into the cabin. He kept the light away from him like this. He gestured to the little fellow to come and hold the boathook steady, and ran up to the stern. From there he had a clear view of the inside of the cabin, and couldn't be seen himself. The light hung at the entrance would be dazzling the man. Its metal screen was this side, so it didn't dazzle him.

Once again, he wished he'd had the old man's shotgun with him. For whatever need arose. A shotgun is essential on all parts of the river. Some will have a shotgun with the barrels sawn off short. But to carry one of these you must be halfway to a killer.

He nestled at the stern and looked.

He was stretched out on the starboard couchette. Lying on his back and with his head towards the bow, he leaned back against the bulkhead of the deck. He had his eyes wide open and it seemed as if he watched him there and didn't show alarm, yet there was no way he could see him. He wasn't really lying down, but almost sitting upright, his legs half-off the couchette and with one laid on the other. He was a tall and bulky man who filled the cabin and seemed confident, in spite of how things were. His face was that of someone who had spent a rotten night, but who still retained his humour. He held his stomach with his hand; a redness lined the gaps between his fingers, and blood oozed out beneath it. The blood had left a wet patch on his jacket and his trousers. The clothes he wore were strange. A three-piece suit just like the kind that's worn by thugs, thin white stripes on black cloth, and the jacket very long. One jacket sleeve was half torn off. Protruding from his trousers was a pair of low-cut boots. The man had mud up to his knees. His other hand hung off the couchette, covering a part of what was certainly a hunting knife, its handle carved from antler, that he'd stuck into the floor.

There was an air of cold resolve in him. It overlay the tiredness and pain set in his face, but he was finished. Boga saw he'd had it, and that he tried to hide the truth. He jumped into the cockpit and he slipped up to the door. Once the man could see him there, perhaps he'd change his temper. He wouldn't know who he was dealing with. He had to see him standing there. As for him, he didn't know the man's face.

He took the lantern from the hook and let him see his face, with the light held up above him.

He tried to keep his voice firm.

'We don't want any quarrels, pal.'

The hand took up its grip around the handle of the knife.

'Come on, just keep calm . . . you can't take anyone on in your state . . . keep calm, that's all.'

A silence.

He was absolutely finished, but his face remained impassive.

'We've got no quarrel with you,' he said.

And then he added, amiably:

'We're going to fix you up, pal, one way or another.'

The man relaxed his hand.

'I've had it, pal,' he said, his voice exhausted.

'Yeah, that's how it looks,' he said.

And he went into the cabin.

And so, with the first signs of the change, the man arrived, and stayed there on the *Aleluya*. In the month of August, that curious month that lay between two seasons and two lights. At first he didn't notice, and it seemed to him that nothing much had changed. It was only some days later, when he saw the man stretched on the deck and taking in a bit of sun, he saw the weather changing. But that was all he noticed.

That night they took his jacket off and pulled away his shirt, and when he saw the wound he scratched his head. The best thing they could do, he said, was take him down to San Fernando. But he wouldn't agree to that, not for anything in the world, and so they patched him up as well as they knew how and spent the whole night listening to his moaning. It was anything but easy. He scratched his head and shrugged a lot. And somehow the man got through it.

He stayed there several days, lying on the same couchette. They couldn't get his boots off without jostling him around too much, so they washed them with a rag instead, and then they washed his trouser legs and left him as he was. His eyes began to brighten and his beard began to grow, and he stood a lot of pain, from what they saw. He gave off a bit of smell. But he was tough and didn't moan. He remembered Sagastume. The man was just like that, his body wracked in pain, picking at the hours against his stomach.

There were days he went out fishing, but he left the little fellow behind and then he kept a distant lookout on the boat, now less apparent on the coastline. He wouldn't have been upset if in the end the man had died, but it would be less complicated if he lived, now he was there.

Fourcade brought him bandages and alcohol and ointment of the kind that has no salt, but he didn't tell him why he needed them. The man had told him:

'Don't say a word.'

'Don't worry.'

'It's all I'm going to ask you.'

He wouldn't have, regardless.

When he came back, close to night, he rested on the door frame and watched him for a good while. There he was with his pain. It was the only thing he had. Himself and his pain in a silent struggle to the death. His eyes shone brightly in the dusk, and yet they didn't see him or the strip of August sky, because their silent gaze was inwards, to his pain.

He stood before those eyes when he returned one afternoon. And the man at last said something after many days of silence, as if he'd just awoken from a monumental sleep, his tired voice arriving from a distance.

'My guts are burning up.'

'Yeah, that's what I figured.'

'But now it's getting easier . . . '

He spoke about his pain as if he spoke about a person, with anger and with pride.

Now he spent the hours lying stretched out on the deck, smoking nice and slowly. He pretty much ignored them. He seemed to be kept busy by whatever he was thinking and by taking in the sun.

Boga thought that he'd move on once he was feeling well again, for there was nothing of this life in which he showed the slightest interest, and because it also made sense that he should leave. But he came to feel much better and he stayed there, on the deck, stretching out and smoking slowly.

Boga thought he'd have his plans.

He had some money and he liked to ask for things.

'I'd like a bottle of brandy if you go up to the store. Or maybe I'd like two. Here, take some money, and pick up something for yourself as well . . . I can't just lie around like this. Just spend what you need to, it's what the money's for.'

He began to feel a bit annoyed. The man was the type who liked to overstep the mark. He seemed completely at ease when giving others orders.

He saw them one day, in the distance, alongside the *Juanita Florida*.

'Who's that?' he said.

'He lives around these parts.'

'Who is he?'

Boga looked at him a long time.

He was stretched out on the deck and had his hands behind his head. He turned and looked towards him. His face was slow and hostile, with a rather glassy look. He looked out from under his raised eyebrows, and as if he might be joking.

'His name is Long Fourcade, of the *Juanita Florida.*'

He seemed to think it over.

'I don't know who he is.'

'I don't believe he bothers folk.'

'The better for him.'

He was starting to consider how he'd get him off his hands, or, as a last resort, how he'd free himself. It wasn't just the man, in truth, but something else he felt. Something hatched by summer and that ripened, like a fruit, by time, this time that weighed with curious tensions. Yes, things were tangling in an unfamiliar way.

The end of August came. The days grow slowly livelier. Small events take place, they gather and produce the change. The willows start budding. The line of islands darkens. They felt that vague restlessness that accompanies the change. A physical anxiety. A vigilance.

He wondered what would happen, what this summer held for him.

The man was still around.

Sometimes he remembered the thing the little fellow had brought behind him.

Now he brought the little fellow to mind, he saw he'd been quite captured, taken over by the other and administered at will. He made efforts to ignore it, but it really drove him mad. He was going out on the river one day and called the little fellow on board. The little fellow looked back uncertainly. Then the other turned his head and, looking with that half-smile, said:

'Leave the man in peace, why don't you?'

The dog had jumped aboard by now. Boga stood there in the middle, with the seat between his legs. He looked at one and then the other, but he didn't know what to say. Caught by surprise.

Then the man continued.

'Now we're on the subject, why don't you stop this fucking about, this thing you call a business? It's a stupid waste of time.'

A silence.

He shrugged and gave a bitter smile.

'Do what you like.'

'It's my affair,' he said, and that was all.

The days passed and the man stayed on, whatever he might think.

He knew nothing of this man. Not that it was worrying him. He'd have his story, just as all the rest. He hadn't even asked him how he'd come to get the wound.

He never thought he'd stay. Perhaps he had some claim on the boat. But he wasn't going to argue. If it came to that, he'd simply disappear himself. There was nothing here to keep him. Nor was he proud. As for the *Aleluya*, he didn't want the boat like this, with him here on deck.

When there was something that was bothering him, he generally moved on. He had put up with a lot just lately. Why? What was the point? Things had got all tangled and he hadn't tried to stop them. Now he was annoyed with things and thought it was enough, time to solve things, so that one of these fine days he wouldn't come back to the boat.

He was right out on the Bajo. From there he could keep going, towards Punta Morán. He'd stop off for the night out

in the shelter he'd built when the summer was just starting. Now, and with more time, he could organise things
better. In this way he could see the man's arrival as a sign.
The summer on its way. The time that drives it on . . . the
previous year, for instance, the old man's death had been
the sign, and then the dazzled eyes of the fisherman who'd
spoken of the north.

What happened was he went back to the boat and stayed
on it, watching how things tangled up. He wasn't set on leaving. He wasn't set on anything. Time was going to choose for
him. Or, perhaps, the man was.

September chose for all of them.

He was returning from the river, just as other days. He
heard voices on the boat. He heard one voice above all, one
that didn't belong to the man, nor to Cabecita. You heard
them from a long way off, at this hour of the day and in this
solitary place. He had the dog there with him. It ran up to
the bow and started barking at the boat.

'What's the matter, Capi?'

He looked across his shoulder. That was when he saw a
tower of smoke behind the boat, on the shore.

'What is it they're up to?'

He said it in a low voice, with some bitterness.

The dog barked still more fiercely.

He couldn't work it out.

He turned the boat around and led the way in with the
stern. The tower of smoke was very tall and black. It would
be visible far off. He couldn't see them yet, because it seemed
they'd gone ashore, behind the boat. He heard that voice and
then he heard the man's. And some screams from Cabecita.

Then the man was there, up on the deck. He seemed immensely tall and wide. He must have seen him too, because he shouted something to the rest and soon he saw the three of them, stationed on the boat, above him and in silhouette. Between that of the man and the other of Cabecita was a third he didn't know.

As he neared the boat, the man called out.

'Ah, here comes the businessman!'

He must have found it funny for he started laughing wildly. The other laughed as well. Cabecita screamed and jumped about. He gave a little smile.

He could see the fellow, now. He was rather on the short side, but very wide and brawny. He had a grey, high-neck sweater, linen trousers stiff with dirt, a pair of basketball shoes and a checked cap, a bit small for his head. He had a hostile look. His face was flat and wide, his lips hard and crushed; he had a squashed nose, the kind you see on fighters, and eyes that were half-closed and slanting. He looked younger than them. He didn't think he knew him.

'What's going on there?' he said, with a look towards the smoke.

'Stop screaming, you little wretch!' the man said, to Cabecita. 'What's going on where?'

'The smoke.'

'Nothing to worry about,' he said, and slapped the other on the back.

He'd arrived from the coast. He was from the coast. Boga knew his kind.

He got here in a rowing boat that was half-rotten, which he smashed to bits and burned once he'd spoken to the man.

He seemed to know the man, but their meeting now was by chance.

He had been fleeing from the coast and simply came upon the man and boat. So now they were four in their little group. Four good-for-nothings with nothing in common, each with his story, and brought together by the river.

This last arrived from San Fernando, bringing violence and hate ingrained in his clothes, from the look of him. Boga didn't know who he was, or else he didn't remember, but he knew his type from many that he'd seen along the coast. The man referred to him as Chino, maybe for those eyes, but to many on the coast his name was Rubia. Never to his face, though; if you called him that he'd have you by the throat. Rubia for his hair, which was extremely blond and long and straight, and which he wore combed back across his head.

He'd fought in the Boxing Club, the middleweight division. Hence the boxer's flattened nose. He'd not been too bad at it, either. But yes, he was tricky, from the start. He got to fight in two or three preliminary bouts, in Martínez, at the Ebro. Then he had two fights on the support bill at the Boxing, the first with Nino Basciano, the other with Bebe Galindo. In the first he lost on points, and the second was a draw, when he should have won on points. Bebe Galindo was finished by that time. This messed him up a bit. He tried to prove himself by standing up to Fredy Lobianco, when Fredy was at his peak. Fredy, in those days, was trying to make the bill at Luna Park, and fought with real savagery when he went in with a tough guy. He saw that Rubia wanted to look good by showing he could last against him, getting through the fight. Proving he could take it would be enough for him. And so he worked him slowly and with measure, taking him to pieces bit by bit. He went down in the eighth, in the middle of the ring. He stayed there on his knees like a dope. He didn't go down in one go, but in stages, bit by bit, and holding on to Fredy, who simply watched him go. Then the moment came when he stayed on his knees, still holding Fredy's legs.

Then came the business with the *liga*. Where all the dirty stuff wound up. A *liga* forms to seize upon surplus goods sold at an auction. If someone in the *liga* wants to buy a certain lot, the others block the bidding. They manipulate the game. No one can stand up to them. Anyone who takes them on does so out of sheer perversion; he'll end up paying twice the price. And then, if he insists, there can be other repercussions. It's a bad affair all round. There are many different *ligas*, and each one, as a general rule, goes after certain lots. Looked at just in principle, they're not entirely bad. But Pepe Ulloa's *liga* was something quite distinct. They named their group a *liga* just to give themselves a name. In fact, it was a *liga* to begin with, long ago, when they bought one lot of engines and another of jeep bodywork, and then, in another sale, they bought a lot of lifeboats. This was the foundation of the group. Then they turned to other matters, leaving the majority without the least idea of why they still spoke of a *liga*. Some presumed a kind of joke. Others, that the name was there to give the thing some punch. As for him, he didn't ask. It was something bad, that's all. And he was something bad. There are many like this on the coast. Blind to things, and harmful. It's not a case of trying to make their way. Not in the least. They're blind to things, and harmful.

And now this man was here. There'd be some filthy stuff behind him. And now he was here.

*

He'd become aware of something bad inhabiting the river. It's indifferent, in general. But at times it's truly bad. He remembered Sagastume. He recalled a thousand stories more. It was something in the spirit of this river that dragged its tons of mud. A force lodged in the old man and the cream-coloured dog, in Old Bastos and La Rocca, which is to say, in other words, in the river and all its things, and because of that, in him. It was also in him. It was one half of a man, or, and better, it was a man's final substance and the blind and unchecked element that drove Rubia; the kind of joy or fury that at times broke so insanely in the ways of Cabecita.

There was no way in the world that this old and battered boat could have withstood it. And the badness that had finally destroyed the *Aleluya* had now brought them all together, these four good-for-nothings with nothing in common but the hate and violence that formed the incredible bond which would hold them fast until the end.

Coming close to summer, or, and better, to the new time, when the days began to take a different rhythm, violent, in a way, he'd seen unequivocal signals of this badness. It came in from a long way off, had ripened in the torpor of winter.

Now it had arrived, in these men aboard this beaten boat, and wasn't a complete surprise. And he'd expected it, in some way. Not exactly fearing it, for he was also blind and dark. He'd been expecting, even reckoning, that finally this force would drag him with it.

Summer has returned.

The colour of the islands is now hard and doesn't change, and they lie there in the daylight like the slats of a blind. The thrush sings while the day lasts and is taken for the day, at last, as if it were the pulsing of this light. The weeds grow tall, they overflow and darken; finally they grow corrupted. The fire bell sounds out on the coast; it breaks out at an unfixed point and spills along the distant shore, and then dies in the middle of the water. The river drops, opaque and heavy . . .

But then, and above all, is the sticky, humid light that goes on beating overhead; this gleaming like a hive of fire bees buzzing in your ears, this fretting light, that hounds and hunts you down, and stirs up your blood.

The man aboard the *Aldebarán*, on opening his eyes, thought he was hearing Black Carrasco. He'd sailed all through the night and was utterly exhausted. He was waiting for the black man.

He opened, and then closed, his eyes. Lying on a couchette, he could see the ample cockpit through the open cabin door, lit up by the thickened light of summer. Everything seemed still, asleep. The air or else the light, or perhaps it was the silence, was humming in his ears. He closed his eyes again. He'd sailed all through the night, with the glare of the position lights forever in his eyes. He was still wrapped round and covered by the silence. After several hours like this, his grasp of things had drifted. It didn't seem quite possible he'd planned to reach somewhere by simply sailing through the night and dark, suspended just below the sky, or moving through a tunnel, with that glare ahead of him and the stars behind, and with that soporific throbbing of the engine.

He could sleep a few more minutes while the black man came on board and tied his vessel to the boat. This is what he always did. And this is what he tried to do again.

But instead of dozing off, he began to feel uneasy, and then, his eyes still closed, he was absolutely certain there was someone in the cabin doorway looking at him lying there, someone who was not the black man. Opening his eyes, he saw the three men standing and looking, one there in the doorway and the other two behind and in the good light of the cockpit, and studying him hard. The blood thrashed in his temples. He didn't try to say a word and neither did the men, and as if, in a second, he had found that he was standing on the edge of an abyss, he saw as clear as daylight what it meant.

His hand went for the Winchester that hung there on the side, but the man had leapt towards him and he heard the wallop land and then he felt a gentle numbness and just after that the pain, all this in a second, and still he tried to get up and the fist smashed into his face again, and smashed and smashed again, like a swarm of livid wasps.

Boga saw him hit the man as he stood there in the cockpit, and felt a strange arousal. Watching someone be punched left him feeling out of breath. He got a bit worked up and his mouth was getting dry. He knew what was to come or he sensed it at the least, but he couldn't have averted it. He felt the urge to jump the man and take his turn to hit him. His fists clenched in his pockets. The whole thing was disgusting. He heard the punches landing and he listened to the moans. Then the moaning stopped and the punches landed more spaced out, but harder and more considered. He looked across at Rubia. The flanges of his nostrils flared. Cabecita rubbed his hands and punched the air erratically, as if he were a spectator at the ringside.

At last the man was done. There was a silence on the boat. Then he turned around and went back slowly to the cockpit. He tucked his shirt in and ran his hands through his hair.

He often seemed agreeable and kind and even calm. But this was him.

'I've wanted to do that for a long time,' he said.

He'd been thinking all about it, all this time. He'd pictured the surprised expression time and time again, and the look of desperation in his eyes. And the punches. Every one, until he'd bust him up.

He took out a cigarette. His hands were trembling slightly. He took a lengthy draw.

'Come on, let's go,' he said. Before he left he looked down at the man stretched on the cabin floor.

Boga worked together with Rubia to cast off the *Aldebarán*. The man had got the engine going. The noise made them uneasy. Perhaps the man felt just the same, for now he stopped the engine and came up into the cockpit.

'We'd better use the pole until we get onto the river.'

Working with the pole and with the branches of the trees, they got the boat out from the stream.

The man knew very well that the *Aldebarán* would come back here at some point or another. The stream was very sheltered, and also good and deep. It was where they did the transfers. He thought that, when they reckoned that he'd really disappeared, they'd come round here again. And that was how it was. But they miscalculated badly.

They came out on the river and the man went back and started the engine once again. Boga sat down in the cockpit, where he lit a cigarette. There was a thermos flask of coffee standing on the cabin floor. They drank some of the coffee. The bloke was on the floor and he couldn't take his eyes off him. His face was just a mess. The man made signs to Rubia, who went to take the helm. They exchanged a little talk, but the racket of the engine meant he couldn't hear a thing. Some instructions for their course. Rubia took the tiller and the man went to the bloke and started searching through his pockets. Then, back in the cockpit, he called to Boga to gather all the lifebelts. He didn't know why he wanted them, but took them off their hooks and brought them back in to the man.

'Shit, these weigh a ton!' he said.

The man just gave a smile. He opened up his penknife and began to cut the seams. Each one of the lifebelts carried several dozen watches, all without the straps. It was a clever piece of thinking. The man took out the watches and he laid them on one side, all together on a couchette.

When it seemed he'd finished that, the man went to the bow, and, opening the locker, he leaned in to his waist. He finally backed out with a canvas-covered demijohn. He glanced at him and smiled again. He turned the bottle over and unpicked the canvas sheath, which sprouted yet more watches. Then, clowning about, he pulled out the rubber stopper and took a drink of water. It had a false bottom. Another clever dodge.

The rumour of the engine and the swelter of the day began to send them all to sleep. Cabecita screamed a bit, rejoicing in the trick. Watches on the bottom, water on the top.

They came on to the open sea.

They sailed along the channel now, and felt the sombre pressure of the water underneath them. The day was clear and bright. The sun shone overhead, the most intense life in this vastness. It seemed extremely close, and the light it shed immersed them in a soporific buzzing.

They didn't cross a single boat. They saw some on the channel, dark and very large, and sailing in a convoy to the west. But these were out of sight now and the River Plate surrounded them, flat and bright and lonely. A river built of glass, or rather, wood glue used by carpenters, with millions of hardened pleats that didn't appear to move.

They came alongside buoy K40, black and lit up, and the man told them to tie the *Aldebarán* up to the turret. They gathered all the watches in a single canvas bag, and passed them to the little fellow, who'd jumped down into their rowing boat.

'Don't go touching anything,' the man said to them all. 'It isn't worth your while.'

He'd piled the couchette blankets in the centre of the cabin, together with the demijohn and all the other lifebelts. He brought a can of petrol from the locker in the stern, and poured some on the blankets.

'Get into the rowing boat,' he said.

They jumped across.

The man used what was left inside the can to douse the cabin walls. Boga saw the bloke there when he looked in through the portholes, still stretched out on the floor, with his ruined, bloody face.

The man came out and stood up in the cockpit. He saw his shadow, short and black, frozen for a moment in the tall light of the morning.

He was working very quickly, but nimbly and precisely.

A Cessna 172 passed a long way overhead, grazing against the sky as it travelled on north-west.

The man leaned over the gunwale, holding out the empty can. He dipped it in the water and then waited as it filled. Then he spread his fingers and allowed the can to drop down to the bottom. Boga fancied it would go down with a gentle sway. It wouldn't go down vertically, but drifting on a bit, transported by the current.

The warm sun made him sleepy. He held on to the oars as if to hold on to reality. The man jumped on the boat, and then he was awake. Something he transmitted wiped away their peace of mind. He made them tense and nervous. He had a strip of canvas soaked in petrol in his hand.

'Untie her now,' he said.

Rubia untied the rope that held the *Aldebarán* to the turret of the buoy. The man still held the gunwale of the larger of the vessels, to keep the small boat with it.

'Hold on to her now,' he said, when Rubia had finished.

Rubia held the boat in place, helped by Cabecita. They were drifting and the larger boat was crossing into their path. The man remained standing. He looked around them, out into the distance. There was nothing to be seen. It was a thick and silent moment, governed by the river and the light.

'Right,' he said.

He struck a match and played the flame against the length of rope. Then, and with a flick, propelled it through a cabin porthole, thrusting hard against the boat to push the two apart.

'Let's get out of here!'

He hadn't rowed many metres when he saw the first small glimmer. It rose and fell according to the rhythm of the oars, and with the man in front of him, it gleamed above his shoulders. He still felt he was quiet, in some way. The pair of portholes lit up as if someone was inside, and had just switched on a light.

They were quite a way off now and the light grew up and flickered. A pair of yellow tongues abruptly danced out through the portholes. Cabecita screamed. The flames leapt out still further.

'Stop screaming, you fucking little shit!' said Rubia from the bow.

'Don't shout,' the man said, mildly.

The flames were four long plumes that were swaying rather nervously.

'What do you see now, boys?' said the man, and lit his cigarette. He was watching them with eyes half-closed, watching him and Rubia, the match close to his face, where he held it.

It was Rubia who answered.

'It looks like something's burning.'

Cabecita gave a scream and slapped his hands together.

'I've told you not to shout. What were you saying?'

'I'm sure that something's burning.'

'A fire on board's the worst thing that can happen to a man.' He said it calmly, squatting in the bottom of the boat. 'It's not everyone who understands that . . . you're straying off course.'

They'd now come to the sandbank off Isla Zárate. The *Aldebarán* was drifting fast towards the black and unlit buoy. Its cabin roof was burning.

'It's going to hit the buoy,' said Rubia.

The flames began to riot as they reached around the mast. It rather looked as if the boat was crossing through a bonfire, instead of being the source of the bonfire. The stern and bow emerged from either end, calm and white. He felt he heard the constant rustle coming from the flames, urged on by a secret rage, as if their brilliant light was dictated by their brevity.

'What the hell does *Aldebarán* mean, anyway?'

'No idea. I've never thought.'

'I've no idea what most of these names mean.'

'What about the Ale? . . . What was it?'

'*Aluya.*'

'No, *Aleluya.*'

'No idea.'

'What does Chino mean?'

'What's that got to do with it?'

'Does it have a meaning?'

'I've no idea.'

'Every thing has its name. It's enough for me they sound nice.'

'I'm not sure that I like it.'

'It does have something, though.'

'I don't know . . . '

Then something more intense and brilliant shot up from the flames, and erased the boat completely. A second after that, as if the two bore no relation, they heard a sound like the long dark bang of thunder.

The man didn't even turn to look, just signalled his farewell.

'I don't think it's going to hit it,' Rubia said.

'Who wants to do some rowing?'

'You've only just started.'

'Yeah, and I'm fed up with it.'

'We'll all be fed up, soon.'

'Someone take over.'

'Is it going to hit or not?'

'Come on, one of you!'

'You're straying off course.'

'We're all fed up with it.'

'That's funny.'

'I'll row.'

He changed places with the man.

The *Aldebarán* had gone. It was just a little bonfire that was moving with the water. It looked extremely odd.

'What's it going to look like from a distance?'

'We are quite a distance.'

'No. A greater distance.'

'Then you won't be able to see it.'

They were coming to the island.

After the business with the *Aldebarán*, they made their way along the coast. They didn't go back to the boat.

They wondered if they ought to and the man at last said no.

'It's better if we don't, for now.'

'I was counting on it, going back.'

'We will go back.'

'To get some things, at least.'

'No, it isn't worth it.'

He wasn't from the coast, but found he felt much better off here at the moment.

The coast is neither land nor river. Nor simply something in between. It's an unclear world of shadows on a backcloth of neglect, of badness and despair. The man who's from the coast feels that he's tied down by the river. If he touches it, it takes him. But this is where he finds himself, on neither land nor river, in among dead boats and ancient stories.

They moved along the coast from San Fernando to beyond Vicente López. It's a pleasure in the summer. You see the river differently when looking from the coast. They came on other groups of drifters, going in one direction or the other. It's a route favoured by wanderers. Above, on the embankments, the electric train appeared and disappeared from time to time, with its thunderous drumming sound. They saw the vacant, cryptic faces, peering out from or pressed up against the windows. Faces that perturbed them. That looked as if they wished them ill. Cabecita shouted when the trains came into view, attacking them with stones. He yelled with all his strength, but they only saw his lips move. They turned in from the coast when they came to certain stretches, and walked along the rails. Somehow here the sun felt closer, more alive, much closer to the ground. The pair of gleaming lines and the sleepers and the ballast and a long unbroken silence like a tunnel through the morning. And there below, the coast. And the flat and sleeping river.

The air began to hum a little. Then a sombre hammering began inside the rails.

'Here it comes!'

They moved away to one side and the train went past them bellowing darkly, grim, with all those empty faces.

It's not a lengthy stretch of coast, but changes face so often that it seems extremely long, and even different, as if you made your way down several coastlines. Once you pass Olivos, after all the mud and weeds and areas of broken ground, the beaches are exposed and long, and infinitely sad in winter. Here the river looks just like the sea. There's something of a fundamental sadness in the likeness, this seeming and not being the sea. Now, in these summer days, the bathers leave the land behind and set themselves up here, on this sand that has a smell of fish, as if they were awaiting something. When the sun goes down they leave. Once they've disappeared, and the water goes out far enough, some fellows begin to wander round and round across the sand, their faces to the ground.

'What is it they're doing?' he'd said, squinting at the roaming shadows.

'They're looking for bits and bobs.'

They looked for objects lost there in the water by the bathers. Watches, rings, earrings, penknives, glasses and false teeth.

'What use are they to them?'

'They're drifters.'

He didn't really get it.

They heard a sand boat's siren as it moved into the port. Some barges sailed the channel. Rubia and Cabecita went to comb the beach.

'It's contagious,' said the man.

They walked this way and that, moving slowly and deliberately, stamping on the sand from time to time. The dog strayed just behind them, looking rather lost.

Night came slowly from the east, just above the water, while the light drew up its last glow to the heights, above the trees, above the houses. It was strangely still and peaceful, with those shadows raking through the sand. The buoys out on the channel started winking in the night. The sand boat pressed its dark lament and then they heard the tumult of the chain run through the hawsehole like a waterfall of steel. A DC-3 was gaining height, coming from the airfield, and only seconds later it was flying overhead, the blinking of its lights up in the twilight. A restless breeze blew over from the river now and then.

Rubia and Cabecita came back from the beach, still immersed in silence. They all set off towards the port, one behind the other as they walked atop the breakwater, looking at the sand boats that unloaded at this hour. It was a lively spectacle. Scarcely had the boat docked than a line of lights switched on, right above the hold, and then came the washing of the sand with hoses plumbed in to the sides. The growling of the diesel engine pumping round the sand was heard a long way through the night. The sound grew ever clearer and it also grew more lonely, a soft beat in the silence. A noise born of the water.

Now and then a gust of wind brought music from the nightclubs, the Cuba Libre mainly, being nearest, on a pontoon. The little coloured lights were slowly climbing through the night, daunted by the river and the darkness. But the lights along the breakwater fell straight into the water, chilly and quiescent. There were one or two men fishing.

They left this stretch of coast after the man adjudged that stripping all the swimmers of their things at once, not waiting till they lost them on the beach, made better sense.

'We're going to raid the huts,' he said. 'I'm fed up with these people.'

Beyond the stretch of limestone ground, secluded by the trees, between the high embankment of the tracks that keeps the world away and the river there below, runs a string of wooden dwellings with their Ruberoid-membrane roofs. The larger part of all these huts is fashioned out of boarding from Mercedes-Benz packing crates, mounted on a tall brace frame, and sagging, as a rule, either one way or the other. When the river gets too high the water gets beneath the huts, and sometimes undermines them more, and always carries something off, or moves it round at least.

They came through in the afternoon, along the silent street that keeps the two lines of huts apart. They walked out in the light, slightly blinded by the sun. Their slow-moving steps, which patted lightly on the ground, sent up a little cloud of dust. The sun was coming at them from the far end of the street and they appeared to float, swept on with the flowing of the light. Once, the train went by above them, past the edges of the roofs of all the huts along the left. They saw the shifty faces, quickly snatched off by the curve, and the dog began to bark again, seemingly at nothing, not even looking at the train.

They saw several boats lying underneath some huts, and a cabin cruiser up on blocks and in between the trees. Its hull was painted yellow with the rubbing strakes in red. Boga stopped a moment and he studied it with interest.

The man gave him a look, although he barely turned around.

'What is it?'

He only shrugged his shoulders.

'It's been there for a while, several summers,' Rubia said. 'I think it was the other way before. Red hull with yellow strakes.'

'It's not the same.'

They saw an old man working on the caulking of a rowing boat. He left off with his hammering and peered at them a bit.

They knew that they were being watched from inside the huts.

A young boy crossed the street. He stopped out in the middle, to observe them. But he was not more than a fluctuating mark against the sunlight.

When they reached the far end of the street, they stopped when they were opposite a hut set on the right. The river was in sight between the framework of the braces, and a buoy out on the channel. A sand barge made its turn as it approached the Olivos docks. The buoy they could see was black K17, the barge was rounding K15, not visible from here. The man gave this a bit of thought, as if it were important. He knew the Costanera Canal quite well.

When they had come through here more hurriedly, south-east to Buenos Aires, they walked along the rails. All they saw from up there were the undulating roof lines of this shabby string of huts, sticking out between the willow crowns.

Rubia had said, stopping there between the rails:

'I've got a friend down there.'

'What kind of friend is that?' said the man without much interest, and walking some way past before he stopped.

'A beautiful little whore.'

The night was coming down. They heard the long lament of a sand boat on the river. The man stood and waited for the tumult of the chain as it tumbled through the hawse-hole, but the boat was too far off. The hour was very peaceful.

'A woman who is any man's does nothing for me,' he said, before he started on his way again.

They carried on walking.

Now, on the other hand, the sticky, fated summer sun had heated up their blood.

'That's her place,' said Rubia.

'I don't want any trouble,' said the man.

The old man with the rowing boat had come out and was watching. They looked at him in turn, with a kind of cold displeasure. He went back to his boat.

They heard his blows redoubled in the quiet afternoon.

'I don't see what the problem is,' said Rubia.

'And if her man's there?'

'It's how he makes his living.'

'They don't take to it kindly if it's done right there in front of them, however dumb they are.'

'He isn't going to be there . . . and even if he is,' said Rubia, and laying bare his teeth.

'I don't want any trouble 'cause I don't.'

Rubia crossed the street, going in and out of shadow. The rest of them remained there on the other side. The man took out a cigarette and leaned against a fence.

Rubia went around the house and called out at the door that stood behind a hessian curtain.

'Rosa!'

They waited there in silence.

'Hey, Rosita!'

The old man stopped his hammering. Rubia turned and looked across the street, lit up by the sunlight, to the others. They stood there, still and vacant.

His mood began to change.

'Rosita!' he was shouting, and kicked out at a strut.

Then he heard the rub of naked feet along the floorboards.

There she was, Rosita. The curtain moved a little and her head came into view, and she looked across a distance there was no way to negotiate, as if she looked into a well, or simply at the stillness of an empty afternoon, with no one there.

'Rosita . . . '

At last she seemed to know him.

'Hi . . . '

He gave a little wave, and then unleashed a giant smile towards that quite indifferent face. She noticed there were other men, installed across the street, and then she smiled in turn, rather weary and complicit. The man was always maddened by this willingness of whores. There's nothing quite so chilly nor more distant than a whore.

She smoothed her hair a little and came out to the veranda. That was when they saw that she was pregnant. She wore a simple cotton dress, with nothing underneath. Her skin was smooth and bright and dark.

The man now crossed the street.

'This is Rosita,' Rubia said.

'I'm glad.'

He looked into her eyes that had that empty look that stretched away behind you.

'Now I want you to go inside, Rosita.'

He thought he felt her body heat, worked up by the pregnancy. She looked at them, each one in turn, and didn't understand him. She took at the other two, now crossing through the sun, and went inside.

'I don't like things like that.'

Rubia gave a shrug.

'It's when they're at their best.'

'No, it's not my thing. I can't get up on top of that.'

'Ok, I'm sorry.'

The other two had crossed.

'And what do you two want?' said Rubia, just a bit put out.

'They haven't said a word. It's me who tells you what's what.'

'Don't give me that.'

'Leave the girl alone.'

'I'm sorry, it's my decision.'

'The coast is full of whores,' the man said. 'Leave the girl alone.'

'I'm sorry . . . I'm going in. Who else is coming in? . . . Aren't you going to come in, pal?'

It took Boga some time to answer.

'No, I won't come in. It's not the way I like it either.'

Rubia stared at them a moment with his eyes lit up by fury. He seemed about to speak. But then he shrugged and quickly climbed the steps.

The man took out a cigarette.

Four barges joined in tandem, and driven by a tug, were advancing in the middle of the channel.

'We'll have to buy some things,' he said.

They stood and watched the barges.

It was the first time that he'd felt something different for the man. Something very subtle. He wasn't quite sure what it meant.

The night would not be long, now. They heard the little noises that came down from overhead.

'We could find a bar to eat in,' he said after a while.

'I don't know.'

They heard some silly laughter, and after that some moaning.

'I'm going to have to buy some cigarettes if nothing else.'

The man saw Cabecita then, underneath the hut. He gathered up a piece of wood and threw it at him, hard. Then he shook his fist at him. The dog began to bark.

They made their way a bit inland and walked along deserted streets, between deserted houses. At the far end of a street, now and then, they saw the river. The presence of the sun was even stronger on the asphalt. Boga put his boots on. He preferred to go barefoot when he was walking on the coast. He laced the boots together and he hung them from his shoulder.

They went through empty playgrounds, through empty stations, with the tireless train that came and went, and empty too. They walked between long lines of tables set beneath the trees. There were bits of fires and bits of food and, out among the trees that were the furthest from the path, some contraceptives. All of this was hellish if you saw it at the weekend, but now it had the look of something dreamlike. Especially the billboards, announcing things to no one.

They went back to the coast when they arrived at San Isidro. Things looked very different here. They left the rails behind and carried on along the roadway that went off between the trees.

He'd been here just the once, in '47 or '48, when the *Republicano* sank and they killed Lalo Centurione. He saw the ancient shipyards and the silent ships again, and that special breed of men who have their lives bound up in boats.

The bare hull of the *Ráfaga* was still there at the entrance to the shipyard of the YCO. Taller than its sheds, or just as tall, at least. The planks set at a man's height were completely covered with numbers and with sketches that belonged to other ships.

'Still there . . . '

'Who is?'

'She is.'

'They've still a lot to do.'

'It's a lot of draught for round here . . . '

'It must cost several fortunes to fit out a boat like that . . . '

'It is a lot of draught . . . '

'An arm and a leg . . . '

'They're always about to get the work underway . . . '

'Two arms and a leg.'

'There's always one like this, as long as I've been round here.'

'The day will come it's useless.'

'Maybe it's already come.'

'Yeah, maybe so . . . '

It was, in any case, condemned to die a long way from the sea, on the land, among the men so busy and so silent, watching other boats be born and die. It would take a while to happen, for the boat had been well built. And perhaps the men would only see she'd died a long time afterwards. Not these men, but others. These men couldn't think of her nor see her any other way. Waiting for her day to come. He thought about the *Aleluya*. Was she dead already?

The man went through the gate into the Astillero América shipyard, and asked to see Machito. It was the second time he'd asked to see Machito. They'd heard him ask the first time in Olivos, in a bar. Has Machito been round these parts? he'd asked. And now he asked the same thing.

He crossed the yard between the boats and came out at the gallery that stood below the office, with templates hanging on the posts and woodwork benches set against the tin partition wall. There were a few blokes perched on crates and playing cards, next to the bandsaw.

'Does Machito come round here?'

The roof was very high and half its stanchions were now rotten. The dust was floating in the light, a light which had grown old. There were boats here that were new, but the majority were ancient, and some completely useless. He was pretty sure he recognised at least two or three, from '47 or '48. One there in the courtyard that was lying on its side, the *Slocum*, with its YCA plate visible from here.

They waited in the dusty light, silent, in a group, the man a pace in front of them. It seemed as if the other hadn't heard him. But they were pretty sure he had, and was thinking how it was he ought to answer. The man could guess what he would tell him.

The other played his card and then he gathered up the trick, was still gathering the cards when he turned halfway to the man.

'Who was it you said?'

'Machito.'

He spread the cards into a fan and studied them at length.

'No, it's a long time since I've seen him.'

Now he turned right round and took a close look at the man, peering out through half-closed eyes.

'And who are you?' he said.

'Machito knows who I am.'

'Yes, I'm sure he does. It seems to me I know you too, from some place or another.'

'No, I'm sure you don't.'

'It seems that way, in any case.'

They spent a couple of days like this, going round the boat-yards. And the man asked for Machito, not that it concerned them much. He had something in mind, though.

He liked the coast on this side. The boats knocked down in corners of the boatyards left him saddened, but he liked it all the same. At one point he considered ditching the other three, and finding shipyard work. He didn't like feeling tied to things in summer. But it wouldn't have taken much for him to choose to work in a shipyard here, on this side of the coast.

They spent a couple of days like this. Rubia complained on a couple of occasions.

'I'm sick of going in circles.'

'I've got a plan,' the man said.

And they kept going round among the boats.

For Sale, *Skum*, five metres R, designed by Harry Becker – Honduran mahogany – 1937. For Sale, Río de la Plata sloop full rig. For Sale, *Melgacho*, auxiliary cutter 12.80 × 1.60 × 1.50, Bermuda rig – 18 h.p. engine. *Palomita* – double prow – Frers design – 15 h.p. Brooke engine – 10 Ratsey sails . . .

'Let's get going.'

'They look as if they're sailing on the air.'

'What do?'

'The boats.'

'Fuck the boats! Isn't there anything else to look at?'

'Half of them are useless . . . '

'Let's get out of here.'

'I said I'm on to something.'

'Yeah, that's right, you're on to something . . . '

'Have you seen this bloke Machito?'

'Yeah, that's right, have they seen him . . . '

It wasn't just the boats that were getting on his nerves. There was the little fellow and dog as well.

'They're nothing but a nuisance.'

'I don't see why,' he said.

'He's a halfwit . . . and the dog's not all there, either. Why don't we do things properly?'

'I know exactly what I'm doing.'

'They're nothing but a nuisance.'

'Just leave them alone.'

When the man made his decision that the time to leave had come, he said there was a little job to do. They always finished up with a little job. This time they took a magneto, a Paragon gear lever, two chrome-plated windows, a Danforth, a time bomb, a full set of position lights and one Exide battery.

And the clinker-built dinghy that belonged to the *Bermejo*.
Boga was the one who swam across to the *Bermejo*, and used
the old man's gift to him, his rigging knife, to cut it free. The
night was very cloudy and the water thick and still.

The drizzle was beginning when they sailed out from
the port. Rubia went to light up but the man said that he
couldn't. They all craved a smoke now, the man was no exception, and they all became bad-tempered. They had to wait
a while, until they'd moved away a bit, although they'd left
the port behind. The man rowed and the rest of them lay
in the bottom, sullen and not speaking. When the moment
came to smoke, they found the cigarettes were wet. Rubia
cursed the rain.

'It's an advantage in a way,' the man said.

It really did rain now, and the rainfall on the river left them
feeling indescribably alone. The little fellow got underneath
the canvas.

'I'm not sure all this is worth it,' said Rubia, and loudly.

'The Paragon alone is.'

'We ought to do things better than this.'

'We're doing them just fine.'

'This isn't the way to do them.'

'What? . . . '

'I'm only saying, this isn't how it's done.'

'This is just to pass the time,' the man said.

He'd put the oars aside and was trying to light a cigarette.
The little fellow began to laugh.

'What's wrong with that little shit?' said Rubia.

'Who bloody knows! But where's the harm in it anyway?'
And then he turned to Boga: 'Why *is* he laughing?'

'I don't know.'

The rain hissed in their ears and they seemed to hear the laughter far away.

After San Fernando, and just beyond the factory, they came upon a rotten hull, lying in the entrance to a stream concealed by reeds. The man had seen the hull before, quite a while ago, and thought they might still find it there. They carried all the things aboard and Boga took the boat out to the middle of the river, swimming back to join them. It would be taken by the current, far away, beyond their starting point, perhaps, if the water wasn't turning. It wouldn't, more than likely, until morning.

The boat smelt like the sodden earth, or, to be more exact, like the mud that lay and rotted in the bottom of the ditch. When the daylight came, they saw the deck had sprouted weeds.

Boga went to fetch the dinghy brought down from the islands, and the man went down to Tigre, to get rid of the things. He left the Paragon and the battery on the boat, and took the rest as best he could. He'd probably go asking for Machito. He came back as the night arrived, bringing them some food and a pair of Negretti & Zambra binoculars with a tilt-compensated compass built in.

'We can live off this, easily,' he said, suggesting the binoculars in some way or other. 'These sods are so damn slack, they can't even hold on to whatever's in their hand.'

He meant people from the coast, no doubt.

'There's no point in just lifting a little something here, a little something there,' said Rubia.

'This isn't a little something,' said the man, as he waved the pair of binoculars in his face.

He smelt a bit of wine.

Rubia went on and on about the need to get organised. In that case, the man said, the best thing they could do was to open up a boatyard, as this was where you found that theft was organised the best, out here along the coast. A sense of humour wasn't one of Rubia's gifts, and he wasn't really sure what was meant.

The man sold the Paragon for 2,500 pesos. He haggled over a price as if he bargained for his life. And Rubia got nervous.

'What's the need to argue so, I wonder.'

'I'm not going to throw the things away.'

'As if they'd cost a fortune!'

'You've got no head for business.'

It was right when the man said you could do this for a living, and they did so for a while. They stole a thing in Tigre which they sold in San Fernando, or else in San Isidro. They stole in San Isidro and then sold in San Fernando, or in Tigre. There were occasions when they even stole the same thing for a second time, and then they sold it twice, of course.

The man bought a 32 Beretta, second-hand, and a power-driven screwdriver, and this was them established. The screwdriver was used to strip the fittings from the boats, grim work at the best of times. Rubia had the knack for it. They stripped out two or three boats in a night, if things went well.

He was good with his hands, like Rubia, when he wanted, but his heart wasn't in it. He was more like a spectator. He looked on at himself as he looked on at the others, from an incredible, exhausted distance. He'd been taken by the river. The summer. It would end one day. He could have broken free with just a little bit of effort. But he couldn't make an effort, big or small. Things had got all tangled up in one way or another, and him there in the middle. He thought about the islands, and Punta Morán, he thought about the boat, about his point of setting out, just the summer before, when the cream-coloured dog had at last dropped out of sight, and of the face of the old man, the face of that fisherman he met on the Anguilas, with his gaze being dazzled by the sun as he spoke, and of the old woman's face that was further off again, and all mixed up and overlaid, forming in his memory a single, cryptic face.

'What's up?' the man once said to him, and giving him a look.

'Nothing's up,' he said.

'You're always somewhere in the clouds.'

'What with this one and the little boy, we're going to fuck things up.' It was Rubia.

'There's no need to exaggerate.'

'You just can't work like this.'

'There's no need to exaggerate . . . '

The truth is that the man's mind was on other things as well. There was something else. Something in the man that was stony and relentless, a mechanism working away.

Twice he disappeared and was absent for a day. The third time it was two days. And then when he returned he decided they must leave.

He arrived back with the last light and he leapt onto the boat. The rest of them were on the deck, stretched out half-asleep, and he came back in a fearful rush, and landing on the deck he said:

'Is everybody here, boys?'

They gave each other puzzled looks and then they gave a shrug.

'We're leaving right away.'

'What's all this about?'

'I'm the one who needs to know what this is all about. Collect up all the bottles you find and put them in the dinghy.'

It had to be a big job. Or else it was Machito.

They loaded all the usual things and then a roll of steel cable, 8-mm gauge, a drum filled up with petrol and a packet that the man had brought back with him. And they set out on the river in the dimness of the twilight.

They rowed the boat all through the night, and barely said a word. One did the rowing while the others got some sleep down in the bottom of the dinghy. The man remained awake all night. Boga saw his cigarette, its red point in the darkness as it climbed and then it fell, and now and then he saw his face, lit up by the glowing when he pulled. They reached the Arroyón at dawn and halted in its narrows, just behind a bend. They put the dinghy in a ditch and waited out the day sitting in among the trees. The man, helped by Boga, stretched a length of steel cable out from one bank to the other, letting it hang slackly so it rested on the stream bed. In the morning three barges travelled by on their way out to the coast, and only one upriver. They lay on the ground until the vessels were away. The little fellow restrained the dog and made it lie down at his side. They could hear them coming easily, and well before the bend. One of the same barges which had gone out to the coast sailed back in the afternoon, and four more travelled one way or the other.

The man went in among the trees and used the can of petrol, the things inside the packet and the bottles to assemble, with the necessary care, nine Molotov cocktails. It seemed that he enjoyed it.

'They might not come down this way,' said Rubia.

'Maybe not,' the man said. 'But I've got a hunch. They're going to leave the Honda fast.'

'I don't know that they will . . . '

'They'll go in search of hidden water . . . anybody would.'

'How many of them are there?'

'I don't think more than two.'

They spaced their remarks widely, then they spoke as if it bored them, with the light exploding silently around them in the trees.

'It won't be all that easy.'

'No, this time it won't.'

Somewhere up above them a cicada started tuning up, and then released its strident screech.

'There isn't another way?'

'No.'

'All hell is going to break loose.'

'As soon as they feel the blow.'

It was midday. They caught sight of the little fellow, at the edge of the scrub, followed in and out of the light by the dog. Boga slept against a tree, his cap across his eyes.

'One of us is going to have to go the other side.'

'You two. I'll stay over here with the boy.'

'He's going to be a nuisance.'

'No, no he isn't.'

The cicada started tuning up again.

'So how does it work?'

'It couldn't be easier.'

They were practising a good while with a bottle filled with water. They practised more when Boga woke. They had to get to know the weight and calculate the swing. All in all, it turned out fun. They marked themselves a circle in the middle of a clearing and then took turns to throw, making wagers.

The river started rising as the evening came upon them.

Cabecita started with his screaming once again, and Rubia punched his head. He clapped his hands or screamed every time they threw the bottle, and sometimes both together. The man held up his fist up in threat, but Cabecita soon forgot.

'I'm going to beat you to a pulp!' said Rubia ferociously, turning for an instant at the climax of the game.

But he couldn't help himself. He couldn't help himself when the bottle fell off target. Rubia punched him in the neck and then the dog was off again, barking like a thing possessed and nobody could stop it. Rubia ripped away a branch and chased it through the trees, which only made things worse. The dog barked even louder every time he gave up the chase. It was barking at a distance, its head and neck down low, switching to another spot as soon as Rubia moved. When it seemed that it was going to stop, it started up again. He couldn't make the slightest movement.

'You shouldn't have chased it,' the man said, fed up with it all.

'I'm going to break its skull!'

He said the words with feeling, his voice contained, and mostly to console himself with the anticipation of his revenge.

'I don't know what the hell made you chase it in the first place.'

They sat among the trees, and looking at the river.

The final barge went by and they lay on the ground, and the dog gave up its barking.

The reddish evening sun sent its light between the trees, bearing off the shadows to the far bank of the stream. They couldn't look behind them. The glare had wiped out everything that lay behind their backs, and they sat there now against the light. Then the sun went down and an endless stillness followed. The shadows brought a wet smell as they lifted from the ground, a smell of old leaves. They saw the water rising, slowly and determinedly, while they sat on the riverbank, and now he couldn't recall why they were there. A little light remained out in the middle of the river. The water carried some branches off. And brought along some weeds that they'd been cutting down upstream, and then a cardboard box. They drifted on in silence, their motion very steady, as if they'd been arranged on a conveyor. They were all still and silent, and feeling rather sleepy; the river, on the other hand, seemed to be enlivened by a secret obligation. The cardboard box came up against the length of steel cable, it hovered for a moment, as if to feel it out, and then it tumbled round it and away. He was drifting into sleep. He heard, far in the distance, the growling of a river bus. Closer, overhead, was the gentle agitation of the birds come to roost in the treetops. A scrub-hen started squawking somewhere out there in the bushes. The silence after that was more intense and seemed to hammer in his ears.

That was when they started at a sound that was much quieter, much closer. The man had taken out the clip of bullets from the pistol. He cocked the gun and fired it and then replaced the clip.

The scrub-hen squawked, closer now.

The man was just in front of him, resting against the tree with the steel cable tied around it. He looked into his face, hard and wide awake and somehow foreign to his body, as if it floated over it, removed from what was going on, from all of the activity and feelings in his body, gathered up and fixed on just one single point, perhaps on just one instant.

He got to his feet, took a look up at the light and slowly went over to him.

'You're going to go across to the other side with Rubia.'

He lifted his gaze with annoyance, and tried to read this face that was lost inside the shadows.

'I'd rather take the little feller.'

The man looked at him in silence.

'Whatever you say.'

'I can understand him.'

'Whatever you say.'

'When are we going across?'

'Right now . . . I don't mind.'

The man got to his feet.

'It seems to me we need another one of those,' Boga said. He referred to the Beretta, which the man held with the barrel pointing down towards the ground.

'Perhaps we do. We'll be all right.'

The man's words came with absolute assurance. He always spoke like this. And then Boga was surprised by a fleeting sense of hatred. Something short, intense and stabbing. One gun didn't amount to much. The man had thought it through. He preferred that no one else should have a weapon. He'd decided for them all and he'd decided he preferred to put the rest of them at risk.

'It isn't enough,' he said after a while, returning to the matter.

'You're still going on about that?'

'We could find ourselves in trouble.'

'Don't be getting scared.'

'I'm not getting scared . . . but it could happen.'

'It isn't going to happen.'

He wasn't one to argue much. When all was said and done, he should have thought about it earlier. The man knew this as well, because he looked at him with infinite annoyance.

'What's brought this on now?' he said.

He shrugged.

He didn't even know what he'd got into, in reality. The man had something in his head and now he was involved. He couldn't go against things now they'd gone as far as this. The man had pinned his hopes on him. And even if it meant his life, he didn't count for much, he was a secondary element, without the right to fail, because the man was looking at him with infinite annoyance.

'I'm thinking that it's best if the three of you go over,' said the man.

He'd been thinking the whole time.

'I'll be just fine with the feller.'

'It'll be better this way.'

They pulled the dinghy from the ditch and put six bottles into it. The dog stood and waited until Rubia had settled, and then, after many calculations, jumped aboard and ran up to the bow, while the man gave them instructions, crouching on the bank.

'When I give the word, you pull the cable tight.'

'We can pull it tight right now.'

'No, when I tell you.'

'How?'

'I'll give a whistle.'

'Make sure you give us time.'

'Don't you worry yourself.'

'Yeah, I know . . . '

'The moment that you see it snag, start to throw the bottles. Exactly as I'm telling you. Not before the boat snags, if you do they're going to throttle up and anything could happen.'

'It could work out even better.'

'No, I've done the thinking.'

'It could though . . . '

'The *Caporale* has a big engine. Please, just as I'm telling you.'

This was when the dog jumped on the boat.

'I won't throw any bottles if there isn't any need to. If you all hit the target then there won't be any need . . . and, if it comes to that, if I have to throw them, I won't need to light them first . . . you get what I'm saying? It's for you to keep them busy so they'll leave this side exposed.'

'I can't see how we're going to get the stuff out from the boat if we burn it,' Rubia said.

'The tank is set in the bow,' the man explained, and with his tone a little snappy. 'What you have to do is land the bottles in the cockpit. You can let things run their course once the fire starts at the bow. They'll try to moor the boat before they land it on the bank. They've got no space to turn in. And anyway, it wouldn't help . . . they'll try to save the things and so they'll break in through the hull and then they'll drag it onto the bank, so it won't sink more than necessary. Not onto your bank, though. They can take you on from this side . . . at least, that's what they'll think . . . they won't know that I'm waiting for them . . . '

After that, the silence.

'I don't know that it's going to run as smooth as that,' said Rubia.

'I've thought it through,' the man said. 'I've gone over every detail. Stop worrying so much.'

'I just don't know . . . and after what happened with the *Aldebarán* . . . '

'For fuck's sake, what's the matter? All you have to do is hit the target with the bottles and then get down on the ground.'

'I don't know . . . '

They sat a while in silence, undecided.

'I'm only saying it won't be easy,' Rubia said, still grumbling on, his stubbornness apparent.

But as the man said nothing more, just lit himself a cigarette and waited with an air of scorn, Boga set to row towards the other bank.

They hid the dinghy in a ditch, just forward of the cable, and took out all the bottles. The dog leapt from the boat before they'd touched the other shore, and Rubia cursed the creature from the bottom of his soul.

'That dog is going to mess things up for all of us!' he said, through his teeth.

He turned and gave the little fellow a clout, as if he were the dog.

'Don't start with the dog!' the man was shouting from the other bank.

It was now completely dark and they stumbled round a little, and had a bit of trouble trying to come upon the tree to which the cable had been fixed.

The *Caporale* turned up late, and long after they'd given up all hope it would arrive. They heard its engine beating with a curious kind of clarity, punching through the silence of the night.

They were feeling very sleepy after all those hours curled up there in the shadows, without speaking. At first it was mosquitoes that had come out to torment them. He could put up with mosquitoes, but they got to him tonight. He listened to Rubia griping in the darkness, slapping at his body hard. Some say if you're nervous then you'll feel them all the more. He didn't think he was nervous. But this is what they say.

The moon had come up early and was early going down. He saw the figure of the man there, standing on the other bank, and lit up in the brightness like a statue. Everything had lost its relief, and appeared clear and flat. A few birds shuffled in the trees, as if dawn were arriving now. He heard the thrush's song as it rippled in the night, there, just behind him, somewhere in the trees that looked as if they were moving slowly away. The river was a shining ribbon always on its course. After watching it for a while he couldn't say where it ran anymore. There was a moment when it seemed as if it floated right over him, a few metres overhead. With this light, so white and even, this restless, sighing world had become completely fabulous.

Then the moon had gone, and until his eyes adjusted the darkness was intense. From time to time a match flame lit the man's face for a moment. He always felt his face, despite the darkness and the distance.

A limpkin started calling in the middle of the scrub. At first he just ignored it. But when an hour had passed, he longed to have the old man's gun to blast it in the middle of its squawking. Its cry was tired and whining. First there came a lengthy cry, then four to seven shorter ones. Between the cries, the silences themselves became unbearable, wondering if the thing would start again. He couldn't time the silences. Ten, fifteen, twenty seconds. The pause was absent sometimes, and the cries just ran together in a line of three or four. He thought that an opossum must be prowling round its nest. He thought of this each time, to feel some pity for the creature. But even so, its crying seemed to sound inside his head. One long, four short . . . one long, six short. When the bird had finished, everything he heard seemed further off.

Until he heard the *Caporale*'s engine. At first he'd been impatient as he waited for the boat. He didn't know what was coming, but the simple fact of waiting for it made him feel impatient. When several hours had gone by, he'd convinced himself the sound would never come. Anything might happen, but they'd never hear the boat. In some way it was up to him to goad the night and use his will, or maybe his impatience, whatever else it took, to summon the *Caporale*'s sound. But then, it was his will, or his impatience, that presented the greatest difficulty.

Still, there was that face lost in the shadows, quite assured, hardened by a wait that had been considerably longer.

And so they heard the sound, and he knew that something in the man had still to finish waiting, had worked out every move they made with absolute assurance.

From over on the other bank, the man produced the whistle.

He didn't whistle back at once. He'd lost the thread a little. It was the engine all the same.

Rubia had gone to sleep. He bent down quickly over him and shook him into life.

The engine noise grew louder.

He set to raise the cable. The man had said to steady it just slightly off the water. He waited there for Rubia to come across and hold it. Then he bent to try to see its distance from the water. He looked towards the other bank.

'I think it's right,' he said.

They tied the cable firmly.

He'd brought a tin they'd packed with tow and then filled up with alcohol. He levered off the lid and set the tin down on the ground, just in between himself and Rubia. Cabecita only had to light a match and drop it in. Nothing more than that. Rubia wanted either one of them to light the match, but he'd said no, it's better this way. They'd argued on the other bank, before they crossed the stream. Now they argued once again, their voices taut and smothered, listening as the engine noise grew steadily towards them.

'His hands are better out of it . . . '

'He's not a fool.'

'I'm telling you it's better . . . '

'It will save us time.'

'There's no way I can trust him.'

'He's not a fool.'

'He damn well is! And now he's going to fuck us up!'

'It's not the time to argue.'

'He's going . . . '

'Enough!'

'Fuck it!'

All at once the engine noise grew distant.

They left the quarrel there, and listened.

'It's in the bend,' he said, and felt a little startled.

The boat was in the first bend. When it came out from the bend, its noise would be much greater, right on top of them.

They were hanging on the engine sound. They couldn't argue now. Everything now ran on at a certain pace.

He looked out to the other bank. He couldn't see a thing.

'Stay exactly where you are,' he said to Cabecita, quietly.

'Don't strike the match until they're right beside us,' Rubia said, his voice a little shaky.

'I'm going to tell him when . . . '

Rubia grabbed a bottle, and rearranged the rest to hand. Boga did the same. He placed the other two between his legs. He only had to bend to pick them up. Cabecita waited, standing in between them. He could feel his body close to him, shrunken by anxiety and fear.

He tried to see the cable. Nothing. Would they see it?

Now the *Caporale* turned. At any moment it would appear just metres off, with the final bend behind it.

They were tense and didn't move. With that sound, which collided with the pumping in their ears, advancing through the night.

He heard it when the man released the safety catch.

Now.

Then the noise grew suddenly loud and the two position lights appeared, coming straight towards them.

The boat now had to veer twice rather quickly on the stream, which meant at least one man aboard was busy with the steering.

And then, out from the shadows, came the dark smudge of the vessel, very close, its mast in silhouette against the sky at night, lengthening alarmingly and right above their heads as it arrived.

He tried to see the man who was standing at the tiller. The glare sent by the lights made this impossible. They came on, one green, one red, at the level of his eyes.

He reached a hand to Cabecita.

'When I say,' he whispered, almost breathless.

They were completely in the noise now.

The prow was all but up to them. He squeezed the bottle's throat.

'Now!'

Almost as he shouted, the boat snagged on the cable. The tree shook to its roots. First he saw the quick and vivid flaring of the phosphorous and then the soft blue flicker of the alcohol in flame as it sprouted from the ground with a snort. He quickly bent and set light to the tow inside the bottle, then threw it hard away towards the middle of the river, to where he gauged the cockpit was. The plumes of fire flew parallel, but only Rubia's bottle hit a bullseye in the cockpit. His fell on the housing. They sent up dull, suppressed explosions. Then the plumes inflated with a buzz. He saw the man there at the tiller. His silhouette was bright and inky, leaping at the night as if lit up by the flashing of a magnesium lamp.

They threw another pair of bottles, this time both on target in the cockpit. But now the man had gone. They heard the desperate howling of the engine revving flat out, and the shaking of the tree beside them. And then they also heard the shots. One man started shooting at them, aiming through a porthole. They threw the last two bottles fast and dived onto the ground. One of these two bottles hit the boat along the side, and a stream of fire ran down towards the water. The bullets fizzed above their heads and rapped against the leaves that hung a little way behind them.

One of the position lights exploded with a stunted bang. The engine kept on straining. Perhaps they didn't know that they were dealing with an 8-mm steel cable.

The flames inside the cockpit caught and swelled and gathered height. The man had thrown his pair of bottles. Not that they were needed, and this was when he understood the man had other plans. The boat could burn for all he cared.

The two men made their way out from the cabin. The fire had blocked the entrance. The black, cramped silhouettes danced between the flames. They clambered up on deck, crouched behind the housing and began to shoot towards them. They fired away quite blindly, their backs towards the other bank. He'd overturned the tin of tow.

It was what the man had waited for. There in the shadows, he aimed at the head of one of the two men with care, and pressed the trigger. The man's head hit the housing and he sat down on the deck. He fired again at once, at the other, but this man had dropped down at the first shot and escaped towards the bow. He saw him when he half-stood and dived into the water. He fired towards the splash and then a little way ahead. The fire lit up the water and he caught sight of the man's back, then his arms as they were turning in the air. Now he aimed carefully, taking his time, and fired. He fired off several shots, and one of them at least produced a dead sound as it landed, as if it had hit a bag of sawdust, something of that sort.

It had all been very quick. The man was still there letting fly and Rubia and Cabecita had got up on their feet. That was when it happened. They heard the virile roaring of an engine leave the bend and a blinding light erupted in the middle of the river, off the *Caporale*'s stern. He'd raised himself a little when the man began to shoot. Now he was beginning to stand. He hadn't made it yet when the light burst in the darkness and he heard the shots and felt that something punched him in the shoulder and the belly and elsewhere, and he fell and hugged the ground. A thunderstorm of bullets made their way above his head, and he felt Rubia fall with a thud against the earth. Cabecita ran off with the dog barking in a frenzy at his feet. They were followed by the bright light and he saw the little fellow leap up in the centre of the beam, with a convulsive shudder. The dog turned round and barked at the light and then a gun-burst lifted it a little off the ground, and dropped it near him. There was a moment when he saw a strange gloss shining in its eyes, dilated by the light, and now he watched its paw as it contracted in spasms. Rubia was groaning in the darkness.

There were several weapons firing and at both banks. One of these at least, the one that fired above their heads, was automatic.

He caught sight of the man, still over on the other bank, standing stiff in the beam of light. He caught sight of his face, which had hardened in his rage, but which still, in spite of this, continued chilly and impassive. The man emptied out his gun in the direction of the light, facing down the brilliance, and when he paused to change the clip Boga saw him spin around as if a thousand wasps had stung him, and fall down with a bounce against a tree.

They switched the spotlight off, and the vessel toured around the boat. Two men jumped up on the other bank and began searching it hurriedly. He saw the torchlight circle nosing nervously about inside the shadows.

The dog had stopped its trembling. He looked out at the vessel in the brightness of the flames. The river here is tight and the boat was just downstream of him, not many metres off. It was a four-seater Chris-Craft launch; the chrome of its fittings shone splendidly. A man was standing at the wheel and looking at the other bank. The burning on the boat gave out an ever-louder crackling. The heat had turned his face red. He thought back to the *Aldebarán* and what was going to happen when the flames got to the tank. It seemed to him they'd cut the petrol feed.

The pair up on the other bank had stopped beside the man. One nudged him with his foot. There couldn't be much doubt that when they'd finished checking him, they'd search the bank where he was.

Then Rubia gave a moan and the man still on the launch turned round and looked to where they lay. Boga saw his face there, reddened by the glare. He didn't know who he was. His face was completely ordinary. He couldn't have described it at all.

He raised himself a bit more and, not really thinking why, he whispered towards the face.

'Hey there, Machito!'

The man appeared intrigued; he gave a frown and searched the shadows. Then quickly, without aiming, he fired towards the voice. The bullets whistled by his head, once, twice and then, after a long pause, for a third time. He crushed himself against the earth. Now he couldn't see a thing. A long silence followed. He heard the crackling flames. When would the tank explode? Then he heard the men jumping back onto the launch. Their talking sounded livelier. He barely raised his head and saw them standing on the Chris-Craft in the swaying of the firelight. The boat burned end to end. It would blow up at any moment. The engine throttled up and the launch sprang into life, and moved ahead a little. He saw that they were going to go ashore a little further up, in fear of the explosion. Now. This was the moment. He held on to his stomach and began to roll towards the ditch, to where the dinghy waited. Now he felt the other wound. In his left thigh. Woken up and furious.

He was rolling on the ground and spitting curses at the pain when the petrol tank exploded. He felt a blast of heat and saw the treetops high above his head ignite, and then go out, with a flash that hurt his eyes.

He fell into the ditch. He landed on his back and tried to lie there without moving, in spite of his repugnance. He felt his body sinking gently in the mud. And that stink of rotting leaves. He saw the light above his head, fainter now, and against this glow, the tangled weave right by his face, of weeds along the ditch edge. He was sticking to the bottom.

Rubia saw the men who ran towards him on the bank. They halted when the tank blew up, covering their faces. They moved in from the bank, and he lost them for a while. But he heard them when they spoke and when they moved among the trees, not far away. Now he saw the disc of light projected by the torch, skipping like a lark mirror.

He knew that he was done in. He couldn't stir himself at all. Even so, it gladdened him that things had turned out badly for the man. He'd always tried to tell him that it wasn't the way to do things.

The footsteps came towards him.

He saw the men's feet stepping in the circle of the torch-light, walking all round Cabecita's corpse. Then the light began to rake close to him.

It leapt across his feet and stopped a little further on, as if it were alive, and could stop and think things over. Then it made its way back, and beginning at his feet it made a full examination of his body, to his face.

He was leaning against a tree and he squinted straight into the light, without blinking.

Then one man came up quickly. That was when he closed his eyes and let his body slump down to the ground and pressed his face against his arm, and held his breath. The man put the barrel of the gun against his head, and fired. His head bounced just a little.

He heard the shot. And then he heard them go into the scrub. He heard their words and footsteps and the sound of parting undergrowth, moving away towards the centre of the island. They'd jumped across the ditch on their way to check on Rubia. But then they went into the scrub, before they'd seen him. They had to come back anyway, and then, and almost certainly, they'd see him. He'd hug one of the side walls. It was all that he could do. He tried to lift his leg up. It was stuck there in the mud. The sensation was repugnant. He had to try to move, though, to roll himself over and hug the wall. The water dug away along the bottom of the ditch walls, and often left a cavity. He reached his hand along the wall to see.

Now he had the feeling that his other hand was resting on a plank, not on his stomach. One moment the pain would surge terribly, the next it faded just as quickly. The burning in his shoulder was far more constant, but his death was in his stomach. He felt along the cavity.

Just as he was going to move, he sensed a man's presence, very close. He could feel the proximity of a body, keeping guard, and could feel himself being watched. He looked up to the light. He expected every instant that the quiet face would show itself, bending down over his death.

This was how he waited, with one hand resting on the wall and one against his stomach; he waited without moving.

He lay there for a while, feeling absolutely nothing, watching how the glowing from the flames began to fade. It was only when the time had passed that he understood he was gazing at another light, out between the branches, high up in the sky.

The day was beginning. The thought of it inspired him with an odd sense of assurance. It came to him that a deadline had passed, or something of that nature, and that what distance hadn't managed, time had brought about.

Even so, the men were there, and obstinately searching on. They had to clean up everyone. He thought: So they expected this . . . they know us. So they knew one was missing. Me. I'm missing.

That was when he heard the roaring engine of a barge, on its way from the Dorado.

Someone close by whistled.

The voices and the footsteps grew, hurrying from the scrub.

'Let's go!'

'There's nothing here.'

'Tough shit. Come on!'

'The whole thing is a fuck-up.'

'We haven't got the time.'

'We're just about to find him.'

'They're going to land at any moment and we'll still be here.'

'Come on, let's go!'

They jumped across the ditch.

Someone cried:

'The ditch!'

'There's no time. Let's get out of here!'

Not long after that he heard the growling of the launch, and knew that they were going by the Honda Canal, because the noise crossed right in front of him, was muffled in the bend and then faded on its way towards the north.

The boat arrived and throttled down on seeing what was floating in the middle of the river. Motionless inside the ditch, watching the day as it grew up among the treetops, he imagined it all unfolding. It was probably a barge. He heard the sound of voices and the engine throttled up again. It returned to the Dorado. Others would be coming now. And some would come along the bank, for certain.

He must have gone to sleep. He thought he'd closed his eyes and then had opened them again, nothing more than that. The truth was that he didn't have a clear idea of anything. All of him was reducing by the minute, to a very small point. And what remained of his body was also something still and stuck against the ground. Something strange, that had fallen there across him, preventing him from moving.

At first the sensations were clear and distinct. The mud, and the dampness that was wetting all his clothes. The fierce pain in his shoulder and the sick void in his stomach and the throbbing in his thigh. The smell of staleness in the walls. And then there was the day. But then he started losing any sense of where the limits were. The fact of being motionless was really what had numbed him, or rather, had bewildered him. Now and then the pain returned and brought him back to life. Pain returned his feelings to a certain kind of order. The thought he couldn't bear was that he wouldn't be able to move. He hadn't really tried to, but his hand still rested against the wall, alien and cold.

He opened up his eyes and saw the ditch was bright in places. One half of his body was now lying in the sunlight. But there was something else. The water was submerging him. He raised his head a little, and noticed that his body was now partly underwater. The toe-ends of his boots protruded, and seemed further away than usual. The river had been rising for an hour, more or less, and on arriving at the level of the ditch, had started filling it. Now the water trickled round his neck. It was hard to hold his head up, but it seemed to him he wouldn't be able to move himself again if he dropped it in the water even once more. He made a real effort and got up onto his elbows. His intestines seemed to empty out. Now he saw his stomach with its dark stain in the middle, and a thread of blood that slowly turned to water. It was best to do it all at once, given his suffering. He rested on his good side, on the leg that wasn't injured, and tried to get up on his knees. The water swelled his clothes and, when he made it to his knees, it fell out in a flood. When he moved he'd churned the mud that lay down in the bottom, increasing his disgust. Now up on his knees, his eyes were level with the ground. He smelt the heavy stench of grass, the damp warmth of the earth with its successive beds of rotting leaves. He looked away in front of him and saw the river shining, as if at the end of a tunnel or a passage. The dinghy was still sitting at the entrance to the ditch, the water had refloated it and pinned it to the wall with its pressure. He couldn't hear a thing. Neither boats nor people. Nothing but the humming of the light on a summer's day, obstinately rising. He rested on one knee and placed his whole weight on the other leg. Once again the water flooded out from his clothes, and he almost let his body fall. He leaned against the wall. The edge of the ditch was at his chest now and the weeds brushed at his head. He didn't see a way that he could struggle from the ditch. His feet sank gently down into the mud, with noisy gurglings. And he also had the thought that he was dying. I'm dying . . .

He didn't feel surprised. He only felt annoyed at all the things he'd have to go through in the meantime.

He heard a barge far off and tried to move towards the dinghy. Everything would be simpler once he'd made it to the boat.

It seemed somewhat bizarre that he could tolerate such pain. The water reached his knees now. He centred all his efforts on not falling on his face. The thought that he would die buried in one of these ditches was repugnant. This was how Old Nardi died; they'd found him sunk so far down and in such a state of ruin, that they'd left him where he was.

Every time he pulled one of his feet out from the bottom, the mud gave back an irritated snort.

At last he reached the dinghy and he held on to the side and closed his eyes. Then, and with his eyes still closed, he threw his body forward and fell down into the vessel.

The sound of the barge was growing louder in the morning, as if it were increasing with the light. It had left the Dorado and was entering the Arroyón, because the sound was boxed-in now. Things were better here, in the bottom of the dinghy, but he'd had it all the same, and the only thing that mattered much now was getting there. In one way or another, he'd always circled round this thing. And still he hadn't got there. He listened to the noise with his face against the bottom planks, and almost fell asleep to its beating in the morning. It went into a bend and the sound changed again.

He got up on the seat, and with a push against the ditch wall he went out onto the river and the morning, which was sparkling on the water.

The current wasn't strong, but he felt that it would carry him a while. He'd hardly left the ditch when he felt it start to take him, pushing him along against the bank. He got an oar into his fist and tried to turn the boat towards the middle of the current. The light was blazing silently. The middle of the current was the middle of the light, in a way. The river and the light one force. It snatched him from the shadows of the scrub to take him off to die elsewhere.

The *Caporale* lay there tilting over to the starboard, a large part of the boat now underwater. If the river went on rising it would cover it completely. The explosion must have opened up a hole below the waterline, and so the boat had sunk. Something of the other side was showing through the surface, blackened by the fire. At first sight it seemed to be the belly of a fish. The end-piece of the mast, with its crosstrees still in place, was lying on the other shore, and from the way it lay he saw the fire had eaten through its base, starting from the mast-hole, and nothing but the rigging now attached it to the hull.

He heard the voices moving down the shore.

He saw one of Cabecita's arms hanging down, pointing at the water, and part of his head that was showing through the grass. But this was all he saw. The three of them would be there, and Capi, stuck to the ground, as if they were asleep. And he'd broken free at last, even if a little late.

He began to turn the bend, and the voices and the panting of the barge moved away.

The water helped him onward, and almost all the time, for the *bajante* took him with it once he'd reached the Paraná, and, with an oar just to keep the boat on course, the current took him right across and on into the Sueco, and swept him along it to the Bajo del Temor.

He was rowing with his arms alone, setting up a stroke that used a minimum of effort. He watched his hands go up and down, the skin a perfect white where there wasn't any mud, as if these hands were not his own. His left arm didn't exist. His shoulder was the limit of his body on that side, a limit made of pain, and which at times appeared to hold a massive weight. He felt his other arm was growing longer in some wondrous way, and at a place he couldn't fix it ceased to be his own. The wound in his thigh wasn't leaking blood for now, but he couldn't bear its throbbing. On the Honda Canal, he stuck a finger in his trouser leg and ripped the fabric open all the way down to the knee. Then he leaned across the rail and washed the wound a little. His shoulder went on bleeding, perhaps because he moved it. A sluggish line of blood ran all the way beneath his clothing, and joined with the haemorrhage that, when he moved from time to time, still welled up short and sticky from the hole in his stomach.

The sun had dried out the mud that was covering his body and he felt it pulling at the skin on his neck. Once he tried to smoke, but he found the cigarettes and the matches had got wet. He laid them down beside him, spaced out on the bench, and waited for the sun to dry them out.

He saw the debris from the *Caporale* floating on the water in the middle of the current, to the outlet of the Arroyón.

In the end he was numbed by the sun and the fever.

He seemed to be advancing with his head inside a blazing cloud. The river fired relentlessly into his eyes. At times it seemed to glitter like the scales of a fish that was leaping on the beach before it died. He saw things floating round when he let his eyelids close, shifting greenish patches on a dark and sticky ground, dissolving in the cloudy murk. He often drifted off, but the pain was always stabbing him, waking him again. The whole of his body coalesced in this pain, was reduced to nothing else. There was something, even so, that stood apart in him and watched as he died, that lay beyond all suffering, as if this couldn't die.

On the Honda Canal he was tormented by the barges. They buffeted the dinghy and his stomach bled again. He felt the wave approaching once the barge had travelled by and, guessing how the boat would move, he tried to ride the rolling, but he never quite surrendered, and it didn't end well.

He sailed on to the Paraná and rounded Isla Nueva, going round the long way, otherwise he ran the risk, between Isla Nueva and Isla YCA, that the current would get hold of him and carry him away beyond the Sueco. He saw a group of barges, black, and, as it seemed to him, motionless, there in the light. In fact, they were sailing to the Serna Canal.

Once he'd passed the island, the wind and the smell that recalled the smell of sea made him feel a little better. The pain had stopped its nagging, but he knew, with strange lucidity, that death would come before the night. The river shone intensely in the fullness of the summer as he died in this splendid isolation.

He could see the Cangrejo, just make out its inlet on the far-distant shore, a scarcely darker point set in the lengthy bed of reeds, and remembered how the fishing there was excellent. He had been there, once, a couple of summers ago, or maybe three, and had always thought of going back.

A little boat was going across the river to the Víboras. He heard the pitter-patter of its engine as it sailed, and only some time after saw the trail of white advancing bit by bit across the river. He was watching how the boat sailed at the time he fell asleep.

It must have been a while, because the entrance to the Sueco was before him when he woke. The heat was still intense but the sun was going down. It felt even hotter once he'd sailed into the Sueco, sheltered from the wind by Isla Lucha. He'd made this passage many times, downstream, with the trembling curve of the head rope between him and the shore. Now, without the trammel, he was running down more quickly. The sun had dried his cigarettes, but he no longer wanted to smoke. And he wasn't sure he could.

He'd kept hard to the coast when he came into the Sueco, fearful that the stream would bring him out onto the Bajo on the far side of the Chaná. The reed beds closed his way and he was held up for a while in the middle of the channel.

He was patient in his waiting for the tide to lift him out. He didn't have the strength to move the oars inside the reeds. And so he watched the river through the curtain as it swayed with a slightly troubling sigh. He was up beside the channel that ran in between the islands, with its shelter for the fishermen standing there on the bank. At the end of the channel he saw the open sea, a different colour. The afternoon was beautiful. I'd like to have the boat rigged and go out onto the river, he thought. It's one of those afternoons . . . what was going to happen to Old Froglia's little boat? he thought straight after. How would it end up? It had another year still in it, maybe two. One never knows.

The water didn't lift him out, but sent him further in. He lay across the starboard rail and reached out to the reeds. He used them to pull the dinghy out gradually. He felt no pain at all now and his stomach wasn't bleeding, unless he moved too roughly. He could hardly move at all, though. He felt horribly tired, and emptied.

He was still lying on the rail once he'd left the reeds behind, when the water started pushing hard, and he had one final view along the channel through the islands. He saw there, in the distance, in the softened evening light, the white and slender figure of a sloop out on the open sea, its spinnaker unfurled. It looked just like a giant bird in slow, majestic flight across the sleepy afternoon.

The channel was behind him and the sloop was lost from sight. He tried to sit and take the oars into his hands. He managed with his good arm, but he couldn't do a thing to stem the dark blood from his entrails. He felt a little cold now and he thought this wasn't normal. It isn't cold at this hour, in this season . . . I'm going.

He stayed close to the left bank as he moved out from the Sueco, even at the risk of getting caught up in the reeds again.

The Bajo was before him, still, and then, to reach the Chaná mouth, he would have to fight the current.

Perhaps he had a will that was more obstinate than death. His will had battled death the whole day long. Now he was here.

At this hour of the evening, the still and cloudy waters of the Bajo looked like aged bronze. A curious kind of stillness weighed across them. His big eyes of a dying fish looked all along the distant shore, showing no distress. Towards the east, the highest of the treetops stood up clearly on the dark, uncertain limit of the coast. The slanting sunlight brushed across them, giving them the look of distant feathers up in flame.

He looked out for the Chaná inlet. Then, across the Bajo, curiously still against the last light of the day, he saw the silhouette, long and beaten, of the *Aleluya*.

Going across the Bajo took forever. He always had the boat in sight, and yet it seemed to be moving away from him. The truth is it was getting dark, and in the waning light one had the sense the boat moved away. The water moved him just a little eastwards, even so. He stopped his rowing now and then, utterly exhausted, and stared out at the boat, his face expressionless. I won't get there by looking . . . nor will it come to me . . .

And then the water started rising, pushing him towards the *Aleluya*.

'Who understands this river?' he said. His whisper was touched with gratitude.

He couldn't feel his thigh, nor his shoulder, nor his stomach, just an infinite fatigue. There it was, his body, and perhaps already dead, and something very small in him was beating very weakly on the far side of a tender wall of silence.

The dinghy gently bumped the hull, he lifted out his arms and sought the gunwale in the shadows. His body followed after them, and left him dangling out. I don't think I can hold on, he told himself serenely. I've got no more to give . . .

His face was pressed against the hull, the odour of the boat just like the odour of the ditch.

It's dead from end to end, he said. The river's got inside it.

His hold began to slacken.

He tried to lift his body up before he lost his grip, and the pain came back to life. Perhaps it was what he needed. The pain brought back some life, and with the gunwale for support he found his feet. If he could stand up on the dinghy's bench, the gunwale would be waist high, and all he'd have to do would be to topple forward over it and hang there from the boat. He put his first foot down and then he waited for a while. And then, and with the same intent, he stood up on the other foot and dropped across the gunwale. He didn't try to check the blow, and felt as if his innards burst. He hung there on the gunwale, exactly as he'd planned, and felt the dinghy start to slip away beneath his feet, and that his blood was warm and oily as it rippled down his legs.

Slowly and determinedly, with not a thought of anything, not even of the pain, still vivid and enraged, as if it was a case of simply testing to the limit the extent of his endurance, until it was exhausted, he lifted up his body and fell down onto the deck.

There, he thought, with a smile that never reached his lips. There we are, old chap . . .

He was lying here like this when he heard the tired drumming of an engine from the Sueco entering the Bajo.

It's Lefty, he told himself, his face against the deck planks.

He lifted up his head, and there above the gunwale he recognised the darkened silhouette of the barge, riding on the current through the doubtful light of evening.

He doesn't need to come in on the current with this flood tide, he thought.

He felt no pain at all now, but his body weighed like lead. He tried to sit, and succeeded only in falling and crashing his head against the deck. But he was measured and persistent, and after two or three attempts he sat himself up at last. Now he was sitting on the deck, his back against the housing and the river there in front of him.

The wind blew from the river. That damp and stealthy breeze, like the grazing of a shadow.

The boat released a small complaint.

The night was coming down.

He felt nothing of his body now, not even as a weight, now he felt the boat instead. Himself and the boat, this unhappy *Aleluya*, were now a single body that was dying with the day. The timbers and the stories of the past made their complaints through him.

He watched the darkened river with his big eyes like those of a dying fish.

Something of the day remained across the River Plate, but already it was night around the boat.

Long Fourcade must have passed an hour ago, he thought.

The wind got up again.

He could no longer see the meagre light he'd watched earlier, far off in the distance, but he remained before the night with his big eyes of a dying fish now opened very wide.

TRANSLATOR'S NOTES

It may be of interest to signal where I moored my point of
honest dealing in my translation of Haroldo Conti's Castilian-
Spanish text *Sudeste*. It was the rhythmic sensibility that drew
me into the novel, from its first lines:

> *Entre el Pajarito y el río abierto, curvándose bruscamente hacia*
> *el norte, primero más y más angosto, casi hasta la mitad, luego*
> *abriéndose y contorneándose suavemente hasta la desembocadura,*
> *serpea, oculto en las primeras islas, el arroyo Anguilas.*

In *Rhythms* (Stanford, 1995), Nicolas Abraham describes rhythm
as the origin of the 'fascinated consciousness' that projects
a story forward and produces the sense of enchantment we
know when reading the best stories. My reading of *Sudeste*
was formed by this immediately intuited aspect, the rhythms
ever-present in the novel's style, which are reinforced and
intensified by the cycle of the seasons and the movements of
nature, the intervals of the protagonist Boga's journeys and
the laconic dialogues with those he comes across around the
rivers of the Paraná Delta. Mooring a translation to this sty-
listic feature of the novel was for me the natural choice, but
it required the identification of suitable points of anchorage.

Conti's use of punctuation forms a distinctive 'respiration' in his text, a rhythmic feature that is also pronounced in well-known authors such as Isabel Allende – and often cancelled in the translation of their texts. The difficult interest in writing *Sudeste* into English centred on the presentation of this respiration in a language with a quite distinct music. The work of translating the poetic quality of a text lies in the selection of words and phrases with appropriate *sounds* to convey the relevant meaning, but the flexibility required when structuring such phrases into sentences that present the rhythmic style of Conti's writing brings word *size* into play.

The register of Conti's text is poetic but, at the same time, its narrative is simple and direct. Shorter words are not only more flexible bricks in the building of lines of rhythmised text, they also lend themselves to his plain-speaking register. It is at the level of this bricking that *Southeaster* (*South-East* in the Immigrant Press edition of 2013) is anchored to *Sudeste*.

Not that I was aware of this for many months into the writing: while reading lends itself to the analytical act of interpreting, writing is rather more intuitive work. It was the rhythmic sensibility of the novel at both its underlying, narrative level, and at the surface level of its respiration, that formed the enchantment through which the writing of the translation found its form.

Discussion of the practice of translation is keen in the matter of the basic beliefs, policies or procedures – the theory – a translator works from. For a fiction translation, it requires study alongside the novel in its first language to suggest where the work of translation has been moored, to which aspects of the source text it shows 'fidelity'. But a translator is first a reader, and Marcel Proust has something to say about the unfaithfulness of readers:

> Saddening too was the thought that my love, to which I
> had clung so tenaciously, would in my book be so detached
> from any individual that different readers would apply
> it, even in detail, to what they had felt for other women.*

Were the reading translator able to feel sure of any such ascribed authorial intention, writing its exact reproduction into a new language would still be the commonly argued 'impossibility' of translation.

The concern of the practising translator might better be seen as that of an honest dealer in the work of bringing the source text into a new tongue. Distances will remain between a source and its translation, those natural in the play between the languages involved and, apropos of Proust's lament, those between the readings of the author and translator. What matters is to find a text declaring itself worthy of our company as readers: the faithfulness in that.

I have retained terms from the Spanish text to name particular features of the geography of the Delta where the use of an English term might mislead in what it suggested. The most important of these terms is related to the spectacular movements in the water level of the rivers and streams that are the principal influence on the lives of those who live here. The *bajante* is the fiercest of these, when the rivers can literally

---

* Marcel Proust, *Remembrance of Things Past Vol. 3*, Translated by CK Scott Moncrieff and Terence Kilmartin; and by Andreas Mayor, London: Penguin 1989, pp. 939–40.

empty themselves of water, but the *crecientes*, under the influence of winds from the south or east, are also impressive, and intervene in the novel with particular force. These can reasonably be translated as the kind of surge experienced in other environments, and so I use this term in the text. Local geographical names are also retained, despite the obvious temptation of signalling the Terror Shallows [*Bajo del Temor*], for instance.

Born in the town of Chacabuco in western Buenos Aires province, Haroldo Conti was a keen reader as a youngster and wrote scripts for the school puppet theatre. A second stimulus to writing was his father's love of telling stories, many recounting the events and personalities of his journeys as a travelling salesman. But small-town life in Conti's beloved Chacabuco ended when his parents separated, and his mother took him to the capital city to attend secondary school.

His later schooling included two seminaries, an environment Conti said didn't suit him but where he discovered what he termed missionary novels, tales of preaching the gospel amongst the 'unbelievers' in far-off places. He could never remember if he finished it, but the young author wrote a first novel set in Africa and inspired by this reading. He eventually experienced a crisis of faith and left his studies to return to Chacabuco.

Conti became a secondary-school teacher of Latin and, whether or not he relished the work, he was regarded by his fellows as a conscientious colleague, until the political difficulties in Argentina began to interfere with his attendance. But his passion was writing, particularly for the cinema, in favour of which he considered putting aside fiction at one point. Indeed, *Southeaster* was first conceived as a film script, and directors have brought other of his literary work to the screen, taking advantage of its preference for strongly visual narrative.

Among his many and varied activities, Conti trained as a civil pilot of light aircraft; it was flying that led him to discover from the air the landscape of the Paraná Delta. He rented a small wooden house, which he later bought, sited on a stream in the islands of the Delta, just across from Tigre, and known to most as the Gambado – but names are slippery in these parts, as Conti has related.

Conti's interest in the lives of others wasn't merely intellectual: he became a keen fisherman and decided to build a boat; he spent a lot of time with an otter-hunter at one point – and all of this investigation went into his writing, of which *Southeaster* was the first important published expression.

I met Haroldo in the public lending library in my home town of Úbeda, when I came upon a 1985 edition of *Sudeste* published in Spain by Alfaguara. I blew off the dust of Andalusia and read the first paragraphs on my feet, between the shelves. Deciding to publish a translation was simply the way to ensure the novel would not have to wait another fifty years to be read in English, and that I could do the work.

It was important to visit the world of the novel, to clarify aspects of local and boating vocabulary for the translation but also just to see the place. I experienced two *sudestadas* (southeasterly storms) during a month on the islands. The second *sudestada* was uncommonly severe. The geography of the Delta means that these south-east winds literally pile up the water from the River Plate – the Southern Atlantic, in effect – and send it across the islands of the Delta, where the water level on this occasion was almost three metres above its level on the River Plate. I spent three nights with the water slapping about under the house – just as Boga does in the lean-to.

The first act of every morning on the Delta is to draw back the curtains and look outside, for the activity of each day – quite often of each hour – is determined by the state of the river.

Each of Conti's four novels was awarded a literary prize, culminating in the prestigious Casa de las Americas prize for his last novel, *Mascaró, el cazador americano* ('Mascaró, the American Hunter', 1975).

The protagonists in Conti's first three novels are solitaries, a characteristic that is paired in each case with a desire for the wandering life. In *Southeaster*, Boga's life around the islands of the Delta is forced on him by circumstances: the death of the old man for whom he works cutting reeds and the fact that he doesn't know anything else. Despite the austerity of his life and the discomforts of the solitude it implies, Conti's protagonist finds comfort and takes a pride in his knowledge of boats and engines, in being able to navigate his way around the rivers and in his handling of the simple tools that are the means to survival in his environment. He observes and learns to read the changes in the natural world – in the river above all. These readings give a meaning to his world, but it is a world that cannot be dominated, and here Conti's protagonist is distinct from Defoe's Crusoe: despite the dignity of his daily life, Boga lives with a fatalism that comes from understanding that he lives in a world that has no design behind it.

If the indifference of this world to man is what gives the first part of the novel its tension, the appearance of the simpleton Cabecita and the dog heralds change. Conti's protagonist is irritated at once by this interruption to his solitude, yet he tolerates the odd pair and finds himself, at the last, unable to abandon them. The entry, hard on their heels, of a murderous smuggler confirms a turn in the story towards a more conventional dramatic trajectory.

It is the playing-out of Boga's dreams and ambitions, and his small achievements in the face of his greater errors and the disasters that befall him, that keep Conti's story from solemnity. Its enchantment emerges from the understated prose, which provides the space required for readers to do their own imaginative work, and in the rhythmic nature of Conti's voice.

The matter of how man might best face life was something that conditioned Conti's reading; Juan Carlos Onetti's fictions and the early work of Alan Sillitoe were constants in his preference for writers who expressed a defined attitude before life. As to the nourishing of his writing, Conti held to Guimarães Rosa as the principal stimulus, considering the great Brazilian the figure responsible for renewing the language of Latin American literature; he speaks of reading Guimarães Rosa's work throughout the writing of *Mascaró*.

Politics forces its way into the story of Conti's life but, despite the political turmoil in Argentina during the period of his writing, Conti avoids overtly political subjects until *Mascaró*. Repression in Argentina intensified following the military coup of March 1976, and Conti was warned by someone with links to the military that his life was in danger. But he decided against exile and offered his home in the capital as a place of refuge for others under threat of kidnap and murder. Until he was taken from the streets in the early hours of 5th May.[*]

JON LINDSAY MILES
Úbeda (Jaén),
May 2015

---

[*] The known details of Conti's disappearance were recorded in the CONADEP Report *Nunca Más* ('Never Again', 1984) and can be found at www.desaparecidos.org/nuncamas/web/english/library/nevagain/neva-gain_248.htm.

AFTERWORD

When you set out for Ithaka
ask that your way be long,
full of adventure, full of instruction.[1]

HAROLDO CONTI: VOYAGER

Los lugares son como las personas. Comparecen un buen día en
la vida de uno y a partir de ahí fantasmean, es decir, se mezlcan
a la historia de uno que se convierte en la quejumbrosa historia
de lugares y personas. Esto es, los lugares y las personas se incor-
poran en los adentros y se establecen como sujetos persistentes.

[Places are like people. They turn up one fine day in life,
and start to prance around and boast, which is to say,
they weave themselves into your story, which becomes
the grumbling history of people and of places. Which
means the places move themselves inside you, becoming
what will be persistent subjects.][2]

The *sujeto persistente* of Haroldo Conti's writing, as Jon Lindsay
Miles so eloquently maps the terrain, is the river. *Southeaster*
(*South-East* in the 2013 edition of this translation) was Conti's
first novel, and the chronicle 'Tristezas del vino de la costa, o
la parva muerte de la Isla Paulino' [Sorrows of the Wine from
the Coast, or, the Dead, Unthreshed Grain of Isla Paulino] was

227

his last extensive article, published in April 1976. 'Tristezas' was based on a research trip – camera and tape recorder in hand – to Isla Paulino, close to the coastal city of La Plata, in December 1975 and January 1976. We are immediately, recognisably, in the world of Haroldo Conti: the very precise description of landscapes; an attention to the way things work (boats and engines); a blend of popular culture (a song by the *folklorista* Chango Rodríguez acts as a leitmotif); an analysis of past history and current conditions through the voices of different interlocutors, mainly ordinary people, met along the journey; a sense of loss (*tristeza/parva muerte*) but also a hope for change, and a very strong sense of bringing what is considered marginal – both geographically and in terms of literature – into strong focus. As he leaves the island, Conti remembers the first Spanish explorer and conquistador in the region, Pedro de Mendoza y Luján, who 'founded' Buenos Aires in 1536:

> *Y pienso, antes de girar la llave de contacto, con una punta de la isla en el espejo retrovisor, que si don Pedro de Mendoza le hubiese chingado por unos grados habría fundado Buenos Aires en la isla, lo cual habría sido peor para ésta que la creciente del 40, y yo en este momento estaría partiendo de la tumultuosa ciudad de Paulino hacia un lugar nostálgico y desconocido llamado Buenos Aires.*

> [And I think, before I turn the ignition key, with one tip of the island in the rear-view mirror, that if Don Pedro de Mendoza had been a few degrees out, he would have founded Buenos Aires on the island, which would have been worse news for the island than the floods of 1940, and I would now be setting out from the tumultuous city

of Paulino for that wistful and little-known place called
Buenos Aires.] [3]

This afterword places the work of Haroldo Conti within a broad
account of Argentine literature from its early foundational
moments, before going on to present Conti's views on the
nature and function of writing.

HAROLDO CONTI AND ARGENTINE LITERATURE

Accounts of Argentine literature offer a defining place to
the writings of Domingo Faustino Sarmiento, in particular
his vertebral *Facundo: Civilisation and Barbarism* (1845). In this
hybrid text – part literary evocation, part political tract –
Sarmiento sets out a vision of post-Independence Argentina
which seeks to promote a dynamic export economy linked
to the expanding British Empire. The export trade would
pass through the city and port of Buenos Aires and yield a
high revenue which, he argued, would benefit all areas of
the country. The central city of Buenos Aires would thus
control a process that would encourage foreign investment,
technology and immigration.

Refracted through the Romantic prose of Sarmiento, this
dichotomy between liberalism and autarchy was expressed
in terms of a struggle between civilisation and barbarism.
Barbarism was equated with the backward interior of the
country, with local *caudillos* (strong men) and the Argentine
plainsman – the gaucho – as the inferior social types who repre-
sented introverted nationalism. Despite Sarmiento's sneaking
regard for the gaucho and his accomplishments, he argued

that civilisation could only be found by way of the adoption of European patterns in political, social and cultural spheres. Argentina had to open its trade to the rest of the world, attract European migrants and, at the same time, acquire values of sociability and respectability which would lead the country out of fragmentation into being a well-organised nation.

Rivers – as opposed to the pampas – play an important part in Sarmiento's imagined nation and political project, insofar as they allow a flow to ever-widening estuaries and to the sea, and link Argentina as a primary producer to world commerce.

Sarmiento was an early traveller to the Paraná Delta. He led an expedition there in 1855, and later bought an island and built a house, and he looked to encourage migration to the islands and their commercial exploitation. Unlike the unproductive, feckless gauchos, the local inhabitants – the *carapachayos*, he called them, after a key river connecting the River Luján with the Paraná de las Palmas – were perfectly and productively integrated into the landscape. In Sarmiento's always exuberant, hyperbolic use of analogies, he felt that the Delta could be to Argentina what the Nile is to Egypt, or a Venetian community, or the promise of a Far West, a California, but on one's doorstep.[4] Sarmiento's encouragement did help open the region to commerce and to migration from the late-nineteenth through to the mid-twentieth century, before that economy collapsed.

Haroldo Conti's world is full of traces of the broken memories of those former times: abandoned houses, the shells of boats. His own modest house, built in the 1950s, sits close to Sarmiento's wooden house, constructed almost a century before; both are now preserved as museums.

As Argentina from the 1860s was to develop in line with Sarmiento's project, so the dominant images of Argentine identity in literature would portray the tension between civilisation and barbarism, Europe and America, the port city and the country. There is little equivalence to the foundational novels of the United States – the fishermen and whalers in *Moby Dick* or the Bildungsroman of a nation that is *The Adventures of Huckleberry Finn*. When the Argentine Ricardo Güiraldes rewrites *Huckleberry Finn* in the early twentieth century, he puts his boy-narrator as apprentice to a gaucho, the mysterious Don Segundo Sombra (*Don Segundo Sombra*, 1926), and their journey takes them across the pampas, not down a river akin to the Mississippi.

The River Plate is present in many narratives but primarily as a place for the arrival of immigrants in their millions, mainly from southern Europe, or of travellers and visitors. It also offers the embarkation point for journeys to Europe. Memoir accounts of the early twentieth century would be full of descriptions of elite travellers to Europe. The writer and cultural Maecenas, Victoria Ocampo – who later promoted Conti's *Southeaster* in the pages of *Sur*, the magazine she both funded and edited – wrote engagingly of the way her family would visit Europe almost as a biblical exodus. They would load onto the ocean liner all manner of family, staff and provisions, including cows to give milk on the journey and in their subsequent lodgings in the best Parisian hotels.[5] Ocampo was a lifelong cultural bridge-builder, and it was fundamental to her concerns to bridge the span of the ocean, bringing together like-minded intellectuals from Europe and the Americas.

The city of Buenos Aires became the centre of the nation, both in economic terms and in terms of literary imagination.

Jorge Luis Borges would explore the *orillas* (literally banks or shores) of Buenos Aires in his poetry of the 1920s, but his eccentric view is from the outskirts of the city, where it meets the countryside. Certain writers would share Conti's later interest in marginal figures in a landscape, but these works would also mainly be set in the cities, as in the novels of Roberto Arlt who, in the 1920s and 1930s, would paint the world of the urban poor (see, for instance, his 1929 novel *The Seven Madmen*). When nationalist writers in the first part of the twentieth century questioned what they considered the elite, 'European' liberal values of society, they would look to reverse Sarmiento's formulations and espouse nationalist symbols such as the gaucho Martin Fierro, the eponymous hero of the late-nineteenth-century poem. Conti's views would chime with those who sought to question the cultural and economic dominance of the port city: 'I am from the interior,' he says. 'I always saw Buenos Aires through the eyes of an outsider, and this is the only way that it functions for me.'[6] Yet his vantage point is different: he chooses the ebbs and flows and sudden storms of the river, not the land, and Buenos Aires is always a landscape in the mist, just around a corner, before the Delta opens into the River Plate. Buenos Aires is only a few miles away, but it is in another time, it is another way of perceiving the world.

Conti would witness profound changes in Argentine society. He was five when a military government deposed the Radical party that had emerged in the early twentieth century as a counterbalance to an elite Argentine political system that had ruled the country by oligarchy. He left his religious vocation in 1945 when Juan Domingo Perón and Evita Perón were emerging as political figures. At the seminary he had become the friend of a Jesuit priest, Hernán Benítez, who introduced him to literary criticism and would later become the confessor of Eva Perón. Conti lived between Buenos Aires and the Delta during the Peronist decade of 1946–1955, studying at university and later receiving a grant (in 1952 and 1953) from the Cine Club 'Gente de Cine' (Cinema People), to work on film projects. It was at Gente de Cine that he would have seen independent cinema that offered an alternative to a Hollywood aesthetic, in particular Italian neorealism and French new wave. (In the light of this interest, readers of *Southeaster* might wish to observe Conti's use of description that has the precision of a camera, his attention to images, forms, colours, sounds, and to the ways in which his narrative is 'cut' and edited.)

Conti began publishing in the aftermath of Perón's overthrow in a military coup, and he lived through the many changes that took place as Argentina struggled to find a political system that would exclude or incorporate Peronism, under the ever-watchful eye of the military. He became more politically active around the time when Perón returned from exile in 1973 in a wave of popular euphoria. And Conti published his last novel, *Mascaró, el cazador americano,* when Perón's third wife, Isabel, took over as president following Perón's death in 1974, and government and paramilitary forces became more oppressive, and the political moment more radicalised.[7]

Of course, we should not make easy connections between politics and writing. Conti himself would often warn against such easy links. He would affirm throughout his life that writing to an overt political formula could result in bad literature:

> *Quiero decir que por la sumisión a ciertos universales rígidos, cuya imposición y verificación se convierte en un fin en sí mismo,*

alguna literatura comprometida corre el riesgo de ser pasatista ella también.

[I want to say that, by submitting to certain rigid rules, the obedience to which, and demonstration of one's conformity to which, becomes an end in itself, a literature of commitment runs the risk of becoming frivolous.][8]

For the purposes of this brief overview we can say that, at least at the level of rhetoric, the first Peronist governments gave value to an Argentina beyond the city. Peronist parades would often be lead by gauchos on horseback, and speeches made constant references to *cabecitas negras*, migrant workers from the interior. Radio programmes would broadcast popular music from the countryside, as well as the urban tango. We know that Conti's father, Pedro Conti, set up a branch of the Peronist Party in his home town of Chacabuco, though there is little information about his son's political affiliations at the time. There were aspects of this Peronist cultural project that would chime with Conti's own affiliation to regional cultures. While most intellectuals were opposed to the first Peronist governments, which they perceived as authoritarian, Perón's overthrow by the military, and subsequent military involvement in politics, led to a gradual reappraisal of the political order and, by extension, the social function of intellectuals and writers. These were debates that Conti would enter more vigorously from the early seventies.

While writing *Southeaster*, Conti would have been living at a time of both political confusion and also excitement: how should Argentina become more modern and develop (modernisation and 'developmentalism' were the terms used at the time); how might it embrace the new; how might it react to the imaginative proximity of revolution, with the triumph of the Cuban Revolution in 1959? One of Conti's answers seems to be to step back from the glitter of the new, and shine a torchlight from the brow of his boat on hitherto unexplored spaces of popular culture. In particular he would look to eschew the notion of writer as celebrity, someone – in Tom Wolfe's phrase – leading the vanguard march through the lands of the philistines. As Conti remarked in a handwritten note:

> *No sé si tiene sentido pero me digo cada vez: contá las historia de la gente como si cantaras en medio de un camino, despojate de toda pretensión y cantá, simplemente cantá con todo tu corazón. Que nadie recuerde tu nombre sino toda esa vieja y sencilla historia.*

> [I don't know if it makes sense, but I tell myself these same words every time: narrate the people's story as you'd sing while on a journey, relinquish all ambition, simply sing with all your heart. Let no one be concerned to remember your name, but everything there is of this old and simple story.][9]

The novel that seemed to both represent and guide this optimistic embrace of the new was published one year after *Southeaster*: Julio Cortázar's *Hopscotch* (1963). This novel, in its 'hopscotch' between the cities of Paris and Buenos Aires, was a playful but also sophisticated search for freedom, both existential and profoundly literary. It stressed the need to 'un-write' the novel, to free it from convention and high seriousness – the solemnity and pomposity of much of national literatures – and to play the game with grace and intelligence.

It was the novel's freshness, its limitless cultural breadth and its eroticism that captivated a new audience, who wanted to be Cortázar's active readers: engaged, modern, experimental and hip. It was one of the first 'boom' novels in Latin America, chiming with the literary, modernist experimentation of the Peruvian Mario Vargas Llosa, the Mexican Carlos Fuentes and the Colombian Gabriel García Márquez. These were the writers who would be promoted by publishing houses, critics and cultural magazines, and would be translated throughout the world.[10]

It would be wrong to argue that the attention given to particular writers distorted the market, because the readership for Latin American literature as a whole grew throughout the sixties, both at home and abroad. But it would be fair to say that, in their excitement to promote the boom, publishers and critics in the sixties paid less attention to the quieter, seemingly less ambitious narratives like those of Conti. Readers in Latin America and beyond are today far more likely to bring to mind the trips down the Magdalena River described by García Márquez in *Love in the Time of Cholera* (1985) and *The General in His Labyrinth* (1989), or the Amazon as described by Vargas Llosa in *The Green House* (1966).

If there is one travel image that might be said to represent this sixties boom – and despite the writers' own attested fear of flying – it would be the fast-paced mobility of jet flights that looked to shrink the spaces between Buenos Aires and Paris, Mexico City and New York, Havana and London. By contrast, as Eduardo Galeano puts it: *Para entender a Haroldo Conti hay que estar en el Tigre y ver el río correr despacito. Ese es su ritmo* [To understand Haroldo Conti, one has to be in Tigre and to see the river running slowly on. This is his rhythm.][11]

Let us hope that, fifty years after the first publication of *Southeaster*, this first translation into English can offer a similar place in our imagination to the Paraná River and its Delta.

It is not the intention of this afterword to offer a context for the entire scope of Conti's writings up to 1976, but rather to situate the moment of *Southeaster's* publication and its immediate aftermath. (It might however be of interest to note that the boom writers themselves certainly read and admired Conti's work: in 1971 he was awarded the Barral Prize for his novel *En vida*, and two of the jury members were García Márquez and Vargas Llosa.)

We have looked to place *Southeaster* where it belongs in the history of Argentine and Latin American literature, as one of the most original contributions to what Conti himself would term, in an interview in 1974, 'a stylistically and imaginatively Argentine literature.'[12]

CONTI ON CONTI: A SHIP'S LOG

When the writer Juan Carlos Martini was compiling the interview with Conti from which we have just quoted, he spoke of how difficult it was to get Conti to talk about himself and his own work, and of his phobia about being interviewed.[13] Yet, when coaxed into speaking in interviews, he would give very measured and insightful comments on his work. One such interview, made at the time of the publication of *Southeaster*, is published in the first book-length study of his work, Rodolfo Benasso's *El mundo de Haroldo Conti* (Buenos Aires, 1969). The following pages present Conti's illuminating reading of the novel and its different contexts.

When asked if he felt himself to be a figure in the literary world we have outlined above, he replied:

No sé si, después de todo, he llegado a ser un escritor, pero lo que indiscutiblemente no soy es un literato. Cuando escribía Sudeste, *vivía prácticamente en las islas y, aparte del hecho de empuñar una lapicera y sentarme frente a una hoja de papel, la historia salió de la gente y las cosas, casi a mi pesar. Por ese entonces no conocía a ningún escritor.*

[I can't say if, at the end of the day, I've come to be a writer, but one thing I am unarguably not is a man of letters. At the time I was writing *Sudeste*, I practically lived on the islands and, aside from the act of my picking up a pencil and sitting in front of a piece of paper, the story itself came from other people and things, and almost in spite of myself. In those days I didn't know a single writer.][14]

This isolation would change, of course, and might be slightly exaggerated, for he won a prize for *Southeaster,* and the novel appeared on the bestseller lists in the newly founded *Primera Plana*.[15] But his sense of being marginal to dominant literary currents is further emphasised by his comments on the state of much Argentine literature. He is opposed to:

la pretensión de una novela que abarque y agote de una vez y para siempre una supuesta realidad nacional. Lo que podría llamarse la novela monumento o la literature de bronce. Todo lo que se ha logrado con esto es acentuar todavía más el divorcio entre la literature y el país. La Argentina es una suma de realidades, a menudo incomunicados entre sí, en perpetuo cambio todos ellos . . .

[the pretension of a novel that embraces and exhausts once and for all some supposed national reality. What one might call the monumental, or iconic novel. All that's been achieved through this is to accentuate still further the divorce between the literature and the land. Argentina is the sum of its realities, which often don't speak to each other, and are all in constant movement . . .][16]

This awareness of the diversity of Argentine cultures, and the lack of communication between these cultures, is fundamental to Conti's writing.

He goes on to speak of the writers with whom he finds affinities:

Entre la literatura y la vida, elijo la vida . . . Pocos libros valen una hoja de ese loco vagabundo, de Jack Kerouac, que con su mochila al hombro corre de una punta a otra de esa gigantesca tierra que gime, canta o resopla a través de su sangre . . . Pocos libros valen una página de Hemingway, ni media de Sillitoe, ni una línea de Morosoli.

[Between literature and life, I choose life . . . Few books are worth one printed spread from that crazy vagabond, from Jack Kerouac, who with his pack on his back runs from end to end of that giant land, that howls and sings and snorts through his blood . . . Few books are worth a single page from Hemingway, nor a half-page from Sillitoe, nor a line from Morosoli].

All these references will be familiar to an English reader, except perhaps that to the little-known Uruguayan writer Juan José Morosoli, who had a similar interest in portraying liminal characters in a landscape of rivers and ports. Conti would speak of another Uruguayan writer, Juan Carlos Onetti, whose novels and stories were often set in the invented town of Santa María and its environs, on the banks of the River Plate; Onetti's famous novel *The Shipyard* was published in 1961. Conti would often refer to the Argentine poet of the Paraná River, Juan L Ortiz. Added to this list of admired writers was the Brazilian João Guimarães Rosa, whose complex novels and short stories would, in the main, map the backlands of Brazil, but which moved beyond mere regionalism in their philosophical content and radical linguistic experimentation.

Conti would pay an extended homage to Ernest Hemingway in an article written after a trip to Cuba in 1974. He describes his visit to different sites in Hemingway's Cuban landscape: the room in the Hotel Ambos Mundos in Havana where Hemingway wrote, and the fishing village and the fishermen immortalised in *The Old Man and the Sea*. There he swapped stories about *navegaciones y peces y amigos, todos esos blandos temas que alivian el tiempo, lo tornan a uno vaguedad, espuma, pájaro forastero* [sailing trips, fishes and friends, all those gentle subjects that lighten the time, that turn one to vagueness, to froth, into a strange bird]. The fishermen stories trigger memories, evoke other rivers and seas:

> *De un vistazo veo yo allí, superpuestos tiempos y lugares . . . al Nene Bruzzone del Tigre, al siempre capitán Marcelo Gianelli, al Vasco Arregui que en este momento debe estar pescando la centolla a bordo del Cruz del Sur en el Beagle . . .*

[In a glance I can see myself there again, the times and
the places all superimposed . . . Kid Bruzzone from Tigre,
Marcelo Gianelli, always the captain, the Basque Arregui
who, right at this moment, must be fishing for crab on
the Cruz del Sur, on the Beagle . . .][17]

In this account, Hemingway offered Conti a model for the dis-
cipline of writing as well as a repository of shared themes. On
his final visit, to Hemingway's former house, now a museum,
Conti finds Hemingway's boat, the *Pilar*, marooned on the
'sandbank' of the grassy lawn. He describes in great detail
the dimensions of the boat and its engine capacity, before
remarking:

*Este es el barco que el Viejo amó como a un hijo, condenado in
memoriam a vivir lejos del mar, a navegar nostálgicamente entre
arecas y palmeras sobre el césped bien cortado . . . Saludo al barco
en voz baja, porque los barcos son como personas, entienden a
su manera.*

[This is the boat the Old Man loved like a son, condemned
in memoriam to live far from the sea, to nostalgically sail
between palms and arecas, over the nicely cut lawn . . .
I greet the boat in an undertone, because boats are like
people, they understand in their way.][18]

When Conti spoke specifically about *Southeaster* in the early
sixties, he would explain a writing technique which was also,
by extension, a philosophy of life. He would begin by stress-
ing the autobiographical and almost ethnographic nature of
his work:

El viaje de Boga en cierto modo es mi viaje. Sólo que el viaje del Boga viene mucho después cuando aquello adquirió pasado y se hizo historia para mí . . . Por fin, otro día, todo aquello (su vida en el Delta) me golpeó como ausencia. Y entonces a punto de perderlo, de alguna manera, ya lejano y extraviado, traté de inventarlo de nuevo . . .

[Boga's journey is my own, in a way. Except Boga's comes very much later, when all that it comprised acquired a past and became a story for me . . . And then in the end, on another day, all of this (his life on the Delta) invaded me as an absence. And then, when I felt I would lose it in some way, already far off and gone astray, I tried to invent it anew . . .][19]

Writing is not, for Conti, a description of 'great events':

Me reconozco en las pequeñas cosas y las pequeñas vidas sin residuo de historia . . . los pequeños sucesos de un tipo que ni siquiera tiene nombre se juntan y se pierden sobre ese río-tiempo con otras historias tan insignificantes como la suya.

[I see myself in the small things and small lives, the ones that leave no residue of history . . . the small things that happen to a chap who doesn't even have a name, converge and disperse on the river-time with the stories of others that are as trifling as his.]

And *Southeaster*'s landscape of the river offers the perfect location for such a story:

No hay nada que dure sobre este paisaje de olvido, no hay nada que se afirme y resista. Él mismo cambia de forma, tentando continuamente bordes y orillas distintas. Un río nuevo para cada historia.

[There is nothing that lasts on this scene of forgetting, nothing stands firm and endures. It changes its face, continually trying to draw borders and shorelines. The river is new for each story.][20]

This image of flow and flux is related to perception and to the nature of writing. Writing is re-creation, not simple description, for there is no objective reality: *Lo que existe en todo caso, es una pura fluencia, un caos de estímulos y sensaciones, al que nuestra subjetividad le otorga sentido* [What exists after all is pure flow, a chaos of feelings and stimuli, bestowed with meaning by our subjectivity].[21] There is a tension in the writing, between a desire for precision and an awareness of flux and flow, which talks of wider issues of engagement, the satisfaction of small tasks in opposition to fatalism and subjectivity. The rhythms of the writing and the shifting narrative perspectives are thus essential to Conti's overall purpose, and Jon Lindsay Miles' splendid translation is particularly sensitive here.[22]

This interview from the early sixties ends with a statement that lyrically encapsulates the novel we have just read.

Hay algo erratil en todo el asunto. Los barcos de humor vagabundo, los tipos que vienen y se van, la espera interminable de algo borroso que arguardamos del tiempo o del agua, el viaje que siempre hemos sonado, la ciudad en la espalda, gentes y lugares distintos

243

que presentimos detrás de ese horizonte que en los días grises se confunde con el cielo, pero sobre todo esa sustancia movediza que penetra las horas y los días y que destila ansiedad . . .

Es la misma nostalgia vagabunda de Kerouac . . . el tema del 'homo viator', del tiempo que pasa y nos vuelve ajenos, nos adelgaza en láminas de olvido el esfuerzo por aferrarnos sobre algo sustancialmente movedizo, dejando pistas y rastros de nuestra presencia que se vuelven testimonios de nuestra mayor ausencia, los pequeños objetos poseídos, las cosas que cubrieron o prolongaron o auxiliaron a mi cuerpo, esas pacientes cosas a las que yo he asignado un sentido exclusivo, un uso preciso, inclusive un carácter personal e intransferible: en fin, todos esos vestigios a través de los cuales alguien podrá acaso reconstruir mi rostro, la presión de mis manos, el roce de mis pies, la dirección de mis deseos.

[There is something capricious in all this. The boats with their wandering nature, the blokes who come and go, the interminable waiting for something unclear that the time or the water will bring, the journey we've dreamed of forever, the city behind us, different people and places we feel are there beyond that horizon, which on grey days is mixed with the sky, but, more than all this, that substance like quicksand that runs through the hours and the days and exudes a disquiet . . .

It's the same nostalgia for wandering Kerouac knew . . . the theme of the 'homo viator', the time that goes by and leaves us estranged, that takes our efforts to hold on to something that's always essentially shifting, and thins it to layers of forgetting, leaving tracks and prints of our presence that turn into proofs of our much larger absence, the small objects possessed, the things that conceal or sustain or give aid to my body, those long-suffering things that I've given a personal meaning, a use that's required, a personal nature, even, unique, that can't be exchanged: anyhow, all those remains that someone might use to bring back my face, the press of my hands, the touch of my feet, the course of my longings.]

Thanks to Jon Lindsay Miles's careful translation, readers in English can at last immerse themselves in the subtle, beautifully wrought, journey of the voyager, 'homo viator', whose identity is defined as, and in, movement.

JOHN KING
Leamington Spa,
March 2013

NOTES

1 CP Cavafy, 'Ithaka', in E Keely and P Sherrard, eds., *Six Poets of Modern Greece,* London: Thames and Hudson 1960, p. 42.

2 Haroldo Conti, 'Tristezas de vino de la costa, o la parva muerte de la Isla Paulino', *Crisis* 36 (April 1976), p. 51. In this Afterword, all translations appearing inside square brackets are by Jon Lindsay Miles.

3 Ibid, p. 57.

4 See Domingo F Sarmiento, *El Carapachay*, Buenos Aires: Eudeba 2011, pp. 52–53.

5 See Victoria Ocampo, *Autobiografía, Vol 2: El imperio insular,* Buenos Aires: Sur 1980, pp. 65–75.

6 Quoted in Rodolfo Benasso, *El mundo de Haroldo Conti,* Buenos Aires: Galerna 1969, p. 146.

7 Hernán Benítez, mentioned earlier in this paragraph, introduced Conti to the literary criticism of another occupant of the Seminario Metropolitano Conciliar de Villa Devoto, Father Leonardo Castellani, a controversial nationalist philosopher and writer. (See Haroldo Conti, 'Era nuestro adelantado', *Crisis* 37 (May 1976), p.43.) Conti was abducted and disappeared on 5th May 1976, some thirty years after leaving the seminary and only days after his short note on Castellani appeared in the magazine *Crisis.* Two weeks after his disappearance, General Videla, who had led the military coup on 24th March 1976, invited four writers to have lunch with him, to give the impression that all was normal in a society gripped by fear, assassination, disappearance, censorship and arbitrary arrest. One of those invited was Father Castellani. The magazine *Crisis,* in its penultimate issue before being forced to cease publication and its editors escaping into exile, interviewed Castellani about the lunch, and he replied: 'I tried at least to take advantage of the situation with the Christian concern that I carried in my heart. Someone had visited me days before, who, with tears in their eyes and plunged in desperation, had begged me to intercede on their behalf for the life of the writer Haroldo Conti. I knew nothing more than that he was a prestigious writer and had been a seminarist in his youth . . . I noted his name on a piece of paper and gave it to Videla, who took it from me respectfully and assured me that peace would return to the

country soon.' Padre Castellani, 'Algo más que libros', *Crisis* 39 (July 1976), p. 3.

8   Ibid, p. 156.

9   Haroldo Conti, handwritten note, La Rioja, June 1967, published in *Crisis* 16 (August 1974), p. 44.

10 In Argentina, the highly influential magazine *Primera Plana* would put certain boom writers on the front cover (*primera plana*) and do close readings of their work, often accompanied by interviews placing them *en primer plano* [in the foreground].

11 Quoted in Héctor Guyot, 'Haroldo Conti y el río de la vida', *La Nación* 17th October 2009.

12 Haroldo Conti, 'Compartir las luchas del pueblo', *Crisis* 16 (August 1974), p. 42.

13 Juan Carlos Martini, ibid, pp. 40–41.

14 Benasso, p. 152.

15 See note 10, above.

16 Ibid, p. 153.

17 Haroldo Conti, 'La breve vida feliz de Mister Pa', *Crisis* 15 (June 1974), p. 64.

18 Ibid, p. 67

19 In Benasso, pp. 157–8.

20 Ibid, pp. 158–9.

21 Ibid, p. 153.

22 See also the analysis by Aníbal Ford which helps inform this section: 'Homo viator. El conflicto entre estrategias literarias y etnográficas en *Sudeste* de Haroldo Conti', in Eduardo Romano, compilador, *Haroldo Conti, alias Mascaró, alias la vida*, Colihue: Centro Cultural de la Memoria Haroldo Conti, Buenos Aires, 2008, pp. 245–67.

Dear readers,

We rely on subscriptions from people like you to tell these other stories – the types of stories most publishers consider too risky to take on.

Our subscribers don't just make the books physically happen. They also help us approach booksellers, because we can demonstrate that our books already have readers and fans. And they give us the security to publish in line with our values, which are collaborative, imaginative and 'shamelessly literary'.

All of our subscribers:

- receive a first-edition copy of each of the books they subscribe to
- are thanked by name at the end of these books
- are warmly invited to contribute to our plans and choice of future books

BECOME A SUBSCRIBER, OR GIVE A SUBSCRIPTION TO A FRIEND

Visit andotherstories.org/subscribe to become part of an alternative approach to publishing.

Subscriptions are:

£20 for two books per year

£35 for four books per year

£50 for six books per year

OTHER WAYS TO GET INVOLVED

If you'd like to know about upcoming events and reading groups (our foreign-language reading groups help us choose books to publish, for example) you can:

- join the mailing list at: andotherstories.org/join-us
- follow us on Twitter: @andothertweets
- join us on Facebook: facebook.com/AndOtherStoriesBooks
- follow our blog: Ampersand

This book was made possible thanks to the support of:

Aaron McEnery
Adam Butler
Adam Lenson
AG Hughes
Ajay Sharma
Alan Cameron
Alan Ramsey
Alasdair Thomson
Alastair Dickson
Alastair Gillespie
Alastair Laing
Alec Begley
Alex Martin
Alex Ramsey
Alexander Balk
Alexandra Buchler
Alexandra de
   Verseg-Roesch
Alexandra Georgescu
Ali Conway
Alice Nightingale
Alison Bowyer
Alison Hughes
Alison Layland
Alison Smith
Allison Graham
Alyse Ceirante
Amanda Dalton
Amanda DeMarco
Amanda Jane Stratton
Amanda Love Darragh
Amelia Ashton
Amelia Dowe
Amy Allebone-Salt
Amy Rushton
Anderson Tepper
Andrea Davis
Andrew Lees
Andrew Marston
Andrew McCafferty
Andrew van der Vlies
Andrew Whitelegg
Angela Thirlwell
Angus MacDonald
Angus Walker
Ann McAllister
Ann Van Dyck
Anna Demming
Anna Milsom

Anna Vinegrad
Anna-Karin Palm
Annalise Pippard
Anne Carus
Anne Claire Le Reste
Anne Lawler
Anne Marie Jackson
Annie McDermott
Antonio de Swift
Antony Pearce
Aoife Boyd
Archie Davies
Averill Buchanan
Ayca Turkoglu

Barbara Mellor
Barry Hall
Bartolomiej Tyszka
Belinda Farrell
Ben Schofield
Ben Smith
Ben Thornton
Benjamin Judge
Benjamin Morris
Bianca Jackson
Blanka Stoltz
Bob Hill
Bob Richmond-Watson
Brendan McIntyre
Briallen Hopper
Brigita Ptackova
Bronwen Chan
Bruce Millar

C Mieville
Calum Colley
Candy Says Juju Sophie
Caroline Mildenhall
Caroline Perry
Carolyn A Schroeder
Catherine Taylor
Catrin Ashton
Cecilia Rossi
Cecily Maude
Charles Lambert
Charles Rowley
Charlotte Holtam
Charlotte Murrie &
   Stephen Charles

Charlotte Ryland
Charlotte Whittle
Chris Day
Chris Elcock
Chris Fawson
Chris Stevenson
Chris Watson
Chris Wood
Christine Luker
Christopher Allen
Christopher Terry
Ciara Ní Riain
Claire Brooksby
Claire Fuller
Claire Seymour
Claire Tranah
Claire Williams
Clarissa Botsford
Claudio Guerri
Clifford Posner
Clive Bellingham
Clodie Vasli
Colin Burrow
Courtney Lilly
Craig Barney

Dan Pope
Daniel Arnold
Daniel Carpenter
Daniel Gillespie
Daniel Hahn
Daniel Hugill
Daniel Lipscombe
Daniel Sheldrake
Daniel Venn
Daniela Steierberg
Dave Lander
Dave Rigby
David Archer
David Gould
David Hebblethwaite
David Hedges
David Higgins
David Johnson-Davies
David Roberts
David Shriver
David Smith
Dawn Hart
Dawn Mazarakis

Debbie Pinfold
Deborah Bygrave
Deborah Jacob
Denise Jones
Denise Muir
Diana Brighouse
Duncan Marks

Eddie Dick
Elaine Rassaby
Eleanor Maier
Eleanor Walsh
Eliza O'Toole
Elizabeth Bryer
Emily Jeremiah
Emily Taylor
Emily Williams
Emily Yaewon Lee &
    Gregory Limpens
Emma Bielecki
Emma Teale
Emma Timpany
Eric E Rubeo
Eva Tobler-Zumstein
Ewan Tant

Fawzia Kane
Finnuala Butler
Fiona Graham
Fiona Quinn
Florian Andrews
Floriane Peycelon
Fran Sanderson
Francesca Bacigalupo
Francis Taylor
Francisco Vilhena
Freya Carr
Friederike Knabe

G Thrower
Gabrielle Crockatt
Gavin Collins
Gawain Espley
Gemma Tipton
Genevra Richardson
George McCaig
George Sandison &
    Daniela Laterza
George Savona
George Wilkinson
Georgia Panteli

Gill Boag-Munroe
Gillian Jondorf
Gillian Stern
Gordon Cameron
Gordon Mackechnie
Graham & Steph
    Parslow
Graham R Foster
Gregory Conti

Hannah Perret
Hannah Vincent
Hanne Larsson
Harriet Mossop
Harriet Owles
Helen Asquith
Helen Bailey
Helen Brady
Helen Collins
Helen Weir
Helene
    Walters-Steinberg
Henriette Heise
Henrike Laehnemann
Holly Johnson
    & Pat Merloe

Ian Barnett
Ian McMillan
Irene Mansfield
Isabella Garment
Isobel Staniland

J Collins
Jack Brown
Jacqueline Crooks
Jacqueline Haskell
Jacqueline Lademann
Jacqueline Taylor
James Attlee
James Beck
James Cubbon
James Portlock
James Scudamore
James Tierney
James Wilper
Jamie Richards
Jamie Walsh
Jane Brandon
Jane Watts
Jane Whiteley

Jane Woollard
Janet Mullarney
Janette Ryan
Jason Spencer
Jeff Collins
Jen Hamilton-
    Emery
Jennifer Hearn
Jennifer Higgins
Jennifer O'Brien
Jennifer Winter
Jenny Diski
Jenny Newton
Jeremy Weinstock
Jerry Lynch
Jessica Kingsley
Jessica Schouela
Jethro Soutar
Jillian Jones
Jim Boucherat
Jo Harding
Joanna Flower
Joanna Luloff
Joanna Neville
Joe Robins
Joel Love
Johan Forsell
Johannes Georg Zipp
John Allison
John Conway
John English
John Fisher
John Gent
John Hodgson
John Kelly
John Nicholson
John Royley
John Steigerwald
Jon Lindsay Miles
Jonathan Evans
Jonathan Watkiss
Joseph Cooney
Joshua Davis
Josie Soutar
JP Sanders
Julian Duplain
Julian Lomas
Juliane Jarke
Julie Gibson
Julie Van Pelt

Kaarina Hollo
Kapka Kassabova
Karan Deep Singh
Katarina Trodden
Kate Beswick
Kate Gardner
Kate Griffin
Katharina Liehr
Katharine Freeman
Katharine Robbins
Katherine El-Salahi
Katherine Jacomb
Kathryn Lewis
Katie Brown
Katie Smith
Keiko Kondo
Keith Dunnett
Kevin Brockmeier
Kevin Pino
Kinga Burger
KL Ee
Kristin Djuve
Kristin Pedroja
Krystalli Glyniadakis

Lana Selby
Laura Clarke
Lauren Cerand
Lauren Ellemore
Leanne Bass
Leigh Vorhies
Leonie Schwab
Leri Price
Lesley Lawn
Lesley Watters
Leslie Rose
Linda Dalziel
Lindsay Brammer
Lindsey Ford
Liz Clifford
Loretta Platts
Lorna Bleach
Louise Bongiovanni
Louise Rogers
Lucia Rotheray
Lucie Donahue
Lucy Caldwell
Luke Healey
Lynda Graham
Lynda Ross
Lynn Martin

M Manfre
Mac York
Madeleine Kleinwort
Maeve Lambe
Maggie Livesey
Maisie & Nick Carter
Malcolm Bourne
Marella Oppenheim
Margaret Davis
Margaret Jull Costa
Maria Pelletta
Marie Donnelly
Marina Castledine
Marina Lomunno
Marion Cole
Mark Ainsbury
Mark Lumley
Mark Waters
Martha Gifford
Martha Nicholson
Martin Brampton
Martin Hollywood
Martin Price
Martin Whelton
Mary Nash
Mary Wang
Mason Billings
Matt Oldfield
Matthew Francis
Matthew Lawrence
Matthew O'Dwyer
Matthew Smith
Matthew Todd
Maxime Dargaud-Fons
Meaghan Delahunt
Melissa da Silveira
    Serpa
Melissa Quignon-Finch
Michael Harrison
Michael Holtmann
Michael Johnston
Michelle Bailat-Jones
Michelle Dyrness
Miles Visman
Milo Waterfield
Mitchell Albert
Monica Hileman
Monika Olsen
Morgan Lyons
Murali Menon

Nan Haberman
Nasser Hashmi
Natalie Smith
Nathalie Adams
Nathan Rostron
Neil Pretty
Nia Emlyn-Jones
Nick James
Nick Nelson & Rachel
    Eley
Nicola Hart
Nicola Hughes
Nina Alexandersen
Noah Birksted-Breen
Nuala Watt

Octavia Kingsley
Owen Booth

Pamela Ritchie
Pat Crowe
Pat Morgan
Patrick Owen
Paul Bailey
Paul Brand
Paul Hannon
Paul Jones
Paul M Cray
Paul Miller
Paul Munday
Paul Myatt
Paula Edwards
Paula McGrath
Penelope Hewett
    Brown
Peter Armstrong
Peter Law
Peter Lockett
Peter McCambridge
Peter Murray
Peter Rowland
Peter Vos
Philip Warren
Phyllis Reeve
Piet Van Bockstal
Piotr Kwiecinski
PM Goodman
Polly McLean
Pooja Agrawal
PRAH Recordings

Rachael Williams
Rachel Kennedy
Rachel Lasserson
Rachel Matheson
Rachel Van Riel
Rachel Watkins
Read MAW Books
Rebecca Atkinson
Rebecca Braun
Rebecca Gillam
Rebecca Moss
Rebecca Rosenthal
Rhodri Jones
Richard Ellis
Richard Jackson
Richard Smith
Rishi Dastidar
Rob Jefferson-Brown
Robert Gillett
Robin Patterson
Robyn Neil
Ros Schwartz
Rose Cole
Rose Oakes
Rose Skelton
Rosemary Rodwell
Rosemary Terry
Ross Macpherson
Roz Simpson
Ruth Diver
Ruth F Hunt
Ruth Van Driessche

Sabine Griffiths
Sally Baker
Sam Cunningham
Sam Gordon
Sam Ruddock
Samantha
    Sabbarton-Wright
Samuel Alexander
    Mansfield
Sandra de Monte
Sandra Hall
Sarah Benson
Sarah Butler
Sarah Duguid
Sarah Pybus
Sarah Salmon
Sarah Salway
Sasha Dugdale

SE Guine
Sean Malone
Sean McGivern
Seini O'Connor
Sheridan Marshall
Shirley Harwood
Sigrun Hodne
Simon James
Simon John Harvey
Simona Constantin
Sioned Puw Rowlands
SJ Bradley
SJ Naudé
Sonia McLintock
Sonia Overall
Steph Morris
Stephanie Brada
Stephanie Carr
Stephen Bass
Stephen H Oakey
Stephen Pearsall
Steven Sidley
Sue & Ed Aldred
Sue Childs
Susan Tomaselli
Susie Roberson
Suzy Ceulan Hughes

Tammy Watchorn
Tamsin Ballard
Tania Hershman
Tasmin Maitland
Thomas Bell
Thomas Fritz
Thomas JD Gray
Tien Do
Tim Jackson
Tim Theroux
Tim Warren
Timothy Harris
Tina Rotherham-Win-
    qvist
Todd Greenwood
Tom Bowden
Tom Darby
Tom Franklin
Tony Bastow
Torna Russell-Hills
Tracy Northup
Trevor Lewis
Trevor Wald

Tristan Burke
Troy Zabel

Val Challen
Vanessa Jackson
Vanessa Nolan
Vasco Dones
Venetia Welby
Victoria Adams
Victoria Walker
Visaly Muthusamy
Viviane D'Souza

Wendy Langridge
Wendy Toole
Wenna Price
Wiebke Schwartz
William G Dennehy

Yukiko Hiranuma

Zoë Brasier

Current & Upcoming Books

Haroldo Conti was born in the province of Buenos Aires in 1925. He studied at a Salesian school and a Jesuit seminary before graduating with a degree in philosophy from the University of Buenos Aires. In his professional life, Conti was variously employed as an actor, a bank clerk, a Latin teacher and a screenwriter.

After the publication of *Southeaster* in 1962, he went on to write three more novels as well as several short story collections. He is the recipient of a number of important literary prizes, including the Casa de las Américas Prize. Conti was arrested in his apartment after the military coup of 1976, and is currently included on the list of the permanently disappeared.

Jon Lindsay Miles lives and works in southern Spain, also publishing as Immigrant Press. The translation of Conti's *Southeaster* (2013) followed a hybrid guide-novel of Úbeda (*Along the Way. Walking in Úbeda,* 2009) and a bilingual collection of mediated stories of migration (*Desde las Américas a Jaén/From the Americas to Jaén,* 2011). He pays for this life by teaching English conversation at an outpost of the University of Jaén.

John King is Emeritus Professor of Latin American Literature at Warwick University. His research focuses on the cinema and literature of Argentina and Mexico in particular, and he edited *The Cambridge Companion to Modern Latin American Culture* (CUP, 2004), among other publications.